THE SECRET ORDER OF THE
SCEPTER & GAVEL

NICHOLAS PONTICELLO

THE SECRET ORDER OF THE SCEPTER & GAVEL

MURDER CAN HAPPEN ON MARS TOO

BOOLEANOP, LOS ANGELES, CALIFORNIA

To Kenji and Sara—for everything

CHAPTER 1

SURELY BY NOW you've heard of the Order of the Scepter and Gavel. Either you've heard the stories passed down in common lore or you've read the exposé written up in the May 2041 issue of *Vanity Fair*. For those of you just tuning in, put quite simply, Scepter and Gavel is a collegiate secret society. *Was* a collegiate secret society. It was officially dissolved after the scandal of '41. Before its demise, its members moved among the highest echelons of Martian society. Martian royalty.

I was inducted into Scepter and Gavel in November of 2040, less than a year before a state judge condemned the society to oblivion. In condemning Scepter and Gavel to oblivion, the state judge effectively condemned me to oblivion, too.

Go figure.

I now work as a janitor in A-Block on Mars. I make my

living cleaning up the messes of scientific researchers—physicists, geologists, botanists, and so on. I make thirteen credits a week, enough to scrape by.

Pretty much everybody scrapes by on Mars. Even the top politicians and diplomats making a hundred credits a week scrape by. Mars is not an easy place to live—not for anyone.

I've been here for almost three decades, enough time to get used to the gravity sickness and seasonal disorientation that all new recruits experience when they first arrive on Mars. We say here that you have to get your sea legs, even though there is no natural water to speak of anywhere on this godforsaken planet—except at the poles in the form of cold, hard ice.

And thank god for that cold, hard ice. It's what keeps us alive here on Mars. It provides us with drinking water, and irrigation for our crops, and slop with which to mop the floors of the A-Block labs every day, including Sundays.

Goddammit.

And to think this lonely janitor was once a member of Scepter and Gavel! A gavelman, they used to say. The women, too, were called gavelmen.

My wife was not a member of Scepter and Gavel, was never a member of any secret society, at least not that I know of. Her name is Cady Palminteri, née Pinkleton. All during the time I was dating her, I had to hide the fact that I was a gavelman.

Turns out she was hiding something, too.

We are all hiding something.

THE SECRET ORDER OF THE SCEPTER & GAVEL

Until the scandal of '41, nobody except other gavelmen knew with any certainty who was in Scepter and Gavel. Membership was a closely guarded secret. Cady only found out after *Vanity Fair* published all of our names in the famous piece that proved to be the undoing of the whole society. After that, the university demolished the Tomb—the society's official meeting place. All gavelmen were put on academic probation and closely monitored up until the moment we were sent up.

"Sent up" is what we say when graduates of Vanderough University take off for Mars. I was sent up in June of 2044, three years after *Vanity Fair* published my name in its famous exposé. That list of names might as well have been a prison sentence. After that, the only jobs gavelmen could get here on Mars were the lowest of the low. The pittiest of the pits. The turdiest of the turds.

My pal Surge—a former gavelman—is a waste disposal operative in F-Block. Mickey G. is a handyman at central command. And Howie Van Bruggen, probably the most notorious gavelman from my day, shovels shit at the landfill in Sector 3.

Cady has a nice job as a botanist in the Exotic Garden in E-Block. It's where folks who've won the lottery like to host their children's birthday parties and where Governor Harding had his inauguration ceremony in January of 2067. He is currently running for a second term.

Cady says she is considering voting for him. I certainly will not. That fool of a man is part of the reason why I'm cleaning out the latrines every day while he has tea and scones off a silver platter in the gubernatorial palace.

"A decent person," Cady says, having met him once for five minutes. Anyone can be a decent person for five minutes. Why, I can be a decent person for up to six or seven minutes if I have to be. And I do have to be, because that's how much time I spend with Yuji Ishida, my boss, down in the boiler room at the start of each workday.

Yuji tells me what needs doing that day. I say, "Aye-aye, sir." Then off I go to scrub manure off the walls of the biofuel lab, all the while cursing Yuji Ishida and Governor Harding and even my dear Cady, depending on my mood.

My name is Herbert. Herbert Hoover Palminteri. I graduated from Vanderough University in 2044. And if it weren't for the scandal of '41, I'd be ambassador to Europa for all I know. But, fuck it all, I'm a janitor in A-Block on Mars.

CHAPTER 2

MY PARENTS NAMED ME Herbert Hoover Palminteri after the thirty-first president of the United States. President Herbert Hoover, a Republican from Iowa, served only one term before he was defeated in a landslide by Franklin Delano Roosevelt. President Hoover was responsible for the Hoover Dam. Some say he was also responsible for the Great Depression.

Go figure.

During his brief tenure as president of the United States from 1929 to 1933, Herbert Hoover supported prohibition and the efficiency movement. Prohibition forbade the sale and consumption of alcohol. The efficiency movement sought to eradicate waste in business and production. My father believed Herbert Hoover was a misunderstood genius of his time. So I inherited his name.

It would seem I also inherited his bad luck.

Bad luck. That's how I came to spend the bulk of my days scrubbing toilets and mopping floors.

Yesterday there was a chemical spill in the synthetics lab. Chemical spills are a nightmare to clean up. I pulled on my hazmat suit and set to work mopping up the mess with special antichemical slop. Meanwhile, the researchers were champing at the bit to get back into their lab, and Yuji Ishida was yelling at me like a dogsled driver: *Mush, mush!*

Yuji was not a gavelman. He landed his pitiful job the ordinary way: by getting low marks at university.

I usually had pretty good marks. I was never the best in the class, mind you, but I had to keep my grades up if I wanted to stay on the cross-country team. Not that I did get to stay on the cross-country team after what happened.

My event in college was the 5K. I could knock out 3.1 miles in fifteen minutes and six seconds. That's fast enough to get you noticed by the admissions board at Vanderough University but not fast enough to make you a captain of the team. The captain of the team was a tall, skinny boy named Leo Offredi—a fellow Italian.

My mother and father were Italian, so I identify as Italian, although I've never set foot on Italian soil in my life. Martian soil, yes. Italian soil, no. I had plans to travel all over Europe with one of my college roommates the summer of 2041. But things didn't go so well for us that year, and we never made it to Italy.

I'm getting off track. Where was I?

Oh, I made it into Vanderough University because I was a runner. In high school, I was the New York State titleholder in cross-country two years running. I had a 4:16 mile. I was a champ. A pro. A specimen to behold.

Those days are gone.

Today I'm lucky if I can make two laps around C-Pod, which is equivalent to a mile, or 1.6 kilometers. It takes me roughly twenty minutes, which is almost five times the time it would have taken me in the golden days of my youth.

The captain of the VU track team, Leo Offredi, was the real champion. He could knock out ten kilometers in twenty-seven minutes and seventeen seconds. He had a 4:06 mile. Now and then I see him running around C-Pod. We nod to each other politely, but I don't think he remembers me. I was a freshman when he was a senior. And he was the fastest boy on the team. So while the rest of us had our eyes trained on Leo Offredi's back, Leo Offredi might as well have been the only runner in the world. From his point of view, there wasn't another soul in sight.

The runners lived with the other athletes in Owens Hall, named after Samuel Owens, the founder of Vanderough University. As far as I know, Owens Hall is still home to the athletes at VU. It sits perched atop a hill overlooking the lacrosse field. I lived on the second floor at the top of a broad wooden staircase and shared a suite with three other boys: a basketball player named Jake Harrington, a swimmer named Lee

Knowles, and a golfer named Ling Ling Ng.

Jake the basketball player was a raging Republican. Like my father, he would vote for Garrett Dougherty in that November's election, and he believed that all the country's problems would be solved if only we did away with social welfare.

He'd say, "We're only enabling them!" when referring to things like food stamps and welfare checks. By "them" he meant poor people.

Jake also thought the US should build a wall along its border with Mexico. "A great big wall," he'd say. "Like the Great Wall of China. It should be visible from space."

Jake Harrington was a complete and utter asshole.

Lee Knowles was even worse. He didn't know *what* he believed. When Jake and I would get into it, Lee would sit nervously on the fence and say things like "You're both right."

Insufferable.

Ling Ling Ng was an international student from Beijing who didn't speak much English, so I never learned his political persuasion. He wasn't home often since he preferred to hang with other international students from China at the International Co-op on the Huntington Turnpike.

Incidentally, Ling Ling is now one of the foremost landscape architects on Mars, having designed the Sector 2 Promenade, Joshua Beach, and the Exotic Garden.

Cady says he is a visionary.

I say, "Dumb luck."

And it was dumb luck that landed me in a suite with Jake,

Lee, and Ling Ling that first year at VU. If I hadn't met Jake Harrington the raging Republican, I might never have been inducted into Scepter and Gavel.

* * *

I first heard about Scepter and Gavel in my second week at VU. Jake had invited me to a party at his older brother's co-op down on East Main Street. Main Street is one of the oldest streets in Bridgeport.

I ought to have said before that Vanderough University sits squarely on 128 acres of land just west of Beardsley Park in Bridgeport, Connecticut. The estate once belonged to a silent film actress named Hattie Howard Hunt who had made her living stripping naked for cameras in the early twentieth century. During the First World War, Hattie's films played on rotation at seedy theaters across the country, where men and sometimes women went to get their kicks for ten cents an hour.

Hattie was a notorious eccentric. At least that was how the *Bridgeport News* described her in 1926. Today she would probably be diagnosed with schizophrenia and prescribed antipsychotics and SSRIs. But back in 1926, Hattie was left to her own devices.

Hattie had a powerful suspicion that secret agents from the Soviet Union were out to get her. So she had her contractors build multiple manors upon the 128-acre property, thinking that she could somehow escape the Soviets by moving from house to house. And Hattie didn't just build ordinary manors. These were huge, confusing buildings with stairways leading to nowhere and doors that opened onto brick walls and long, winding corridors that looked like something out of an M. C. Escher drawing.

In total, Hattie Howard Hunt commissioned fourteen mansions. The last two went up in 1946, simultaneously, because Hattie was superstitious about the number thirteen. She lived a long life despite her declining mental health. She did not die until 1986, and then it was only because she stepped through a third-story door that led to nowhere. Well, I suppose you can say the door led to the rose garden, but only after a twenty-five-foot drop.

Kerplop.

After Hattie Howard Hunt died, the estate went to ruins.

Then in 2033, the buildings were restored and converted into classrooms and dormitories, and Vanderough University was born. Just like that.

So it was that I found myself walking down the hill from Owens Hall in September of 2040, a newly anointed freshman at VU, with Jake Harrington and Lee Knowles, all of us drunk as sailors, headed for a party at Jake's older brother's co-op. The co-op was called Wilde House after Oscar Wilde. And in the spirit of Oscar Wilde, it hosted an all-night rager at the start of term every year.

Freshmen were not usually invited to this exclusive event,

unless they had an older brother who lived at Wilde House, which Jake did.

We had started drinking in our suite at Owens Hall, and because none of us were very experienced with alcohol, we found ourselves wildly intoxicated before we'd even set foot out the door.

A pint of beer on Mars costs two credits. The exchange rate for one Martian credit is US $30.77, so drinking up here is an expensive habit. But back on Earth in 2040, beer flowed freely through the corridors of Owens Hall.

Hallelujah!

When we arrived at Wilde House, we encountered a huge boy in a black suit guarding the front door. His name was Surge, and he was a sophomore. It was his job to keep out the riffraff, like Saint Peter at the Pearly Gates of Heaven.

Standing outside we could hear the music thump, thump, thump.

"Names?" asked Surge.

We gave our names, and Surge checked a list on a clipboard.

"Okay," he said, and stepped aside.

Open sesame!

Suddenly the crowd swallowed us up. I was pushed one way. Jake and Lee were pushed another. And there I was alone in the mob, music thumping.

Thump, thump, thump.

While I was trying to worm my way back to Jake and Lee,

I came across the bar and ordered a vodka and soda. The next thing I knew I was sitting on a couch between two senior boys who were discussing with great vigor their most recent sexual conquests.

Apparently, the boy on my right had only yesterday shared his bed with two redheaded twins named Molly and Mike. The boy on my left wasn't impressed. He'd slept with Molly and Mike during his freshman year. He was more interested in telling the story of how he had made love to a librarian in the main stacks, in the fiction section, just behind Robert A. Heinlein and Joseph Heller.

The two boys didn't seem to notice me, and I was glad of it. The most exciting tale I could tell was about the time I made out with Sally Schwartz at her bat mitzvah and prematurely ejaculated into my shorts.

Finally the two senior boys got up to get more beer, and a lean, tall boy with a distinctive mustache took a seat on the couch. He looked at me, extended his hand, and introduced himself as Prescott Harrington.

"Harrington? Are you Jake's older brother?" I asked.

"That's right," said Prescott. "I suppose you're one of his friends."

"We're roommates," I said. "I'm Herbert."

"Tell me this, Herbert. Do you also think all the country's problems stem from social welfare? Do you think we should build a big wall along the border with Mexico?"

"Uh . . ."

"Go ahead," Prescott said. "Tell the truth. Are you a raging Republican like my dear little brother?"

"The opposite," I said.

"How do you mean?" Prescott asked.

"I canvassed for the Holden campaign."

Tamara Holden was the Democratic nominee for president that year.

"Aha! Well, that settles it." Prescott laughed. "Herbert, I think you're going to be a good influence on my little brother."

"Hmm," I said.

"I like you, Herby. I like you a lot." Prescott's breath smelled of whiskey.

"Thank you," I said.

"Speak of the devil!" Prescott stood. "Here's the little pip-squeak now!"

He was of course referring to Jake, who had just stumbled out of the crowd and into an armchair across from where we were sitting. Lee was with him.

"Jakey!" Prescott said. "What a charming friend you have."

Jake rolled his eyes. "Hi, Prescott."

Prescott went on. "We were just talking about you. Do you still believe that climate change is a hoax?"

Jake folded his arms across his chest. "I don't want to get into this right now, Pres."

"Why not? Your friend Herby here doesn't mind talking

politics." Then Prescott turned to me and said, "Do you think climate change is a hoax, Herbert?"

I shook my head.

"There! See?" said Prescott.

Jake snorted. "You're both drunk."

"C'mon, Jakey. We're just having a little fun."

"I gotta use the restroom," I said to break the tension.

"I'll go with you," said Lee.

We left Prescott and Jake to work out their brotherly differences on their own.

The line for the restroom wound like a snake through the kitchen and out onto the back patio. Two sophomore girls were in front of us in the queue. They were whispering back and forth. I could just make out what they were saying above the din of the party.

"I'm sure of it!" said the first girl.

"Scepter and Gavel? You really think so?" said the second girl.

"She disappeared in the middle of the night," hissed the first girl. "And when she got back the next day, she barely said a word about it. She'll never tell us straight out, but I'm sure of it."

"What would Scepter and Gavel want with Melissa?" said the second girl.

"She got top marks in all her classes. Don't they always pick the smartest kids?"

"I thought it was more about who you know."

The line moved forward and the girls' conversation shifted out of earshot.

I turned to Lee and asked, "What's Scepter and Gavel?"

"You've never heard of Scepter and Gavel?"

"No. What is it?"

"It's only the most notorious secret society in the country," Lee said, glancing around to see if anyone was listening. "They say members of Scepter and Gavel go on to become the most influential people on Mars."

"Hmm," I said.

"Yeah. Rumor has it that Governor Roswell was a gavel-man. And Andy Eaton, the media mogul. And Iris Crump, the architect."

"Those are some pretty big names," I said.

"Exactly," said Lee in a low whisper. "Gavelmen rule the planet."

The planet Lee was referring to, of course, was Mars, the red planet.

That was a long time ago. I think I ended up kissing a girl at that party, but I don't remember her name or what she looked like. Jake went home with a sophomore girl from Alpha Gamma Phi. Her name was Ursula Beal.

Lee, the nervous nelly that he was, went back to the dormitory shortly after our conversation. I found him snoring in bed when I crept in at three o'clock the following morning. Ling Ling was also there, snoring away.

I tried to sleep, but my head was spinning. I ended up down

the hall in the coed bathroom barfing my brains out in a toilet. And I remember thinking, *Thank god I don't have to clean toilets for a living.*

CHAPTER 3

THE WAY MY JANITORIAL schedule works is this: I get two days off for every seven I put in. Cady's schedule is a bit different. She gets one day off for every four she puts in. So it's rare to have a day off together.

Yesterday was one of those days.

We'd been looking forward to it for some time. Cady had plans for us to go down to Joshua Beach, which is really just a stretch of pavement on the east side of the big reservoir. You can't go in the water since we use it for drinking. But people like to sit on the pavement with their tops off and pretend they're at the ocean. It gets quite humid during the daytime when the sun beats down on the glass dome and water evaporates off the reservoir. But it's still better than having no beach at all.

However, we didn't get to go to Joshua Beach after all. Yesterday morning, a body was discovered in the residential pod next door to us—a young man named Adolf Dussel who worked over at city hall doing something related to the Martian census. He was only thirty-five.

Initial reports said he died of natural causes, but the police were here questioning Cady and me for several hours after the discovery. How well did we know Adolf Dussel? When was the last time we saw him? Now I hear the police are treating the incident as a homicide. Adolf's body has been taken to the coroner's office to be thoroughly examined for signs of foul play.

Cady says he probably had an aneurysm. Aneurysms are common on Mars due to the reduced gravity. But maybe it was a homicide like the police say. There has never been a murder on Mars. Crime on Mars is almost nonexistent. Probably because there's nowhere to hide.

Joshua Beach was closed by the time Cady and I were done with the police, so we went to the movies instead to see the latest flick sent up from Earth. It was about a deep-sea diver who sets out to find the bottom of the Mariana Trench, the deepest part of the ocean. When he gets to the bottom of the Mariana Trench, he finds a thriving metropolis of microbial life-forms that, when acting together, create a vast deep-sea network that behaves like a human brain. The deep-sea diver befriends the giant brain and together they find a way to communicate using Morse code.

The giant brain says it can detect things happening on the other side of the planet by reading the shifting water currents, which respond to shifting air currents, which respond to any movement anywhere on Earth. It says it is so sensitive that it can detect a snowflake falling upon a cherry blossom.

The deep-sea diver asks if it knows who won the most recent World Series.

The brain says yes and proves it by telling the deep-sea diver it was the Tampa Bay Rays.

And then the brain says it has a message for humanity. It says that all the human activity up on the ground resonates so loudly down in the Mariana Trench that the brain has a constant headache.

"Could you please make it stop?" says the brain.

The deep-sea diver, tasked with this message, returns to the surface to tell everybody what he has found.

Of course nobody believes the deep-sea diver. They all think he's gone off the deep end. Figuratively and literally. They send him to an institution, where he taps out a message in Morse code with his foot.

The message is this: "I'm sorry."

And then the deep-sea diver jumps out the fifth-story window.

I quite enjoyed the film. It speaks to the profound and often devastating impact humans have on other life-forms. Cady found it depressing. After the film, Cady said she was glad to be living on Mars, where she could be certain no other life-forms were suffering because of her.

That's a nice thought, but it isn't entirely true. We still depend heavily on Earth for supplies and fuel. Mars is responsible for at least some of the oil drilling in the Arctic Ocean. So we're not exactly blameless.

Incidentally, when she was just out of high school, Cady went on a cruise through the Arctic Ocean with her family. So she has seen the oil rigs that supply fuel to Mars with her very own eyes. Cady once described them as "beautiful." In fact, Cady grew up in Santa Barbara where, on any given day, she could look out over the ocean and see the Santa Barbara oil rigs at work. Cady says what she remembers most is the way the oil rigs twinkled at night, like little cities in the distance. She used to say that those oil rigs at night made her think of all the remarkable things human beings had achieved.

Now she feels foolish for thinking the oil rigs were beautiful. As a botanist, she knows exactly how badly life all over Earth has suffered thanks to humans' dependence on fossil fuels. Part of why Cady has come to Mars is to try to terraform the planet. She thinks she can save life on Earth by colonizing Mars. I say good luck.

A few of those old oil rigs still stand off the Santa Barbara coast, but they no longer twinkle. They have been devoid of life for many years now, having sucked the seabed dry long ago.

That is how I know the fuel we use here on Mars comes

from the Arctic Ocean—it's the only place left on Earth we haven't sucked dry.

The cruise: In the summer of 2040, Cady's family took a cruise through the Arctic Ocean. The ship set sail from Seattle and landed way over in New York City. The route the cruise ship took—usually referred to as the Northwest Passage—was once impassable due to heavy snow and ice. But ever since things started heating up all over the planet, the ice sheet that covers most of the Arctic Ocean has become as brittle as porcelain. Nearly any ship can get through nowadays.

Cady's family thought it would be nice to see the Arctic this way: by cruise ship. So they loaded onto a massive ocean liner called the *Pearl of the Sea*—even though it was more of a wrecking ball than a pearl—and set out to disturb what had once been one of the most pristine environs on Earth.

And it was while they were slicing through this once pristine environ that Cady met Paul O'Malley, a handsome graduate student from the University of North Carolina. Paul was studying economics in the hopes of one day becoming a professor at a prestigious Ivy League school.

Cady fell head over heels at once.

Paul O'Malley was what you might call a perfect catch. He was tall, handsome, smart as a whip, and Catholic. Cady's parents—the Pinkletons—were devout Catholics.

Paul was on vacation with his granny. Cady told him that she'd be attending Vanderough University in the fall, and Paul promised to stay in touch by phone and email and Skype and FaceTime and whatever else we had going on back in those days.

It was a match made in heaven. Destined to be. Except for one small thing: Paul was headed for an Ivy League school and Cady was headed for Mars.

So it was that when I met Cady Pinkleton in the fall of 2040, she was spoken for. I didn't stand a chance. I was a small, gangly freshman, still undeclared, and Paul was a tall, virile graduate student with a promising future.

Jake Harrington was having more luck. He and Ursula Beal, the girl he had gone home with after the Wilde party, hit it off right away. Ursula was a real groovy gal. She wore Birkenstocks on her feet and horn-rimmed glasses on her face. She didn't shave her legs or armpits. And she called herself a socialist. I have no idea how she and Jake managed to get along so well. Perhaps it was because both of them, for all their talk about what was right and what was wrong, really just wanted someone who disagreed with them.

Ursula was a year above us, and she was very popular on campus. That September she decided to run for student body president. Jake said he would support Ursula in her bid for presidency, but he would not vote for her. He would never vote for a socialist. Ursula was just fine with that. She didn't need Jake's vote to win. Later that month, she defeated her opponents with 58 percent of the student body vote.

At one point during her campaign, Ursula addressed the student body during the halftime show at a football game. Yes, we had a football team at Vanderough University: the Vanderough Voles. A vole is a small furry puffball—a relative of the mouse. A Vanderough Vole was pretty much the same thing. That is to say, our team was no good. Rotten. Lousy.

The starting quarterback was another Italian. Geraldo Gelatti was his name. But he was a real Italian. He had come all the way from Rome to be a Vanderough Vole and to have the crap kicked out of him every Saturday on live TV. Gelatti stood about five feet four inches on a good day. He was covered in hair from head to toe. He was missing a thumb—they said he lost it to a garbage disposal when he was twelve—so he couldn't catch worth beans. All he was good for was chucking the ball fifty yards downfield. It was up to whoever happened to be in the general vicinity of a throw to catch the ball, even if it was a member of the opposite team.

So there weren't many people attending the game that day when Ursula got up in front of everybody and said what she said. Ursula had the cockamamie idea that education should be free for all. And that is what she told the attendees at the homecoming rally.

"Education should be free," she said. "Do we want a bunch of illiterate nincompoops running the country or what? Everyone has a right to an education. Down with tuition bills!"

The crowd went wild.

Ursula was not a gavelman. Her mile time was eleven

minutes and thirteen seconds.

Geraldo Gelatti was not a gavelman either. His mile time was six minutes and seventeen seconds.

Ursula died of leukemia eight months later. While she convalesced in Bridgeport Hospital, Jake Harrington and I hid out in our little suite in Owens Hall, trying to avoid the media frenzy surrounding Freddy Euler's death.

Freddy Euler *was* a gavelman. His mile time was seven minutes and forty-five seconds.

If it hadn't been for Freddy's death, perhaps the Order of the Scepter and Gavel would still be one of the most powerful organizations in the solar system. But Freddy did die, and up went Scepter and Gavel in a puff of smoke.

CHAPTER 4

VANDEROUGH UNIVERSITY abuts Beardsley Park, designed in 1884 by Frederick Law Olmsted, the famous architect of Central Park in Manhattan and Prospect Park in Brooklyn. Beardsley Park was once the winter stomping ground for the Barnum and Bailey Circus. P. T Barnum used to promenade his animals through the park for exercise during the cold winter months. P. T. Barnum was a big name in town. He was even elected mayor of Bridgeport in 1875. Now there is a small zoo in the park—called Beardsley Zoo—that opened in 1922. Outside of Vanderough University, Beardsley Zoo is probably the most recognizable attraction in Bridgeport.

That's not saying much.

We have a small zoo here on Mars, too, but I'm not allowed anywhere near it thanks to my criminal record. Cady goes sometimes, mostly to observe the children. She has always wanted children. I remember her telling me so when we first arrived on Mars.

She said, "Herbert, let's put our name in the lottery straightaway. I want to have kids someday."

So every year we entered our names in the lottery. And every year my dear Cady was disappointed when we didn't win. Now our child-rearing years are past us and we don't even bother with the lottery.

Still, Cady gets a dreamy look on her face whenever I bring up anything to do with children. The zoo is probably the center of the world for children growing up on Mars. As with Bridgeport, there isn't much else to do. For two credits, Cady can get an annual pass.

Step right up and see the children!

When Cady and I were in college, the zoo in Beardsley Park wasn't much of a zoo. It wasn't much bigger than the zoo here on Mars, and its main attraction was a tired, old Amur tiger that suffered from arthritis. The tiger's name was Jinx.

Here is a list of Beardsley Zoo's other attractions:

A miniature horse.
Three white-tailed deer.
Two red pandas.
A giant anteater.
An Amur leopard.
A red wolf.

A bobcat.

Four Mexican wolves.

A Canada lynx.

A two-toed sloth.

A gray fox.

Six North American porcupines.

Four pale-faced saki monkeys.

Seven Chacoan peccaries.

A herd of llamas.

Five pygmy marmosets.

A maned wolf.

Eleven guinea hogs.

Three pronghorns.

Six red-rumped agoutis.

A black-and-gold howler monkey.

Twenty-three vampire bats.

Three San Clemente Island goats.

Fifteen black-tailed prairie dogs.

Fourteen domestic rabbits.

A herd of Dexter cattle.

A herd of sheep.

Two Goeldi's monkeys.

A Brazilian ocelot.

Three African pygmy goats.

Five golden lion tamarins.

Three river otters.

Six bison.

There were also a handful of birds, amphibians, insects, and reptiles. And Beardsley Zoo was home to the last functioning carousel in New England.

That's where I came into the picture. I worked weekends at the zoo, taking tickets for the carousel. Two dollars a ride.

I needed a job to help pay the tuition at VU.

Even though Mother and Father were loaded, they refused to pay my tuition in full. Father said I would value my education more if I had to pay for some of it with my own hard-earned cash. So Father put in 90 percent of the tuition each semester while I was expected to come up with the remaining 10 percent on my own.

The first thing I did upon arrival at Vanderough University was apply for jobs in the area. I was hoping to get something flashy, like an internship at an architecture firm or a temp job in a law office.

As it turned out, the only job I could secure given my limited experience was ticket-taker for the carousel at Beardsley Zoo. They said I wasn't even qualified to handle the cash register.

"Tear and toss," Geoffrey said to me, taking a ticket, tearing it down the middle, and tossing it into the trash bin. "That's your job."

Geoffrey was, for all intents and purposes, my boss. He was twenty-five years old. He attended Housatonic Community College. One of his canine teeth stuck straight out like a tiny pearly toothpick.

Geoffrey sold tickets for the carousel at a little booth next to where I collected them.

Once I had collected all the tickets and the riders had mounted their steeds, I would pull a lever and the music would start up and the horses would go round and round.

Whee!

I probably pulled that lever hundreds of times. But never once did I ride the carousel myself. That would have been un-professional.

Tear and toss. That was my job.

I always suspected that Geoffrey stole from the cash regis-ter. Every week he'd come in wearing some new, hip acces-sory, like a Rolex watch or Ray-Ban sunglasses, things he never should have been able to afford working sixteen hours a week at $13.00 an hour.

I worked eight hours a week at $12.45 an hour.

Minimum wage in Connecticut in 2040 was $12.45 an hour.

Geoffrey's mile time was nine minutes and seventeen sec-onds.

Last I heard, Geoffrey went off to St. Vincent's College to get his associate's degree in nursing. He texted me before I was sent up to show me a picture of his new Porsche. He was the only person from the zoo that would still talk to me after what happened.

What happened?

I'll tell you what happened: All hell broke loose.

And none of it would have happened had I only kept my big mouth shut. But the first thing I said after I was inducted into Scepter and Gavel was that I worked at Beardsley Zoo on the weekends.

I was concerned I wouldn't be able to balance my responsibilities as a gavelman with my duties at the zoo.

Turned out that wasn't a problem at all.

Everyone was thrilled to hear I worked at the zoo.

"Do *we* have a job for *you*," Prescott Harrington said.

Prescott Harrington was a gavelman. He wasn't just any gavelman. He was the Grand Pooh-bah, Master of Ceremonies, King Cobra, Maestro of Debauchery and Sin.

His mile time was four minutes and forty-eight seconds. He had competed in the mile in high school.

He was called King Cobra because the mascot of the secret society was a cobra.

Let me try to describe the coat of arms of the Order of the Scepter and Gavel for you.

Picture a king's scepter lying across a judge's gavel so that you get a capital X. Now picture that X flanked on each side by a writhing cobra. Now envision a jewel-encrusted crown atop the X. And below the X, the words *Fratres in Peccatum* etched across a narrow scroll. Finally, imagine the whole thing encircled by a wreath of thorns.

That's what the coat of arms looked like.

Fratres in Peccatum translates roughly to "Brothers in

Sin."

There were no cobras at Beardsley Zoo. However, there were several boa constrictors and a black rat snake with one eye named Blinkie.

I worked the noon-to-four shift on Saturdays and Sundays. The zoo always opened at 9:00 a.m. and closed at 4:00 p.m. The fellow who worked the earlier shift on weekends was named Lionel Dubois. He was a medical student at VU. He was not a gavelman. His mile time was five minutes and twelve seconds.

Lionel Dubois is Cady's gynecologist now. He's very successful. There is a waiting list a mile long to see Dr. Dubois. There are only three gynecologists on Mars, and Lionel Dubois is the best.

The population of Mars is 10,328. Correction: 10,327 after Adolf Dussel's death yesterday. There are 5,612 women on Mars. Dr. Dubois sees an average of 1,870 patients in a Martian year, which is 687 Earth-days long. That means he treats roughly three patients every Martian day, which is forty minutes longer than an Earth day.

Dr. Dubois is also the planet's only obstetrician, so he is responsible for delivering all the babies on Mars.

Whee!

Lionel Dubois worked his way through college. He came from a poor neighborhood in Los Angeles. His father was a car mechanic from Haiti and his mother was a grocer from

Compton. Lionel had to work seven days a week at the zoo in order to put himself through the medical school at VU.

"Some people have it harder than others," he used to say to me. "Your father is the CEO of GeneTech and rakes in millions a year, while my father is lucky if he makes enough to pay the rent."

This was never meant to make me feel bad. Lionel was simply stating a fact.

Now he says to me when I see him, "How fickle the fates are. I'm making eighty-five credits a week doing the easiest job in the world and you're mopping floors."

Again, he doesn't mean to make me feel bad. Lionel is simply stating the facts.

Lionel Dubois married a man named Brad Dauer. Brad is a different kind of doctor. He is a physicist and he works in A-Block where I clean toilets and mop floors. Brad Dauer handles radioactive waste for a living. Pod City is powered by a nuclear reactor. Waste from the nuclear reactor makes its way over to A-Block, where Brad Dauer pokes and prods it, hoping it'll do something interesting.

As far as I know, the only interesting thing nuclear waste has ever done is mutate cells.

I wear a special hazmat suit whenever I go in to clean Dr. Dauer's laboratory. I empty the contents of the trash bins into a special radiation-proof box. I stow the box on the back of my HG-46 dune buggy, and I drive out to a special disposal site. There a fellow named Frank Gutierrez takes the waste deep into an underground facility, where it will live for tens of thousands of years.

Nuclear waste can remain dangerous to living organisms for up to one hundred thousand years. However, without the nuclear reactor, Pod City wouldn't be able to support 10,327 human lives. We can only get by on so much crude oil from the Arctic Ocean.

That's the way of it.

We just have to hope that Frank Gutierrez can hide the nuclear waste well enough so that future generations of Martians cannot find it.

Incidentally, the results of the autopsy performed on Adolf Dussel's corpse came in today. It turns out young Adolf died of radiation poisoning.

Adolf Dussel should never have had access to radioactive material. He was a paper-pusher in the offices of the Martian Census Bureau. He should never have suffered from anything more than a paper cut.

The authorities suspect foul play.

"One thing is clear," police chief Marisa Gringold told the newspaper today, "Adolf Dussel came into contact with some highly radioactive material before he kicked the bucket."

"What a tragedy," Cady said over breakfast. "Do you think

they'll ever find out who did it?"

She wasn't asking me. She was on speakerphone with Renata Sachs, the rabbi at Temple Beth Hillel over in E-Block.

"How can they not find out who did it?" Renata replied. "There are only ten thousand people on this planet. Surely they'll be able to sort the killer out in due time."

"From your lips to God's ears," Cady said.

Cady grew up Catholic but converted to Judaism in her third year of college. She says Judaism resonates more with her.

I'm an atheist, as were my parents, so none of it resonates with me.

Sometimes Cady can be borderline offensive because she tries to use common Yiddish idioms in everyday conversations, as though she'd grown up hearing such things around the house. She did not grow up hearing such things around the house.

Some of Cady's favorite sayings:

"If the rich could hire the poor to die for them, then the poor would make a very nice living."

"All is not butter that comes from a cow."

"However sweet love may be, you can't make a stew out of it."

"He was Jewish," Renata said, referring to Adolf Dussel. "He came to temple every now and then. Do you remember him? Skinny, tall, not much to look at, but they say he had brains."

"Such a shame," Cady said.

"Indeed," said Renata. "Since he has no family on Mars, his closest friends have invited us to sit shiva with them tomorrow evening. You and Herbert should come."

"Of course."

Cady looked at me out of the corner of her eye as if to say *We're going, whether you like it or not.*

I buried my face in my tablet.

After she got off the phone, Cady wanted to tell me everything she and Renata had talked about, even though I had heard every word of their conversation.

"They're sitting shiva for Adolf Dussel tomorrow," Cady recited. "We should go."

I nodded my assent.

"Good," she said. "God help us rise to our feet; fall we can do on our own."

CHAPTER 5

THAT FIRST SEMESTER at VU, I enrolled in the maximum number of courses, hoping to get my breadth requirements out of the way. Everyone at VU had to take Planetary Physics in their freshman year. And Martian Horticulture. And Interplanetary Law.

The university also required us to dabble in history, literature, philosophy, and art. Something about being well rounded. Like it or not, I found myself in Ancient Philosophy that first semester with a professor named Edward Pham.

Edward, or Eddy as he liked to be called, immigrated to the US from Vietnam at the age of fourteen, leaving his parents, siblings, and friends behind. Eddy explained that his family wanted a better life for their eldest son, so they had pooled together all their money in order to buy him a plane ticket to Los Angeles.

Eddy enrolled in high school in Glendale, California. Nobody knew he was all alone in the world, toughing it out on his own. He worked weekends tutoring students in preparation for the SATs. That was how he managed to afford to eat and pay the rent.

Now, Eddy told our class, he was a successful professor and he could afford to send money back home to support his family.

Why he thought it pertinent to share all this with his students, I do not know. But we certainly didn't want to disappoint Professor Pham after a story like that, so we all worked twice as hard in Ancient Philosophy. As Socrates once said, "Employ your time in improving yourself by other men's writings so that you shall come easily by what others have labored hard for."

That semester, I also enrolled in Intro to Structural Analysis and Intro to Design Engineering. I planned to become a civil engineer.

Not to be. Not to be.

By the end of the first two weeks of classes, I was in over my head with coursework. Plus I had cross-country practice every morning at six. Plus competitions. And I had my shifts at the zoo on the weekends.

Jake Harrington laughed at me whenever I came home from a long day looking haggard and overwhelmed.

"Socrates got you down?" Jake would ask.

"The unexamined life is not worth living," I would retort, even if I didn't quite believe the words coming out of my mouth. Jake was probably the best example of the unexamined life, and he seemed pretty happy. Jake did only enough to get by, getting straight Cs on his midterm report card. He claimed he was injured, so he didn't go to basketball practice anymore. And his favorite pastime was following the 2040 election on Fox News.

I couldn't afford to get straight Cs. My parents would cut me off. They didn't believe in wasting their money on an underappreciated education. So appreciate my education I did. I appreciated it so much I eked out a 3.67 on my first-semester report card.

I'm no dummy.

I managed to get a 3.67 even though I was racing the 5K and working at the zoo every weekend. I managed to get a 3.67 even though I was enrolled in six rigorous classes. I managed to get a 3.67 even though I was inducted into the Order of the Scepter and Gavel.

Yes. That fall I was tapped to become a member of the famous secret society.

Why me?

I'm pretty sure it had everything to do with Prescott Harrington, Jake's older brother.

After the Wilde House party, I ran into Prescott several times around campus. Prescott was a recreational runner, and I'd catch him on the track some mornings, doing laps. He was in decent shape, but I could lap him pretty easily in the 5K. The third time I did this, Prescott stopped me.

"Hey, Herb! Wait up!" he called to me as I ran by.

"Hi, Prescott," I said, slowing to a jog. "What's up?"

"Run with me for a lap or two," he said.

"Uh, okay."

I have to admit, I was totally mesmerized by Prescott Harrington. I had been ever since the night of the Wilde House party. Prescott was a senior. He talked politics openly and freely, he could run, and he had the coolest mustache I'd ever seen.

So I was thrilled when he singled me out and asked me to run with him. My coach would have my head for it, but who was I to deny Prescott Harrington anything?

"I gotta ask you," Prescott said. "How's Jakey doing? I'm afraid he isn't getting out enough."

"He's fine," I said. "He watches a lot of Fox News. But other than that I think he's compos mentis."

Prescott laughed. "Well, that's being generous."

"He has a girlfriend," I said. "She's a socialist."

"No kidding!"

"Yeah," I said. "They're always fighting."

"At least he's socializing," Prescott said. Then, after a pause: "Where are you from, Herb?"

And like a kid with a schoolyard crush, I spilled all the details of my upbringing right there on the track.

I told Prescott that I grew up in Manhattan on the Upper West Side. I was an only child. Like it or not, my father was a Democrat turned Republican. He had grown up poor but had made a fortune when Google invested in his startup, GeneTech. Now he lived in a penthouse on Broadway and 93rd with my recluse mother, and they were both planning to vote for Garrett Dougherty come November.

"A Democrat turned Republican?" Prescott asked.

"Yeah, once he made all his money, he realized he didn't want to give any of it away."

"Asshole," Prescott said.

I thought it was so cool that he could call my father an asshole. I echoed the sentiment, hoping I would sound just as cool.

"Asshole," I said.

"But that's pretty neat that your dad is the CEO of GeneTech."

I went on to explain about the second house in the Catskills, the private jet, the vacations in Aruba. I could tell I had gotten Prescott's attention—and I so wanted to impress him.

When I finished telling him about the dinner my father had hosted for a prominent senator from New York, Prescott was practically drooling.

"You've got some serious connections."

Then my coach came out of the weight room and started barking orders at me. I took my leave of Prescott and ran off to be with the rest of the team. Prescott peeled off the track and headed down the path toward the dormitories.

Later that day, I was tapped.

Tapping is what secret societies do when they want to recruit a new member. They sneak up on the unsuspecting recruit and perform some sort of ritual or ceremony that indicates their desire to have the new recruit in their club. Usually some amount of humiliation is involved.

I was tapped in broad daylight, which was unusual. Typically the tappers come at night and steal recruits from their beds.

Not this time.

They came for me at 2:00 p.m. I was crossing the quad with Lee Knowles, heading for the dormitories. Suddenly, I noticed several shadowy figures emerging out of the shade of an elm tree. There were six or seven of them, cloaked from head to toe in black.

The Grim Reaper–like figures fanned out across the quad. They were moving quickly, some of them running at a clipped pace. Before I knew it, they had encircled me and Lee and were closing in on us like a lasso being tightened.

"What the hell?" I said.

"It's them!" Lee cried out.

Then they were upon us. Lee was lost in a flurry of black robes and I was lifted from the ground and draped over the shoulder of the largest Grim Reaper.

I was so dumbfounded I didn't even think to fight back.

All of the Grim Reapers were chanting, "Unus ex nobis. Unus ex nobis."

I had gone to private school. I knew enough Latin to understand.

"One of us. One of us."

People all over the quad were laughing and pointing. Either they knew all about Scepter and Gavel, or else they thought it was all some big prank. Either way, nary a face registered even the slightest trace of alarm as I was carried off into the shadows of Moses Hall.

What happened to Lee?

Lee was left crouching on the lawn with his hands over his head.

The Grim Reapers carried me halfway across campus, all the while chanting, "Unus ex nobis. Unus ex nobis."

I had dropped my book bag somewhere in all the commotion. I don't know why, but I didn't think to call for help. Everyone we passed looked amused, so I didn't get the sense that I was in any real danger.

We approached a large church-like structure. There was an imposing iron door in the front. The rest of the building was impenetrable. It was one of Hattie Howard Hunt's original fourteen houses. I'd noticed the building before, on my way to and from classes, but I'd never bothered to learn what it was for. I noted, however, that it had no windows, which didn't surprise me because most of the houses built by Hattie

Howard Hunt had no windows. Soviet spies, remember?

"Welcome to the Tomb," said one of the Grim Reapers. It was a woman's voice.

She pulled out a large vintage key and inserted it into the iron door. The lock turned with a clang and the door swung open.

In we went, my hooded friends and I.

Only after my captors had set me back on my feet did I have a chance to look around. The room was cozy, no bigger than an average household parlor. There were beat-up old armchairs and couches scattered about the room. The only light came from a series of reading lamps that rested on side tables and bookshelves. The ceiling was high. A small brick fireplace sat in the opposite wall, its firebox dark and empty.

A plush Persian rug lay draped across the cold stone floor. A coat rack stood on one side of the entrance. A four-paneled Japanese screen stood on the other.

The room was full of Grim Reapers. There had to be at least two dozen of them. They were all standing ominously in the shadows.

The woman spoke again. "Herbert Hoover Palminteri, we summon you today to join the sacred Order of the Scepter and Gavel."

I stood there, bewildered.

The woman went on. "Do you accept our invitation?"

What was I supposed to do? Turn them down? I'd been told this was the most prestigious secret society in the country.

Lee Knowles had said that membership guaranteed future success on Mars. Even I knew enough to know that it was a rare honor to be selected. Surely I had to say yes.

I nodded.

"Unus ex nobis," chanted the Grim Reapers in unison.

"There are several initiation rites you must perform before your induction is complete," said the woman. "The first challenge awaits you."

The woman pointed to the Japanese changing screen. There, draped over the panels of the screen, were a pair of baggy clown pants, suspenders, and a polka-dotted shirt.

"Put those on."

The nearest Grim Reaper shoved me behind the changing screen before I could object.

I stripped down to my underwear and stepped into the big yellow clown pants. I slipped into the polka-dotted shirt and was just hoisting the suspenders over my shoulders when the changing screen was pulled away. Then one of the hooded figures moved toward me, popped a red ball on my nose, and pulled a fluffy rainbow wig down over my ears.

Another hooded figure rifled through the pile of clothes I had left on the stone floor. He produced my cell phone, wallet, and keys to my dormitory.

"You'll be needing these," he said, handing the items to me. I slipped them into the pockets of the baggy yellow pants.

"Now put on the shoes," commanded the woman. She indicated a huge pair of floppy clown shoes. I slipped them on over my bare feet.

"Follow me."

The cloaked woman led me up a set of spiraling stairs. The other Grim Reapers stayed down below. We came to a door just tall enough to fit a small child. The woman opened the door, and the autumn sun burst through, illuminating the patch of stone where I stood. The woman beckoned for me to step through.

I crouched to fit through the door and found myself on a narrow ledge three stories above the ground. A wooden beam no wider than my shoulders stretched across the space between the Tomb and the neighboring building. A door stood ajar at the opposite end. This strange bridge between the manors had to be another of Hattie Howard Hunt's senseless constructions. The catwalk had no rails or handholds of any kind.

The rest of the cloaked figures had gathered on the ground below. They started to chant.

"Cross! Cross! Cross!"

I wasn't about to risk my life for a stupid secret society. But when I turned around to climb back inside, I found the miniature door closed and locked.

"Cross! Cross! Cross!"

I stood frozen on the narrow ledge, looking across the abyss at the opposite door. It was my only escape. I had to cross.

I stepped onto the catwalk and teetered. The giant clown shoes flopped over the sides of the narrow beam. I extended my arms to catch my balance. *Take it one step at a time*, I told myself. Down below, the Grim Reapers were chanting.

"Cross! Cross! Cross!"

I hesitated, one foot on the beam and one foot on the ledge. I was scared to move.

The chanting grew louder. I felt like I had to lose my mind if I wanted to take the next step. But eventually I did just that. I don't remember the rest of the crossing. I just know I made it across somehow. There was another cloaked figure waiting for me just inside the other door. I followed the cloaked figure down an identical set of spiral stairs and into an empty parlor.

"Further instructions are forthcoming," said the cloaked figure. "Do not tell anyone that you have been tapped."

Then he shoved me out the front door.

The chanting figures had vanished. I was alone on the stoop of the neighboring building. The big clock atop Moses Hall read half past two. I waited a few minutes, thinking something else was going to happen. Then it dawned on me that this was it. I had passed the first challenge. Now it was up to me to get back to my dormitory looking like a clown.

I took one step and then another. The unwieldy clown shoes flap-flapped on the concrete. The suspenders made the baggy yellow pants ride up my ass. Students making their way across the campus looked up as I waddled by. I didn't make eye contact. I hoped no one would recognize me under the wig.

It took me fifteen minutes to get back to Owens Hall. The

sun was out that day, and sweat had soaked through my shirt and trousers. I entered the dormitory and darted up the stairwell to my suite.

The worst embarrassment was still to come. Right inside the door, sitting at their desks, were Jake Harrington, Lee Knowles, and Ling Ling Ng.

In I burst, a bedraggled buffoon.

"What the . . . ?" said Jake.

"Don't ask," I said, trying to act casual.

"You've been tapped!" Lee cried out.

"No I haven't," I said.

"Yes. I saw them carry you off. The Order of the Scepter and Gavel."

I couldn't help that Lee had witnessed the kidnapping. They'd taken me in broad daylight. But I knew I had to heed the gavelman's warning: Don't tell anyone.

I decided the best response was no response. I pretended not to hear.

"No way," Jake said. "Not our boy Herbert?"

I disappeared into the bedroom I shared with Lee and stripped off the clown costume. Lee and Jake appeared in the doorway.

"He's definitely been tapped," Lee said.

"I don't know what you're talking about," I said.

"Then why in God's name are you dressed like *that*?"

"None of your business," I said.

"Where are your real clothes?" Lee asked.

I remained stoic as I pulled on a pair of jeans.

"Why did they choose you?" Jake was frowning.

I didn't answer. I drew a T-shirt over my head.

"I have your book bag," Lee said, pointing to the leather satchel just inside the door.

"I can't believe Scepter and Gavel tapped you," Jake said.

I plopped down on my bed and picked up *The Republic* by Plato.

When Jake and Lee saw that I wasn't going to fess up, they both ambled back into the common room and resumed their studies.

Later that evening, I heard the television come on. Jake was watching the latest on Fox News. Apparently, Tamara Holden, the Democratic candidate for president of the United States, had been caught on tape picking a wedgie at a fund-raising event.

So we both had wedgies that day.

Go figure.

CHAPTER 6

OUR POD ON MARS is about the size of a small studio apartment. We don't have running water, so we have to do all our business down the hall in a communal bathroom. Since we eat in a mess hall with the rest of the residents in C-Pod, we don't have a kitchen either. Our little space is occupied by several chests of drawers containing everything we kept from our former lives, a full bed that Cady and I share, two nightstands with lamps, a television set, an air filter to suck up the Martian dust, a couch that is covered with dirty clothes, and a small wooden chair.

Cady and I spend most of our free time in the bed. From there we have a clear view of the television. And that's what we spend most of our free time doing: watching television. We never get anything current, mind you. We can't watch the news or sports in real time. Every week or so, Houston sends up the most recent films or television shows for us to stream on our tiny television sets.

Did I mention the television is small?

Everything is small on Mars. It cost a pretty penny to get a couch in here.

We each have our own tablets for computing purposes, and we're connected to the Martian intranet, which is like the internet but only for Martians. So we can email and chat with other Martians in real time on our tablets. But if you want to send a message to Earth, it first has to go through central command, which then transmits the message back to mission control in Houston, Texas. From there the message is delivered wirelessly to the desired recipient almost anywhere on Earth.

This process is known as earthloading. The delay time can range anywhere from four to twenty-four minutes one way. So it can take up to an hour to hear back from anyone on Earth—and that's if we can get a signal to Earth at all. Every two years or so, we experience a solar conjunction during which Earth and Mars are on opposite sides of the sun. During that time, signals get warped and data is lost so that messages don't get through.

The solar conjunction lasts a few weeks.

As it happens, yesterday marked the first day of the solar conjunction. All earthloading has been suspended for the next fourteen days. That means news of Adolf Dussel's death has not yet reached mission control back in Houston.

It will cause quite the sensation when it does.

FIRST HOMICIDE ON MARS! the papers will read.

Our crime unit is very small and unequipped to handle a murder case, so communication with Earth will be essential to solving the mystery.

That gives the perpetrator two weeks' lead time to cover their tracks.

Coincidence?

Says Cady: "There are no coincidences in murder."

Incidentally, Mars and Earth were in solar conjunction the week I was tapped for Scepter and Gavel. Not that it mattered to me then. I didn't know anyone on Mars yet. Everyone I wanted to talk to lived on the same planet as me. What did I care if I couldn't get a message through to Mars?

Lee, however, was distraught. His older sister was in the hospital on Mars. She had been admitted under mysterious circumstances. Diana Knowles worked in the biochemistry lab in A-Block—I should say she *works* in the biochemistry lab. She is still there now. I have the privilege of cleaning up her shit.

Just before the solar conjunction back in 2040, Lee received a message from Diana:

> In the hospital. Will know more after the lab tests. Try
> not to worry.

Telling Lee not to worry is like telling a fish not to swim. Worrying comes so naturally to Lee, Diana might as well have told Lee that she was already dead in the ground.

Since Diana Knowles still works in the biochemistry lab, I don't need to tell you that she turned out okay. She just needed to have her appendix removed, a standard procedure. But we didn't know that at the time of the solar conjunction, and we wouldn't know anything for a couple of weeks. In the meantime, Lee was inconsolable.

It didn't help that later that week, Jake burst into our suite wearing the black-and-white uniform of a French maid, complete with feather duster. His face was beet red. It was clear he had been running.

"You too?" Lee cried. "I can't believe it."

Lee had deduced, as had I, that Jake had been tapped for Scepter and Gavel. At the time, it seemed like quite the coincidence. And we were stupid enough not to put two and two together. We'd both been tapped thanks to Jake's older brother, Prescott Harrington, who, unbeknownst to us at the time, was the Grand Pooh-bah of Scepter and Gavel. The Master of Ceremonies. The King Cobra. The Maestro of Debauchery and Sin.

Jake was no good at keeping a secret.

"Yeah," he said. "I'm in!"

Lee threw up his arms and said, "I guess I'm just a nobody. A nothing. A zero!" Then he stormed into the bedroom and slammed the door.

Lee should consider himself lucky. If he *had* been tapped,

then he would have been caught up in the scandal of '41, and instead of being Governor Harding's chief of staff, which he is now, he'd be a janitor like me or a plumber like Jake.

Things were never the same with Lee after that. He stayed clear of Jake and me, spending the majority of his time in the library studying interplanetary law. He wanted to become a lawyer. And he did. He was a very successful lawyer for a while. But he quit his practice when Frank Harding asked him to join his gubernatorial campaign in 2065.

Lee has never been particularly political, but he knows how much Jake and I hate Frank Harding, and I think his joining the campaign was his way of getting even with us all these years later. Now Lee is considered the second most influential man on Mars. He isn't particularly outspoken, and he shies away from the limelight, but everybody knows he has Governor Harding's ear.

I haven't spoken to Lee in twenty years. I went to him for some lawyerly advice back in 2050. My father had just died, and I needed help sorting out the will. My mother had died five years earlier, and I assumed I was next in line to inherit my father's fortune.

Not to be. Not to be.

Lee obligingly looked over my father's will and—with a hint of glee in his voice—informed me that there was nothing he could do. The will was ironclad. Foolproof. Impenetrable. My father had left me nothing. And that was that.

All of that money. Lost.

Where did it go? I'll tell you.

A fortune in the amount of $523 million went to a person I had never heard of before, a child named Wesley Krall.

Who was he? I'll tell you.

My father used to frequent a brothel called the Horse and Pony. There he had a favorite lady friend named Martha Mary Mae Krall. In 2045, one year after I was sent up, Martha Mary Mae Krall gave birth to Wesley Krall, my father's bastard son.

This was all in the will.

My father stipulated that the money be put aside in a trust in Wesley's name. Wesley was born the same year my mother died. In fact, he was born two days after my mother's death of a stroke.

You do the math.

Wesley was not even five years old when he inherited $523 million. He was set for life. Martha Mary Mae Krall gave up sex work and moved into the penthouse on Broadway and 93rd. That, too, had been left to Wesley.

Martha Mary Mae sent Wesley to the best schools in New York—first the Dalton School on 89th Street, then to Columbia University on 116th Street. At least that's what Delia says in her letters.

Delia Styles was my nanny growing up. She stayed on to take care of my mother after I left for college. And she stayed on to look after Wesley after my father died. She's been in the family for forty-eight years, if you can call Martha Mary Mae Krall and her bastard son family.

Delia sends me letters from time to time. She is the only person left on Earth who misses me. She was like a second mother to me. In fact, she was more like an only mother to me. My real mother didn't have it together enough to take care of me growing up. She suffered from obsessive-compulsive disorder, which led her to believe that she was going to kill me in my sleep. So she stayed clear of me during my entire childhood.

My mother had a form of obsessive-compulsive disorder called harm OCD. She was plagued with thoughts of harming others. She couldn't drive for fear of running someone over; she couldn't go out for fear of pushing someone into oncoming traffic; and she couldn't be near me for fear of stabbing me with a kitchen knife.

So Delia Styles cared for me as a mother would: bathing me, feeding me, tucking me in at night. Delia is sixty-six years old. She started caring for me when she was eighteen.

She is Nigerian American.

Martha Mary Mae Krall is fifty-five years old.

She is Australian American.

Wesley Krall is twenty-five years old.

He is American American.

Here is Delia's most recent letter, beamed up just before the solar conjunction:

Dear Baby Boy,

I hope you and Cady are well. I'm doing just fine. My arthritis has been flaring up due to the unseasonable cold. The house here is lonely. No more children running around. Ms. Krall is fine. She is strong as an ox.

Wesley just finished his MBA at Georgetown. He's going to work for GeneTech. They hired him straight out of the program. It's no wonder. He is smart as a whip. It's a shame you never had a chance to meet him.

I know you are bitter about how things turned out. But I promise that Wesley is a very deserving recipient of your father's charity.

It was only fair that your father try to put things right after what he'd done, betraying your mama like that and bringing a helpless child into the world with a sex worker for a mother.

You had a good education anyway. Your father did right by you, too, even if he left you out of his will.

Best not to dwell on such things.

Love,
Delia

I will form my reply after the solar conjunction. It will go something like this:

Dearest Delia,

Cady and I are well. We would be much better if we had $523,000,000.

Yours,
Herbert

Delia gets my sense of humor. She will not take offense to my curt reply. She can be sweet as a dove, Delia, but her life hasn't been easy either. She knows what it's like to be bitter.

Delia was the child of a sex worker. She never knew anything about her father except that he was a Nigerian national. Delia grew up with her mother in East Harlem. She was often at home when her mother had gentleman visitors. With all the men coming and going, Delia had to make the best of things on her own.

She was sexually assaulted thrice. Once when she was only nine, and again when she was fifteen. Both men had threatened to slit her throat if she didn't comply.

She complied.

When she was eighteen, a man tried to rape her on the subway as she was coming back from a friend's house in the wee hours of the morning. This time she didn't comply.

Delia snapped his penis. *Snap!*

That was it for Delia. She'd had enough. So she threw back her shoulders and made her way to the Upper West Side, where she got work sweeping floors in a beauty parlor.

That's where my mother met Delia.

Delia came to work for my mother straightaway. Mother said she liked Delia's spirit and could tell a good egg from a rotten one any day. Delia was a good egg.

So they fixed up a room for her at the back of the penthouse and set her to work cleaning and cooking. I came along about a month later. The rest is history.

Delia still lives in that same room at the back of the penthouse on Broadway and 93rd. After she came to live with my parents, she never saw her mother again.

Good riddance, she says.

"To move the world we must move ourselves." That's Socrates.

"The apple doesn't fall far from the tree, but it can roll for miles." That's Cady.

CHAPTER 7

WE SAW LESS and less of Lee Knowles as summer turned to autumn. The trees changed to gold, and cool breezes sent leaves dancing about the quad. It was October 8, 2040, the day of the first presidential debate between Democrat Tamara Holden and Republican Garrett Dougherty, when I got a note under my door.

Dear Sir Herbert:

As you may know, the quarterback of the Vanderough Voles is a young man by the name of Geraldo Gelatti. He wears a silver cross on a chain around his neck. It is his good luck charm, and he will not go anywhere without it. Your next task is to retrieve the silver cross by any means necessary. You have until Friday, whence, should you wish to become a member of our society, you shall present the cross to the Order at midnight in front of the statue of Samuel Owens on Memorial Hill.

Yours,
S&G

The note came in a red velvet envelope with a wax seal bearing the Order's coat of arms. The message was scrawled in thin, slanted handwriting on a piece of folded stationery, also bearing the coat of arms. I carefully returned the note to its envelope.

Geraldo Gelatti was a senior. I didn't know him. I didn't know anybody else who knew him. He was about as far removed from my circle of friends as a person could be.

I considered walking up to Gelatti in the dining hall and simply asking for the cross, but there was no way that was going to work. If Gelatti wore the cross around his neck for luck, then it was highly improbable that he would hand it over willingly.

It was Monday now, so I had exactly five days to figure things out. But the more I thought about it, the more I realized how hard it would be to slip a necklace off a living, breathing person without him knowing it.

I'd have to come up with a plan.

That night, Jake held a viewing party for the first presidential debate in our suite. The debate was to be a two-hour affair in the format of a town hall, with invited guests sitting on the sidelines, questions at the ready. Jake was in the Republican Club—the second-largest organization on campus after the Asian American Association—so he had invited several numbskulls over to watch the debate with him.

Henceforth I will refer to Republicans as numbskulls.

He also invited Ursula Beal, his hippie girlfriend, for good measure.

Vanderough University wasn't a particularly conservative institution. In fact, the vast majority of students on campus identified as progressive. That's how dear old Ursula Beal the socialist could win the class presidency in such a landslide. But where there is a thriving liberal culture, there is apt to be a mob of numbskulls throwing bottles and causing a ruckus. The Republican Club at VU was so robust back in those days because every single numbskull on campus was in it. And there were a lot of numbskulls on campus, despite being in the minority.

The presidential debate was a big deal. For one thing, the candidates were expected to discuss the recent terrorist attack in Milwaukee. A man had run several people over at a farmers' market with a moving van.

The moving van was rented from a local U-Haul. It had not been used for moving. Someone had rented a moving van for the sole purpose of mowing down pedestrians.

The attack had taken place two days earlier, a Saturday, when the farmers' market was in full swing. Eighteen people were killed, twenty-nine more were injured.

The thing that finally stopped the moving van? A watermelon stand.

The driver exited the vehicle and began stabbing the nearest passersby with a hunting knife.

Local police shot him dead two minutes later.

The terrorist was a white American who identified as a neo-Nazi. His Facebook page was peppered with deep state conspiracy theories and calls for violence.

The media labeled him a lone wolf.

The candidates at that night's debate were expected to address the recent spike in "lone wolf" attacks in the US. Jake sided with Republican Garrett Dougherty, who called for increased funding for police, more civilians with guns, and tighter security at large-scale events. I sided with Democrat Tamara Holden, who called for increased funding for mental health care, fewer civilians with guns, and stricter guidelines for hate speech on social media.

Tamara Holden believed mental health care should be free for all.

My therapist on Mars is a woman named Paula Cuevas. Paula believes mental health checkups should be conducted annually on all people in the US regardless of color or creed. She says that she never knew a person that wasn't a little bit crazy.

If you are planning on living on Mars, you better get yourself a therapist. There's no way the mind can function normally up here.

The first question from the audience went something like this: "If elected president of the United States, how are *you* going to keep our children safe from the threat of radicalized terrorists, particularly lone-wolf attackers?"

If I remember correctly, Garrett Dougherty pivoted from neo-Nazis to Islamic extremists. His response went something like this: "It's time Muslim communities held their own accountable. And how do you hold someone accountable? You let them know you're watching them, that's how! As I've said before, we'd be living in a hell of a lot safer world if we had a Muslim registry. The terrorists need to know we're watching them."

And Tamara Holden's response went something like this: "It's not Muslim extremists who are responsible for sixty-five percent of the attacks on American soil. It's white Christian men. We are a great nation made up of great people from all backgrounds. If people had proper access to mental health care, then we could combat the radicalization of our population. Medication and therapy are underutilized in today's advanced society. Let experienced mental health professionals do what they do best: help people who are desperate to be helped."

From there the debate devolved into a lot of quibbling over semantics and some pretty innocuous name calling. For example, Dougherty called Holden "naïve" to think terrorists would sign up for therapy, and Holden said Dougherty was a "first-class ass" for equating Muslims with terrorists.

At the end of the debate, Jake was sure his man Dougherty had won. However, Ursula was equally sure that Holden had made the better showing. There was a lot of bickering. Some innocuous name calling. And Ursula was out the door, slamming it in Jake's face.

The rest of our guests took Ursula's dramatic exit as a cue to get out of there lickety-split. And by a quarter to nine, Jake and I were the only people left in the suite.

"Hey, Herbert," Jake said, turning off the television. "I've been meaning to ask you something."

"What's up?"

Jake went into his bedroom and withdrew a red velvet envelope just like mine.

"Did you get one of these?" he asked.

"Yeah," I said. "Just today."

"Does yours say anything about a silver cross?" Jake asked.

Somehow I wasn't surprised to discover that Jake's note contained the exact same assignment as mine. We lived together. Naturally, the Order would expect us to work together.

After comparing notes, Jake asked, "What's your plan?"

"I haven't got one," I said.

"Well," said Jake, "I say we do this thing together. It's no use both of us going after that cross all on our own."

"Do you have any ideas?" I asked.

"I have one."

The football team practiced three hours every day in the late afternoon. Jake had been a couple of times to watch the team run drills. He was a nut for football, and even though they were crap, he supported the Vanderough Voles through thick and thin.

After practice, all the players would head into the locker room, shower up, and go their separate ways. Jake thought that if we could get into the locker room and slip something into Gelatti's water, we'd have a chance of rendering him unconscious.

"Then we can just grab the cross and go!"

This seemed highly unethical.

"What are you going to put in his water?" I asked incredulously.

"A roofie," Jake said, looking proud of his cunning.

"Where are you going to get a roofie?" I asked.

"I know a guy," Jake said.

Jake was a notorious pothead, so of course he knew a guy. However, getting high on pot was one thing. Drugging an unsuspecting victim was another.

"I don't know," I said.

"Sure!" said Jake. "It'll be easy. We just have to figure out which water bottle is his, slip him the roofie, and trail him until he passes out. Then the necklace is ours. No sweat."

I don't know why, but Jake's confidence in the plan was

reassuring. I made every objection I could think of, and for each objection, Jake shot back a reason why I needn't worry. By the time Lee walked in the door at 11:00 p.m. shouldering his book bag and looking weary, Jake had me convinced.

"What are you two talking about?" Lee asked, placing his book bag on his desk.

"Um," Jake stammered.

"The debate," I said quickly.

"Oh, how was it?" asked Lee.

"Fine. Fine," I said.

"Who won?" Lee asked.

Jake and I looked at each other across the room.

"It depends on who you ask."

Jake could not get a meeting with his dealer until Wednesday, so we had to be patient. On Tuesday, we both skipped class and followed Gelatti around the school, trying to get a sense of his general behavior.

He was a bit of a loner, which boded well for us. It guaranteed nobody would be around to stop us from stealing the necklace. Gelatti proceeded from class to class alone, nodding now and then to someone he knew, but keeping well to himself.

By a quarter to three, Gelatti was in the locker room dressing for practice. It wasn't unusual for Jake or me to be there at the same time since we both had lockers for our respective sports. I pretended to rifle through my locker, all the while keeping an eye on Gelatti. His bag was red with gray stripes, Adidas. After Gelatti suited up, he removed a water bottle from the bag and took a long swig. The water bottle was a blue Nalgene with "VU" printed across its front.

Jake and I followed Gelatti into the stadium, where he proceeded to do warm-up drills. We made our way up into the bleachers. There were several football aficionados in the stands watching the practice, so Jake and I remained hidden in the back, out of sight.

When practice was over, we watched Gelatti return to the locker room, then reemerge twenty minutes later with the red bag slung over his shoulder and the blue water bottle in hand.

We trailed him at some distance, hoping to see where he would go next. We found ourselves at the main dining hall in Carmelo Square. There we watched Gelatti down three cheeseburgers, two bowls of Lucky Charms cereal, two bananas, and an ice cream sundae.

Go figure.

After that, Gelatti made his way back to his co-op on Broadbridge Road, where he stayed the remainder of the evening.

Wednesday came. I refused to go with Jake to meet his dealer somewhere in South Bridgeport—he had to take a bus.

He got back later that evening. Lee was in the common room, so Jake beckoned me into his bedroom.

"Some secret society business?" Lee asked.

"Keep out of it!" Jake barked. He had grown increasingly hostile toward Lee.

In the bedroom, Jake showed me the tiny white pill that promised to bring down Gelatti. I was afraid to touch it. I knew that if anyone found out about what we were doing, we would be expelled from school. But I also knew that if I didn't do what it took to become a member of Scepter and Gavel, I'd regret it for the rest of my life.

Oh, the irony.

"I'm entrusting this to you," Jake said, dropping the pill into my palm.

I flinched. "Why me?"

"Because you're going to put it in Gelatti's water bottle while I keep a lookout."

For some reason, I didn't object.

"Meet you in the locker room tomorrow at three o'clock."

CHAPTER 8

I FIDDLED WITH the pill in my pocket all through Dr. Pham's Ancient Philosophy class the next day—Thursday.

When Dr. Pham called on me to read from Plato's *Apology*, I jumped, and the rest of the class chuckled.

I read, "'You are mistaken, my friend, if you think that a man who is worth anything ought to spend his time weighing up the prospects of life and death. He has only one thing to consider in performing any action—that is, whether he is acting rightly or wrongly, like a good man or a bad one.'"

I looked up. Everyone was staring at me. I could swear they knew what I was up to. They must have heard it in my voice. I felt the pill burning a hole in my pocket.

"Thank you, Herbert." Dr. Pham nodded and then moved on to the next student. I slumped down in my chair in a mixture of panic and relief.

Was I really going through with this?

"You bet you are!" Jake's voice echoed loudly from the phone. I was standing outside Moses Hall, pill in hand, trembling. "It's no big deal. It's not like we're going to rape the guy."

"Wh-what if someone else does?" I stammered.

"Nobody is going to rape him," Jake said. "He'll probably pass out somewhere and everyone will think he's sleeping. If anything, they'll call the campus police."

"The police?" I squeaked.

"Don't worry," Jake said. "We'll be long gone before the police arrive."

By three o'clock that afternoon, Gelatti was back on the field doing drills and I was rummaging through his bag in the locker room. Jake was standing just outside, keeping a lookout.

"It's all clear," he hissed.

"I don't want to do this," I said.

"Hurry up!"

I found the blue Nalgene with "VU" printed across its front. It was nearly three-quarters full. I unscrewed the lid and dropped the tiny white pill into the water.

"Shake it up real good," Jake said.

I shook the bottle, and the little pill dissolved quickly into nothingness.

You know that part of *Snow White and the Seven Dwarfs* where the witch—disguised as an old hag—gives Snow White the poisoned apple?

I was that old hag.

I stuffed the water bottle back into Gelatti's bag and threw the bag back on the bench where I'd found it.

"All right," I called out. "It's done."

Mirror, mirror, on the wall, who's the fairest of them all?

Not me. Not me.

"Let's go!" Jake cried.

Together we made our way up into the bleachers to see what would happen next. Gelatti spent a good hour just running drills with his teammates. Then he spent another hour throwing the ball down the field. And the final forty-five minutes or so were spent scrimmaging with the rest of the team.

Finally, one of the coaches blew a whistle long and hard, signaling that practice was over. The players made their way to the locker room. The football aficionados in the stands started leaving in ones and twos. Jake and I stayed in the bleachers, hiding in the shadow of the press box.

About fifteen minutes later, Gelatti reappeared, sipping from the bottle. My stomach lurched. It was happening.

Gelatti headed down the tree-lined path leading to Carmelo Square. We followed at a safe distance.

Suddenly, Gelatti started to stumble. His shoulders and arms were loose. He staggered.

Sleep, my pretty! Sleep!

"Here it goes," Jake said.

Gelatti continued forward, but he was zigzagging all over the place like a drunkard. He came to a bench on the side of the path and slumped down on it, chin resting on his chest. He was out.

The path was quiet. A few people were headed down from the stadium, but they were still a ways back. We had time to get the necklace and go.

"You get it," Jake said.

"No fucking way," I said. "It's your turn. You go."

Jake nodded. "Okay."

But then a dark form jumped out of the trees on the other side of the path and began sprinting toward Gelatti.

"What the . . . ?"

It was a girl about our age. Skinny, loose-limbed, and fast. Her black hair was braided down her back. Jake and I watched her go, rooted to the spot.

When the girl reached Gelatti, she quickly unclasped the necklace from around his neck and took off again through the trees.

"You're a runner," Jake cried. "Go get her!"

I took off after the girl, but she was already a good two hundred yards ahead of me. I sprinted through the trees, the girl a distant speck in the fading light. Finally I broke into the main quad. The girl was on the other side, unlocking a bike from a bike rack.

"Hey!" I called. "Wait!"

The girl looked up but did not stop. She leapt onto the bike seat and began pedaling away at breakneck speed down the Huntington Turnpike. She turned a corner and disappeared.

"Fuck!"

CHAPTER 9

THE PLOT THICKENS: Today all 127 members of the police squad, with the help of all 23 members of the fire department, evacuated C-Pod of its six thousand residents. The chief investigator in the case of the Adolf Dussel murder—a man by the name of Forrest Dunst—obtained a permit to search Dussel's pod.

You know what he found?

A spent nuclear fuel pellet.

A spent nuclear fuel pellet is cylindrical in shape, one centimeter in diameter, the size of a small grape. The pellet was tucked neatly under Adolf Dussel's mattress.

If Adolf Dussel had been a true princess, he would have felt the tiny pellet under his mattress. But alas, he was not and did not. Now he is dead.

Typically, these pellets are stacked in long tubes called fuel rods, about four meters long. And the fuel rods are packaged together to form nuclear fuel bundles. About 250 rods make a bundle. And about 200 bundles make up the core of the nuclear reactor. The bundles can provide energy through fission for about three years before they need to be replaced. The used-up nuclear bundle then becomes spent nuclear fuel, otherwise known as radioactive waste.

Go figure.

Long-term exposure to radioactive waste can cause serious illness and possibly death. It most certainly caused Adolf Dussel's death.

Radioactive waste is a silent killer. It has no smell, makes no sound. Inspector Dunst and his crew were in Adolf Dussel's pod for nearly an hour before they found the spent nuclear fuel pellet. They didn't know what it was at first. It wasn't until they got the pellet back to the forensics lab that some savvy lab technician recognized it for what it was and went screaming out of the room.

Now Inspector Dunst and his crew and the lab technician are all in the hospital with radiation poisoning. They're lucky to be alive.

The question remains: Who put a spent nuclear fuel pellet under Adolf Dussel's mattress? And why?

When a spent nuclear fuel bundle is removed from the core of the nuclear reactor, it is placed in a pool of water to cool for ten years. After it cools, a nuclear technician removes the bundle from the pool of water and carefully extracts a handful of spent nuclear fuel pellets. These pellets are for research purposes only. The technician stores the pellets in a small radiation-proof box. A nuclear transportation specialist then delivers the pellets to Dr. Brad Dauer in A-Block. There the good doctor toys around with the pellets, hoping they'll do some kind of magic trick.

Presto chango!

As far as I know, the good doctor hasn't been able to make the nuclear waste do any good tricks yet. The pellets just want to kill everyone and everything in the vicinity.

The rest of the spent nuclear fuel bundle is bound in a lead casket and loaded onto a special truck driven by another nuclear transportation specialist who takes it out to my good friend Frank Gutierrez for disposal.

Frank Gutierrez is called a nuclear disposal specialist.

Inspector Dunst wants to know how many people in Pod City have access to spent nuclear fuel pellets.

You do the math: There are eleven full-time technicians working at the nuclear reactor. There are two nuclear transportation specialists. There are four nuclear disposal specialists on site at the disposal facility. There is Dr. Brad Dauer and his assistant, Dr. Edie Moyer.

And then there is the janitor who cleans Dr. Dauer's lab: me.

That makes twenty suspects, counting myself of course.

Did I kill Adolf Dussel?

No. I never had any reason to want Adolf Dussel dead. I *did* know Adolf Dussel. Peripherally. He conducted the Martian census—very literally. Adolf Dussel went door to door collecting information about people. He'd ask things like name, gender, race, age, occupation, number of people in the household, income, etc., etc., etc.

So in one sense, everybody knew Adolf Dussel, at least peripherally, like I did. And, what is more, Adolf Dussel knew everybody back, knew the details of their lives, knew things people didn't want others knowing.

For example, he knew that Cady and I had entered the lottery to have children seventeen times before we gave up. We may have set some kind of record.

He knew that my father had been the CEO of GeneTech and that I had ended up with none of his substantial fortune. He knew that Cady and I lived off forty-three credits a week, which is not very much.

He knew that I was nearly kicked out of college my first year. But everybody knows that. My name was one of the many names listed in the *Vanity Fair* piece that brought the house crumbling down on our heads.

* * *

Jake and I were flummoxed. We could only assume that this girl who had run off with *our* necklace was also pledging the

Order of the Scepter and Gavel. Perhaps there were a dozen such people looking for the silver cross right now.

One girl had it, though. One very fast girl. And I didn't know what that meant for the rest of us.

Jake felt certain we would be denied entry to the club. I didn't think that made a lot of sense, though, since that would imply only one initiate was destined to get into the society. Surely it wouldn't matter which of us brought the necklace to the Order. Surely it was simply a test of our derring-do.

"We can't be sure," said Jake.

He was out the door very early Friday morning. I went to cross-country practice. And then I went to look for Geraldo Gelatti. I was scared we had overdone it. Maybe he had been hurt while unconscious. Or worse: Maybe his heart had stopped. These were the places my mind went. I was not as cavalier as Jake about what we'd done. All Jake could think about was the missing necklace. I, on the other hand, had a much more active conscience. The little angel on my shoulder was saying, "You're terrible. You don't deserve to be in a secret society. You owe it to Gelatti to at least see that he turned out all right."

I couldn't find Gelatti all morning, which aggravated my nervous state. I comforted myself by thinking he was probably home, sleeping off the roofie. But he wouldn't miss football practice, I thought. And sure enough, at three o'clock, when I went to the stadium, I found him dressing in the locker room, looking none the worse for wear.

That eased my conscience. I would like to say that I pledged never to do something like that again. I would like to say that I realized the error of my ways and repented all the way home. But that's not exactly what happened. Seeing Gelatti there in the locker room behaving as though nothing had happened gave me a sick sense of pleasure.

I had gotten away with it! Suddenly Jake's reckless plan seemed like no big deal, like child's play even. Jake was right. You could roofie somebody and not face any consequences. My confidence in my own derring-do skyrocketed.

Jake returned home shortly after I did, carrying a Zales shopping bag. Lee and I were in the common room. Lee was watching TV and I was working on a paper for Professor Pham.

"What's that?" Lee asked, eyeing the Zales bag.

Jake said nothing but motioned for me to join him in his bedroom. He closed and locked the door behind us. We could hear Lee banging around in the common room, making a fuss.

"Look at this," Jake said, producing a silver cross on a silver chain. As far as I could tell, it was identical to the cross Gelatti had been wearing; I'd never gotten a really good look at it.

"You think this'll work?" I asked, taking the decoy necklace into my hands.

"Sure," Jake said, beaming. "Nobody is going to know the difference."

The little devil on my shoulder jumped for joy. We could

pull it off after all!

* * *

As far as I know, the statue of VU's founder, Samuel Owens, still stands at the top of Memorial Hill in the southeast corner of campus. Memorial Hill is named in honor of the first piloted mission to Mars—launched in 2030—which ended in disaster. Four astronauts aboard the *Achilles*—Jim Green, Marcia Henry, Maria Ruiz, and Lenny Rosenthal—made the journey to Mars in just under 230 days. Funding for the journey came from a private company called Space First that had attracted dozens of wealthy investors.

The flight to Mars was successful and Marcia Henry was the first human to walk on the red planet. We all watched the historic event unfold on live TV.

The other astronauts got to walk around on Mars, too. They planted a US flag in the red soil and took turns posing for photos.

Say cheese!

They spent several days on Mars, sampling the Martian soil, testing the Martian atmosphere, and looking for indicators of water and life.

There were telltale signs that water had once covered the planet. But no signs of life, which was pretty much what everyone expected.

All was well and good until the astronauts decided they

wanted to come home. They buckled up for takeoff. Ignition, check. Life support, check. Three, two, one . . .

But nothing happened. The rocket refused to leave the ground. It coughed and sputtered and gave a little shake and then died out.

That's what you get for naming your spacecraft the *Achilles*.

When news of the shuttle's malfunction broke, engineers from across the globe got in line to help diagnose and fix the problem.

After two weeks of futzing around with the spaceship's carburetor, the crew felt sure they had fixed the problem.

They had.

Little did they know there was another problem. We're not sure exactly what the problem was, but many experts speculate that there was a tiny, hairline fracture in the hull of the ship. During the diagnostics testing, the crack must have gone unnoticed.

You can guess what happened next.

Kablooey!

Memorial Hill is a tribute to the four astronauts who lost their lives paving the way for thousands of Martians to come.

And the statue of Samuel Owens that stands at the top of Memorial Hill is a tribute to the founder of Vanderough University. The school was originally called Mars Academy and was located in a warehouse down by the marina. It threatened to go bust after the *Achilles* disaster. Then a semi-anonymous donor poured a fortune into the school, and it was moved to its current location and christened with the only name the donor had given: Vanderough.

The original mission of Mars Academy had not been to send astronauts to Mars and back, as had been Space First's mission. The original mission of Mars Academy had been to send astronauts to Mars to stay. And that's still the mission of the school all these years later.

I was the 928th citizen of Pod City. Hence my ID number: 000928. Pod City has grown steadily since I arrived. And as the city has become more habitable for humans, more and more people are moving out here. When I first arrived, there wasn't a movie theater or a bowling alley or an exotic garden. What is now the Sector 2 Promenade was just an empty bunker where people occasionally gathered to trade belongings. And Joshua Beach was just a stretch of concrete bordering the reservoir.

Ling Ling's arrival on Mars marked the beginning of what has been called the Big Boom. Pod City doubled in size in just five years. Ling Ling introduced the idea of luxury accommodations, designing a number of high-end pods that attracted a whole new wave of pioneers. He transformed the empty bunker into what is now the Sector 2 Promenade: a series of brand-name shops selling the finest wares on the planet. The Exotic Garden went up. And the gubernatorial palace. Ling Ling had a hand in both of these, as well as the redesign of Joshua Beach.

Mars became a destination.

One of the biggest industries on Mars today: tourism.

Millionaires and billionaires will pay a pretty penny for a seat on a transport shuttle to Mars and back. They come to stay at the Westin Resort. They take dune buggies out to the site of the *Achilles* disaster and pose for photos by the American flag. They stroll the Exotic Garden and tour the research facilities. Mostly, they just want to say they've done it, they've been to Mars.

As for the rest of us . . . we're not likely to go back to Earth. The US government incentivizes colonization of Mars by paying for one-way passage aboard a shuttle. It costs thirteen million dollars for a seat home, so unless you have a loaded trust fund or a wealthy friend on Earth, once you're on Mars, you're there to stay.

Interesting fact: Samuel Owens has never visited Mars. He is seventy-four years old now. The fifth-wealthiest human on Earth. He is still provost of Vanderough University, and he claims he suffers from severe motion sickness, so a trip to Mars is out of the question.

The statue of Samuel Owens on Memorial Hill depicts the provost as a young man standing on Martian soil, his hand around the pole of the US flag. It is total fiction. As I said, Samuel Owens has never set foot on Martian soil. Nor can he stand. He has been using a wheelchair since he was thirteen years old.

Samuel Owens was paralyzed from the waist down after an

equestrian accident in his youth. He liked to ride horses. His family was obscenely wealthy, and they had a ranch out in Montana where they spent their summers. It was on this ranch that thirteen-year-old Samuel Owens was thrown from a horse aptly named Dangerous. They called the horse Dan for short.

Samuel Owens became a bit of a recluse after that. He insisted on being homeschooled all through high school. However, his parents sent him off to Ohio State University when he turned eighteen, and there Samuel studied engineering and business.

He started his first business when he was twenty-three: a self-driving car company that took off within a few years. The company was called Samuel Dan Automated Automotives. We now say "I just bought a 2070 Sam Dan" to indicate that we own one of Samuel Owens's newest self-driving models. As you may have already guessed, Samuel comes from Samuel Owens and Dan comes from Dangerous the horse, who is long dead.

Talk about confronting a trauma head-on.

By the time Samuel Owens was thirty, he had his fingers in lots of pies. He was a primary investor in Solar Corp., which had just made its first billion. He was on the board of GeneTech, my father's company, just one year before it was sold to Google. And he founded Mars Academy, which was then one of many private companies racing to put the first human on Mars.

The first class of freshmen joined Mars Academy in the fall

of 2030, but several major investors pulled out after the *Achilles* disaster later that year. The *Achilles* disaster promised to end all research into Mars exploration. But Samuel Owens persisted, and in 2033, Mars Academy was saved from bankruptcy by a donor named Vanderough.

And you know the rest.

Emblazoned across the plinth of the Samuel Owens statue are the Latin words *Usque in aeternum et ultra*, which roughly translates to "Forever and beyond," the university's motto.

Jake and I had never really stopped to look at the statue on Memorial Hill before that night when we delivered the silver cross to the Order of the Scepter and Gavel.

We showed up just before midnight. A floor light lit the statue from below. I think I commented on how weird it was that Samuel Owens was depicted standing when he had been using a wheelchair the majority of his life. Jake said he didn't know Samuel Owens was in a wheelchair.

Classic Jake.

Then four hooded figures emerged from the darkness beyond the statue. I immediately had the impulse to run away. The last time I had encountered these hooded figures, they had kidnapped me and dressed me up like a circus clown and made me cross a plank. I didn't want to stick around to find out what they had in store for me now.

Then we heard the sound of footsteps behind us, and a boy and girl appeared, trudging up the hill at a brisk pace. It was the girl from before, the girl who had stolen the necklace from us. I didn't recognize the boy, but apparently, Jake did, because he said, "Freddy Euler! Fancy meeting you here."

Freddy nodded hello, and then introduced his female companion as Melissa Veracruz, a friend.

We stood there in front of the hooded figures, me and Jake a few feet apart from Freddy and Melissa.

Then a hooded figure spoke. It was the same woman who had spoken before. "Which of you has successfully procured the silver cross?"

Without hesitation, Jake pulled the phony necklace from his pocket and held it out for the woman to take. Melissa gasped.

"No," she said, "that's not Gelatti's cross. This is!" And she produced another cross on a chain that was virtually indistinguishable from the one in Jake's hand.

"No," Jake said, "this is Gelatti's cross. Herbert and I were able to get it off him."

The hooded woman took both crosses in her hands and examined them closely through the black mask over her face. She chuckled.

"Well, it looks like you both did it somehow," she said.

"But his isn't real!" Melissa frowned. "Freddy and I gave you the real cross!"

"Perhaps," said the hooded woman. "Or perhaps *yours* isn't real."

Melissa looked affronted.

The woman continued. "What matters is that Gelatti is missing his necklace. That means two of you were clever enough to get it from him. The other two were clever enough to not show up empty-handed. Congratulations, plebeians. You have all passed the second task."

The woman turned to go.

"Wait!" Melissa cried. "What's our next task?"

The woman turned back. "So eager. That's good. We will send you your next assignment shortly. In the meantime, don't breathe a word of this to anybody outside this circle."

I looked around at the faces of the other initiates. Were we it? The four of us?

The hooded figures turned and started down the hill. The four of us stayed rooted to the spot, eyeing one another suspiciously. Finally, true to form, Jake broke the ice. "So what did they make you two dress up as, you know, when they kidnapped you?"

Freddy Euler spoke first. "I was a ballerina."

"Nice," I said.

Melissa was still giving us a hard stare. Freddy spoke on her behalf. "And Melissa was a sumo wrestler."

Jake nodded. "Bet it wasn't easy walking the plank in a sumo outfit."

"Come on, Freddy," Melissa commanded. "Let's go."

"Good luck," Jake said. "I'm sure we'll meet again."

CHAPTER 10

MELISSA VERACRUZ did become a gavel-man. Her mile time was five minutes and ten seconds. She came from Biloxi, Mississippi, right on the Gulf of Mexico. She ran cross-country in high school, like I did, and we even competed in the same meet one year, although we couldn't have known it then.

Melissa came from a political family. Her grandmother had been Under Secretary for Terrorism and Financial Intelligence under President Joseph R. Biden. Her father was the current secretary of commerce. Her uncle was the lieutenant governor of California. And her older brother had just been elected to the United States Senate.

Melissa had ambitions to become the governor of Mars. Thanks to the scandal of '41, Melissa's political career was over before it started. She is now a dune buggy repairwoman and spends her days covered in oil and grease.

So much for legacy.

If it hadn't been for the *Vanity Fair* exposé in 2041, I would have put money on Melissa becoming governor of Mars. She was accepted to VU on a full scholarship for her academic and extracurricular achievements. She was the top student at Biloxi High School, a national debate champion, president of the student body, a state-ranked cross-country and track runner, and a finalist at the Intel International Science and Engineering Fair. And despite the whole debacle of '41, Melissa still managed to become VU's valedictorian for the class of 2044.

Cady knew her well; they lived on the same floor during freshman year. Cady says Melissa is the smartest person she's ever met.

I don't know if I would go that far. But she is damn smart. With her academic achievements and political connections, it is no wonder she was tapped for Scepter and Gavel. If the Order hadn't been dissolved in 2041, I bet Melissa would have become its next Grand Pooh-bah, Master of Ceremonies, King Cobra, Maestro of Debauchery and Sin.

Melissa never really warmed to me. But she did invite me to her birthday party on October 19 that year. Jake and I were both surprised, as you can imagine, to receive a formal invitation from Melissa under our door two days after we met atop Memorial Hill.

Freddy Euler and Jake knew each other from before college. They had both gone to the same private school in Chicago: Lake Forest Academy. And against all odds, they were both accepted to VU in 2040 and, as you know, both tapped to be in the Order of the Scepter and Gavel.

I can only speculate why Freddy Euler was tapped. As far as I know, he had no political connections. His parents were middle class—Freddy had been on financial aid at Lake Forest Academy and was on financial aid at VU, too. He wasn't an athlete or a performer of any sort. However, he was Melissa's best friend, and it's possible the Order saw it prudent to invite both in an effort to secure Melissa. I don't know.

Anyway, Freddy and Jake were what you could loosely call "friends" from Lake Forest Academy, and Jake guessed that Freddy had coerced Melissa into inviting us to her birthday party. I also think it's possible that Melissa was the kind of person who kept her friends close and her enemies closer. We weren't exactly enemies, but Melissa was a stickler for the rules, and she claimed that Jake and I had cheated in procuring the silver cross. And she never really got over that.

C'est la vie.

Melissa's invitation suggested we should arrive in coat and tie. We would be starting with dinner at a trendy German restaurant in downtown Bridgeport called Wurstküche, which translates to "Sausage Kitchen." Then we would continue on to drinks and dancing at a club I'd never heard of before called the Light Bulb.

At the last minute, Jake backed out because Ursula had come down with the flu, and Jake wanted to stay home to take care of her. So I went alone.

The restaurant was down by the water. I had to take two buses in my coat and tie to get there. When I arrived, most of the guests were already seated at a long wooden table, with Melissa in the middle, flanked on one side by Freddy Euler and on the other by a pretty redhead with long straight hair, a pointy nose, and a cleft chin.

Her name was Cady Pinkleton.

I sat down in an empty seat at the end of the long table. Melissa, deep in conversation with a boy seated across the table, glanced at me once, scowled faintly, and didn't look at me again for the rest of the evening. Freddy Euler was more welcoming. He waved at me emphatically and motioned for me to order off the menu.

I did.

The big, burly guy seated next to me looked familiar somehow, but I couldn't place him. While I waited for my schnitzel, I introduced myself, and he took my hand in a firm handshake. His name was Surge.

Then I remembered: Surge had been the bouncer at Wilde House the night of the party.

I mentioned that we had met before.

Surge said, "I know."

An awkward silence followed. I felt compelled to fill it. "What are you studying, Surge?"

"Robotics," he replied.

"Cool. So you're going to be working with the Mars rovers, then."

"Yes."

Alas, he wouldn't end up working with the Mars rovers after all because Surge was a gavelman—although I didn't know it then—and he would very nearly be expelled by the end of the year, thanks in part to me.

Surge's mile time was twelve minutes and twenty-three seconds.

The conversation stalled. I didn't realize it at the time, but Surge had been the hooded figure who had carried me to the Tomb on the first day of my induction into Scepter and Gavel.

"How do you know Melissa?" I asked, breaking the long silence.

"We're in the same chem class," he said.

That was all he would offer by way of explanation. But there was more to it than that. Surge had been tasked by the Order to spy on Melissa and assess her worthiness as a candidate for the secret society. Every new recruit was being closely observed. Jake and I didn't know it then, but the Order was carefully monitoring us, too.

"Excuse me." Surge rose and reseated himself at the other end of the table.

"That was rude," I murmured to myself.

My schnitzel arrived and I focused on eating. As long as I was chewing on something, I wasn't expected to talk to anybody. And after my encounter with Surge, I didn't *want* to talk to anybody.

Then Cady Pinkleton got up from the table, walked directly over to me, and perched herself on the seat Surge had left vacant.

"How are you doing?" she asked.

"I don't know anybody here," I said.

"I'm Cady. I've seen you running around campus."

"Oh, yeah." I blushed. "I'm on the cross-country team."

"That explains it," she said. "I wondered why anyone would put themselves through that much trouble. But I guess you're used to it."

Cady still says she doesn't get why I run. I don't really get it either. It's something of an obsession, I guess. Dr. Paula Cuevas says I use running to fill the voids in my life. When I asked Dr. Cuevas what voids she was referring to, she said our time was up.

I know there is at least one void. Cady has it, too. Children. We would have liked to have had children.

C'est la vie.

"Isn't this place wild?" Cady said. She was referring to the sausage kitchen. "A little slice of Germany right here in Bridgeport."

"Yeah," I said, poking at my schnitzel. "You want another beer?"

Cady relaxed into the seat beside me. "Sure."

I ordered two Green Flash IPAs. "Are you going to the club

after this?" I asked.

"I don't know," she said. "Are you?"

We sized each other up in that moment. And then Cady said what we were both thinking. "I'll go if you go."

"Sounds good," I said, trying to sound casual. My conversation with Surge just minutes before had turned me off to the idea of continuing on to the Light Bulb. But meeting Cady changed everything.

Everything.

Cady acted boldly in those days. And she acts boldly now, too. When I was nearly expelled later that year, Cady stood by my side. She didn't even hesitate to stand up for me, for my character, at the academic council meeting that would determine my fate. And when we learned that I would not amount to anything more than a janitor on Mars, Cady said we would work it out. She knew she would be making a living wage as a botanist, and she didn't mind supporting us both.

"Glue and paper stick together," she always says when referring to us.

She's the glue, that one.

Cady was really a godsend that night, too. Her company made the whole party worthwhile. Melissa gave me the cold shoulder throughout the evening. But Cady, who knew several people there, introduced me to her friends, and the dinner turned out to be not half-bad.

Around nine o'clock, the whole party got up and staggered the four blocks to the Light Bulb. Someone had converted an old Edison International power plant into a nightclub. In homage to the building's former life, the club owners had installed thousands of old carbon-filament light bulbs in the ceiling. The whole place was alight with an eerie orange glow.

There were three bars, a dance floor, a lounge, and an outdoor patio. People were dressed to the nines. A gin and tonic cost twenty-three dollars. And it cost fifty dollars a person to get anywhere near the lounge. The prices were ludicrous, and I said so to Cady.

"Yeah," she replied. "I don't know why Melissa feels she has to spend so much money to have a nice time."

It was a good thing Cady had that attitude toward money. Because we would never have much of it.

God bless her.

The others coughed up fifty apiece for a seat in the lounge. I said no way, and Cady agreed, so we stayed standing.

"Want to walk around a little?" Cady asked.

"Yeah."

We circled the dance floor once and made our way out to the back patio. Here we could sit down for free, so I took a seat on a brick ledge and motioned for Cady to sit in the only available patio chair.

Trees bright with white Christmas lights speckled the patio. Here, smokers flicked their ashes into little ceramic trays on wrought iron tables, and the conversation stayed at a murmur. Cady leaned back in her chair and smiled at me.

I smiled back.

Then a woman sitting farther down the ledge turned to Cady and me.

"What's your sign?" she asked.

"Excuse me?"

"Your sign," the woman said. She was slurring her words a little, and the right strap of her blouse had slipped down her shoulder.

"What's. Your. Sign," she repeated, punctuating every word.

"Scorpio," Cady said. "I'm a Scorpio."

"Ooh," the woman said. "Jupiter, Mercury, and Mars are in alignment tonight. You should expect new opportunities."

"Come on," I said to Cady. "Let's go back inside."

"What kind of new opportunities?" Cady asked, ignoring me.

"You don't seriously believe this stuff, do you?" I asked.

"It's fun," Cady said. Then, turning back to the woman: "What kind of new opportunities?"

The woman's words slurred as she said, "Someone close to you will come into"—she hiccuped—"some money."

"What's that got to do with anything?" I asked. "So what if someone else comes into money?"

"That's funny," Cady said, turning to me excitedly. "Because Paul is waiting on a job offer from Yale."

"Who's Paul?" I asked.

"My boyfriend."

CHAPTER 11

SHE WAS OF COURSE referring to Paul O'Malley, the dashing graduate student from the University of North Carolina. Paul and Cady had stayed in touch after their fortuitous meeting on the cruise through the Arctic Ocean. Cady still texted Paul daily, and because they were in the same time zone, they were able to talk on the phone most evenings.

Cady explained that Paul would be completing his PhD in economics that spring, and Yale was looking to hire him as an assistant professor for the following year.

I didn't stand a chance.

Paul would have to die. And lucky for me, he did die, eventually.

C'est la vie.

I went home that night disheartened. I'd been played. Cady

had taken me for a fool. All evening I had been certain she was flirting with me. Then she dropped that bombshell. She had a boyfriend! I felt like a first-class ass.

To this day Cady claims she had not intended to give me the impression that she was interested in anything more than a friendship. She says she felt sorry for me because I looked so lonely and out of place. That was why she deigned to speak to me.

I say bullshit.

I looked Cady up on Facebook first thing when I got home. Lo and behold, there was a picture of her and Paul embracing on the cruise ship with a giant wall of ice rising behind them.

Her profile read "In a relationship with Paul O'Malley."

I clicked on Paul O'Malley's profile. He was everything Cady had described him to be and more. He volunteered with terminally ill children in his spare time. He was an author of two books on the US economy. He listed his granny as his role model. And he claimed to be an original member of the Nexus 28.

I'd heard of the Nexus 28 before. In March of 2038, twenty-eight graduate students from across the country banded together to form what became the most influential think tank in the world. The Nexus 28 focused on addressing climate change, rising sea levels, deforestation, population growth, and nuclear waste. Paul O'Malley, though no longer affiliated with the Nexus 28, had been one of the original twenty-eight founders and had contributed to a great many innovations in environmental policy in the US.

For example, the Nexus 28 successfully lobbied to reopen the Yucca Mountain nuclear waste disposal site in Nevada in 2039. The Yucca Mountain site was essentially a deep, deep cave where nuclear waste could be deposited for safekeeping. During his tenure as president of the United States, Barack Obama shut development of the site down for political reasons. Upon reopening, Yucca Mountain became the first and only permanent storage solution for commercial nuclear waste in the US.

Danvers Cavern here on Mars is modeled after the Yucca Mountain site in Nevada. Frank Gutierrez hides all the radioactive waste produced by our nuclear generator in Danvers Cavern, never to be discovered again. The site is highly secure, and only four nuclear waste disposal operatives have access to the underground facility.

Inspector Dunst, who was released from the hospital today, is in the process of interviewing all four operatives in the case of Adolf Dussel's murder. Tomorrow, he interviews the eleven nuclear reactor technicians who work directly with the spent fuel bundles. The day after that, I will be interviewed, along with the two nuclear waste transportation specialists and Dr. Brad Dauer and his assistant, Dr. Edie Moyer. The spent nuclear fuel pellet found under Adolf Dussel's mattress definitely came from the nuclear reactor, so only one of the twenty aforementioned people could be responsible for its appearance in Dussel's pod three days ago.

I wonder who it'll be.

Cady says I'd better hope nobody set me up.

Who would do such a thing?

* * *

We have actors here on Mars, too. Fifty-two of them. They all belong to the Martian Actors Guild, which puts on a new show every three months at the Red Curtain Theater in E-Block. This month's show is called *Man in a Fishbowl*. Cady and I went with Renata Sachs and her husband, Bob, to see it last night. It is a musical in which seven humans are abducted by a four-dimensional alien named Faaaaah. Since Faaaaah exists in the fourth dimension, humans are to him what cartoons are to us—that is, *flat*. From the fourth dimension, Faaaaah is able to manipulate the three-dimensional universe, bending and twisting it to his will. He creates a four-dimensional fishbowl for the seven humans to live in, much like an aquarium.

The way this fishbowl works for the humans is like this: If a human starts walking north in the fishbowl, where north is a purely relative term, she will come back to the place she started after about half a mile. So when a human standing by a tree looks out at the horizon, he can see himself, his backside, standing by the tree. If he looks just beyond this, another half mile out, he will see his backside again, standing by the same tree. In fact, since the human eye can detect a candle flame flickering up to thirty miles away, this human looking out at the horizon will see sixty or so versions of himself progressively getting farther and farther away in all directions.

The seven abducted humans are not on a planet, mind you. They are in a four-dimensional fishbowl belonging to a four-dimensional being called Faaaaah.

The humans find this version of reality to be very disorienting.

In the fishbowl, Faaaaah constructs a little wooden house in the Craftsman style, because that's what he has seen humans inhabiting on Earth. He places a pond of freshwater right next to the house, because he knows humans need H_2O to survive. He plants a garden with vegetables and fruit out back. And he scatters a few trees about the yard to make things look nice.

Faaaaah wants to know what humans will do under extreme circumstances, like being stuck in a fishbowl half a mile wide with only one house and one pond and a few trees. For the humans' part, they are totally baffled by what has happened to them. They can neither see nor hear Faaaaah since Faaaaah exists in the fourth dimension.

One of the humans called Dara gets the idea in her head that maybe they've all died and gone to heaven. They have adequate food, water, and shelter. Perhaps this is what heaven is. This fishbowl. There's a big musical number in which a character called Judy sings about how much she has sinned in her life and how this can't be heaven ("But it can!" sings Dara) because no god would ever send *her* to heaven.

There is a lot of disagreement among the seven abductees, and they find themselves splitting into factions. The first faction, Dara and Julio and Meghan, asserts that they've landed in heaven. The second faction, Judy and Marco and Tom, thinks this place is hell. And finally, there's a character called Herman who suspects they've been abducted by an alien for experimentation.

This, the audience knows, is the truth.

Another number called "Abducted by God" ends the first act, leaving our little band of humans grossly divided and downright irritated with one another.

Did I mention this is supposed to be a comedy?

The second act opens on Faaaaah, who is played by a chap by the name of Alexander Horace Hyde, lamenting that one of his little humans has died. Alexander Horace Hyde is probably the most notable actor in the play. He is the face of Mars whenever people on Earth look through a brochure or watch an informational video about Vanderough University.

Alexander Horace Hyde is famous for his deep baritone voice.

The focus shifts back to the humans. It is Dara who has died, which throws everyone (except Herman) for a loop, since they all thought they were already dead.

Herman makes his argument again for why he thinks they've been abducted by aliens.

Meanwhile, everyone is wondering, who killed Dara?

She was found, they sing, with a knife in her back. *Knife in her back. Knife in her baaaaack!*

The rest of the story proceeds like a typical whodunit mystery, where the trust among the members of the little group erodes, and people start blaming one another for Dara's death. Faaaaah watches with fascination as a second, then a third, then a fourth member of the group is killed. Each human dies in some new and grotesque way. The second human to die, Tom, hangs himself from a tree. The third human to die, Judy, is stoned to death by the other surviving members of the group. The fourth human to die, Julio, drowns unexpectedly in the pond.

We are left with Meghan, Marco, and Herman, and it becomes increasingly clear that each of them is willing to kill to stay alive.

Faaaaah intervenes. He finds the behavior of the humans so repulsive that he decides to wipe them out completely. With a four-dimensional spigot, he begins to fill the little fishbowl with water, and he watches as the humans scramble like ants in a washtub to stay afloat. Eventually the humans tire from treading water and they sink, one by one.

Plop. Plop. Plop.

Herman hangs on until the very end, and—in an about-face—he concludes in a musical lament that there must be a God after all and that the flood is God's way of punishing the humans for being so wicked.

Herman dies, and Faaaaah, drunk on his own power, is left

wondering, "Am I God?"

Renata and Bob loved it. They both believe in God, and they interpreted the fishbowl to be a purgatory-like place where people are sent to atone for their sins. This place in the Judaic tradition is called Gehinnom or Gehenna.

Faaaaah, they concluded, is God after all.

I tend to interpret the play differently. To the humans, Faaaaah might as well be God, he is so far superior to them in every way. However, I think the play also makes the argument that a human might as well be God to an anthill in the sense that humans are so far superior to ants in every way. God is relative. Or more accurately, God is simply those forces you don't understand.

I don't believe in God. Or purgatory. Or anything like that. But I could be persuaded to believe in a four-dimensional alien named Faaaaah.

Faaaaah seems a lot more probable to me.

What does Cady say? Cady says, "Best not to question what you can never know."

CHAPTER 12

PAUL O'MALLEY came out from North Carolina the next week to spend a few days with Cady. This I knew because I stalked Cady on Instagram, where she posted pictures of all their adventures. Apparently, they took a ferry out to Montauk and spent a day on the beach, basking in the late October sun. The following day, Cady and Paul hiked through Montauk Point State Park, taking pictures of themselves at every milepost on the trail. Paul was of course as handsome as his Facebook profile suggested, maybe handsomer on Instagram. And Cady looked as happy as a clam.

Then the weekend came, and I had to report to my job as ticket-taker at the carousel in Beardsley Zoo. Geoffrey, my thieving manager, was in a foul mood because he had spent the previous night partying at a friend's house. I was pretty sure he was still high as a kite when he showed up to work.

Whee!

"Why do you keep looking at your phone?" Geoffrey demanded about an hour into my shift. "Put it away. Guests don't want to see you looking at your phone while you're operating the ride."

The last time I had checked Instagram, Cady and Paul had returned from Montauk and had just finished breakfast at the Dunkin' Donuts on the Huntington Turnpike. I put my phone in my back pocket and gritted my teeth against the urge to pull it out again.

The afternoon passed slowly. Geoffrey sat scowling in the ticket booth. I stood sweating in the sun. The carousel went round and round. The sounds of monkeys drifted over the trees. From where I stood, I could just see the top of the primate center, where Musk the howler monkey sat crouched on a pole. In the opposite direction, I could make out the long, languid form of Jinx the tiger in her enclosure, stretched out in the sun. She was at the end of her life, twenty-six years old, one of the oldest tigers in captivity. She took strong doses of medication to treat her arthritis, and this made her even sleepier than she already was. I watched Jinx's chest rise and fall. Her tail flicked up and down.

"Herbert?" came a familiar voice.

I turned my head, and standing there, tickets in hand, was Cady with her dashing graduate student boyfriend. I stammered, "C-Cady."

"I didn't know you worked at the zoo," Cady said.

I was in a candy-striped vest, the uniform of zoo employees. "Yeah," I said. "How are you doing? How was Montauk?"

Cady furrowed her brow. "How did you know I was in Montauk?"

I blushed. "Instagram."

"Oh, that's right," Cady said, relaxing a little. "It was fun. Herbert, I want you to meet my boyfriend, Paul."

"Hello," said Paul, shaking my hand. His voice was deep and rich.

"Hi," I said, my voice cracking. I sounded like one of the screeching monkeys.

"Herbert saved my life at Melissa's birthday party," she said, turning to Paul. "I would've died of boredom if Herbert hadn't been there to keep me company."

"Then I owe you one," Paul said.

"No, no," I said. "No trouble at all."

There was an awkward silence as the three of us looked around at one another. Then I said, "Did you guys want to ride the carousel?"

"Yeah," said Cady. "We thought it would be romantic, you know?"

"Yeah," I said, tearing their tickets.

Cady and Paul sat side by side, each on a wooden horse. There were two little girls riding a panda and an elephant. I pulled the lever.

The music started up, and the carousel went round and round.

Whee!

Cady leaned over on her horse and kissed Paul on the cheek. I turned away, embarrassed. I fixed my attention on Jinx, who had gotten up and was traversing the length of her enclosure. She moved slowly, delicately, her paws touching down lightly. She stretched. Even at her age, she was magnificent to behold. Her tail dragged on the ground behind her, twitching. She found a sunny spot atop a large rock and lay down again, her tufted belly exposed.

I turned back to the carousel and switched the lever. The music slowed and the ride came to a stop. Cady and Paul hopped off and exited through the gate opposite me. Cady waved goodbye, smiling. I felt something lurch in the pit of my stomach as I watched her disappear around a corner.

Beautiful!

The chemical that makes a person feel like they're head over heels in love with someone—oxytocin—was flowing. I was a walking puddle of hormones, high on my own stupid infatuation.

I practically floated home from work that evening. I remember the date: October 27, 2040. On that date, Cady flipped a little switch in my brain, I think, and I was done for—an oxytocin addict for life.

I tracked Cady on Instagram that night and the next day, Sunday, which was the day Paul got on a plane and flew home.

"What's the matter with you?" Jake asked when I came home from work on Sunday and threw myself onto the bed with an exasperated sigh.

The last picture posted to Instagram that day was a selfie of Cady and Paul kissing in front of the United Airlines terminal. K-I-S-S-I-N-G.

I felt physically ill. And I told Jake so.

"Maybe you should take an Advil," Jake suggested.

Great advice from Jake, as always.

CHAPTER 13

OCTOBER 29, 2040, was the date of the second presidential debate. Tamara Holden versus Garrett Dougherty. Jake had invited several of his friends from the Numbskull Club over to our suite to watch the debate live on CNN. Ursula Beal was there, too, looking smug. Tamara Holden had pulled ahead of Garrett Dougherty in the polls, and Ursula wasn't going to let Jake and his friends forget it.

"Six points," she said for the third time. "Holden is *six points* ahead in the polls."

"Shut up," Jake said. "It's a fluke, you'll see."

"It's not a fluke. Six points is a lot. Your man has got to do some real sweet talking after what happened."

What happened? I'll tell you.

Only a few days earlier, while I was obsessing over Cady's

Instagram, a radio station out of Branson, Missouri, released a damning recording in which a high-school-aged Garrett Dougherty could be heard saying some offensive things about people of color. Garrett Dougherty was born and raised in Branson, Missouri. There, a controversial radio program called *Speak Your Mind* invited listeners to call in and comment on a given topic. The topic of that day was "Racism: Real or Imagined?"

Seventeen-year-old Garrett Dougherty decided to add his two cents to the discussion. Here is a transcript of the recording:

> HOST: And now we have Garrett Dougherty on the line. Garrett is a high school senior, head of the Republican Club, and Branson native. What do you have to say, Garrett?
>
> GARRETT: Well, I wanted to comment on the topic of racism.
>
> HOST: Go on.
>
> GARRETT: Racism ended years ago in this country. Show me one law on the books that blatantly excludes minorities from participating in this great democracy.
>
> HOST: Some listeners have argued that racism is still embedded in our culture—institutional racism. What would you say to those listeners?
>
> GARRETT: Institutional racism is a myth. Blacks and

Hispanics have just as much opportunity now as anyone else. They're just being lazy when they claim institutional racism is holding them back.

HOST: Are you saying that Blacks and Hispanics are lazy?

GARRETT: Well, look at Asians. They're not sitting around crying about past injustices. They're doing fine. Better than fine. In most of our universities now, Asians outnumber white students two to one.

HOST: You think Asian students work harder than Black and Hispanic students?

GARRETT: If the shoe fits.

HOST: Let me ask you: Are there any Black or Hispanic students in your Republican Club?

GARRETT: A few.

HOST: And what do they have to say about your theory?

GARRETT: Oh, they agree with me one hundred percent. I don't think I could get on the phone and say what I'm saying if I didn't know that my Black and Hispanic friends supported me.

HOST: Thank you. That was Garrett Dougherty from Branson, Missouri.

The host of *Speak Your Mind* was a man by the name of

Pete Reynolds, and he was notorious for saying inflammatory things on his program. He eventually had to resign after he used the N-word on the air. But the station let Garrett and Pete get away with calling Blacks and Hispanics lazy. Now, forty years later, Garrett's words were coming back to bite him in the butt. After news of the damning recording broke, Garrett Dougherty's poll numbers plunged six points.

"And it serves him right," Ursula said. "I don't care how young he was when he said those things. He still has to be responsible for his actions."

"But we all say stupid stuff when we're seventeen," Jake retorted. "You know he doesn't still think Blacks and Hispanics are lazy. He said so in his apology."

"Oh, he said so?" Ursula cried. "You mean he can just say sorry and that means he's not a racist?"

"He's not a racist," Jake said. "He was just trying to say that a lot of people use social welfare as a crutch."

"Are you seriously defending him right now!" Ursula screeched. "You're saying that it's okay to say Blacks and Hispanics are lazy?"

"No, no, no," said Jake.

Just then the announcer on CNN introduced the presidential candidates, and Jake was spared from having to explain himself further. This time the debate was in a traditional format where a moderator, Kim Stephanopoulos, would pose the questions, and each candidate would have a minute to respond. The first question out the gate: "What role does institutional racism play in our current political climate?"

Tamara Holden was the first to respond. Racism, she said, runs rampant through our society from overt acts of hate to more discreet forms of racism, often referred to as institutional racism. This, Holden said, needed to be addressed and recognized as very real.

Tamara Holden was a senator from California. She swung as far left as they come.

Of course, Garrett Dougherty started with an apology. He claimed that what he meant all those years ago was that social welfare programs were not helping to educate and train young people of color in ways that would make them successful in the modern world. The system was failing them.

Nice spin.

"That's right!" said Jake.

Ursula shot him a deadly glance.

Kim Stephanopoulos: "How do you propose to address the steady rise in hate crimes across the country over the past fifteen years? Governor Dougherty, you first."

Garrett Dougherty had been governor of Missouri for four years. He only recently declined to run for a second term in order to focus on his presidential bid. His response went something like this: "Actually, a recent study found that since the start of this campaign, the incidence of hate crimes has dropped dramatically."

Kim Stephanopoulos: "What study is that, Governor?"

"A Breitbart News national survey," said Dougherty.

Kim Stephanopoulos: "Governor, you haven't answered the question."

"Well, hate crimes here and across the globe are terrible, terrible threats to our democracy. Not only have Jews and Muslims been the targets of heinous acts of hate, but in many places right now, Christians are under severe persecution. As president, I will take a firm stance against any form of religious persecution."

"What the hell does that mean?" Ursula exclaimed.

"Shh!" said Jake.

"Christians? Are you kidding me?"

"Shh!"

Tamara Holden's reply went like this: "Governor Dougherty would have you believe that hate crimes are on the decline and that Christians suffer from persecution as much as Muslims and Jews. That is simply not true. We need to cut the dangerous rhetoric that the Republican Party has been spewing. As president, I intend to craft a statement of tolerance to be signed by the governors of every state in this great country. We need to tackle persecution as a united front, and we can use all the help we can get from our local governments."

Dougherty: "Are you calling me a liar, Senator?"

"If the shoe fits."

From there the debate devolved into a shouting match, with each side interrupting the moderator to defend themselves.

A shouting match erupted simultaneously in our little suite. Ursula couldn't keep quiet any longer. She launched a full-fledged attack on Jake and his numbskull friends, calling them fascist pigs, racist, self-serving narcissists, stupid beyond belief. I thought for a second she was going to storm out of the room again.

She stayed.

The yelling reached a fever pitch, so I got up and headed for the door. That was when I noticed two red envelopes on the dormitory floor, shuffled in with the other mail. I picked them up. Sure enough, one was addressed to Jake and the other was addressed to me.

I dropped Jake's envelope on the pile of mail and stepped into the hall, tearing mine open with shaking hands.

Dear Sir Herbert:

Your presence is requested on Wednesday, October 31, at 10 p.m. sharp on the stage of the Hattie Howard Hunt Theater.

Regards,
S&G

I read the letter three times over, trying to glean something new with each perusal. There was no task, no challenge. Just show up at the right place at the right time. What could it be? It must have something to do with the theater.

The Hattie Howard Hunt Theater, named after Hattie Howard Hunt, the previous owner of the VU estate, stood at the northernmost edge of the campus. Hattie, who made her fortune stripping naked for cameras, fancied herself a real actress. So she built a theater on the property with the hopes of attracting crowds of adoring fans who would come to see her perform.

As far as I know, the theater was never used in Hattie's time. By the time construction of the theater was completed, Hattie was too ill to perform. Now it hosted the young performers destined for the Martian Actors Guild on Mars. There they practiced acting, singing, and dancing.

Tra-la-la!

I once fancied myself an actor. I can sing quite well. Mother was a singer, too. She used to practice at the piano in the parlor. Do-re-mi! When I was old enough, we sang together—duets. She had a voice like Liza Minnelli: hard, strident, booming. I would stand across the room and pretend I was Frank Sinatra. Mother always said my voice was like Frank Sinatra's.

Mother never let me get too close, for she feared she would stab me with a knife or smother me with a pillow. So we would sing old standards like "New York, New York," "Luck Be a Lady," and "Unforgettable," her sitting at the piano on one side of the room and me standing across the room against the opposite wall.

Mother didn't let me near windows, either. She was sure she was going to push me out. Sometimes I would come home from school to find Mother on the sidewalk below our penthouse, walking back and forth, looking for a body. She would convince herself that she had thrown me out the window and that my body was splattered somewhere on the pavement. She could do this for hours: walk back and forth in search of my body. Only after she saw me alive and well would she be able to move on. And then we would take separate elevators back up to our condo.

Even though Mother was scared she was going to kill me, I was never afraid of her. I adored her. She was so striking and dramatic, like Clara Bow. And the distance she kept from me only heightened my obsession with her. She was elusive, sphinxlike. I wanted to know everything about her.

I knew she wouldn't kill me. From very early on, I understood that her illness made her *think* she was going to do something terrible. But in reality she was as gentle as a kitten.

When I was ten, I auditioned for a musical at the local community theater. The play was called *The Will Rogers Follies*, which was about the real-life vaudeville performer and 1928 presidential candidate of the same name. The director of the show—I don't remember his name—cast me as Will Rogers's youngest child, Freddy Rogers. The character dies of diphtheria midway through the show but complains that the other children get to stay onstage and so is allowed to remain an active part of the play.

It was a comedy.

The show ran a total of four weekends, twelve performances. I was a hit.

Mother mustered enough courage to come and see the musical on the third weekend, after she had heard how well I was doing. She only stayed for the first act. She left early because she was scared she was going to strangle the little old lady seated next to her in the mezzanine.

I was thrilled she had come to see me at all.

I went on to perform in sixteen plays at the local community theater, all before I reached the age of eighteen. Mother never came to see me again, but she helped me rehearse for each and every part, with her sitting on one side of the room and me standing against the opposite wall.

Tra-la-la!

My nanny, Delia, could sing, too. She had a soft, gentle voice that floated through the penthouse. When Mother was having a bad day, Delia would practice singing with me. Neither of us could play piano, so we would sing a cappella.

Will Rogers had a famous catchphrase that was turned into a song for the musical: Never met a man I didn't like. I admire him for that. There are a lot of men I haven't liked in my life. And women, too.

Lee Knowles.

I'm not a big fan of Lee Knowles.

* * *

I was standing in the hallway, rereading the note from Scepter and Gavel when Lee appeared, trudging home from the library.

"What's that?" he said when he saw me. "Another secret

message from your pals in Scepter and Gavel?"

"No," I said. "It's a letter from my mom."

"Sure," Lee said flatly. "Whatever you say."

Lee pushed past me and stuck his key in the door to our suite.

"I wouldn't go in there," I said. "Jake and Ursula are at it again."

Lee rolled his eyes at me and opened the door. Ursula's voice came booming from within. "You rotten, racist xenophobe!"

"You tree-hugging, bleeding-heart hippie!" Jake retorted.

"Out!" Lee yelled over their voices. "Everybody out! I'm going to sleep."

Leave it to Lee to break up a party.

Ursula growled, grabbed her bag, and stormed out of the room. Jake's numbskull friends bid him a weary farewell and followed behind her.

Lee headed straight for the bedroom and slammed the door in our faces.

Jake looked ragged and defeated.

"What a bitch," he said.

"You got a letter," I said, pointing to the red envelope addressed to Jake on the floor. "Open it."

Jake opened the letter. "It says to meet at the theater Wednesday night at ten o'clock. What's yours say?"

"Same thing," I said.

"Here we go again."

CHAPTER 14

THIS MORNING Inspector Dunst pulled me in for questioning. I got up early, around 5:00 a.m., and I went for a run around C-Pod. I may be slow as molasses, but I don't walk. I keep trotting, even if it doesn't feel like I'm going very fast. I was thinking about my pending interview with the investigator—we had set it for 9:00 a.m.—when I ran into Prescott Harrington, who still jogs recreationally.

Prescott has aged, like we all have. He has silver streaks in his hair, and wrinkles around his eyes, and hair growing out of his ears. He's fifty-one or so, only a few years older than I, but he doesn't look so good. He told me he's been on leave from work for a few months because he herniated a disc a while back. He works in construction, so he can't work while he recuperates. Apparently, this was his first run in months.

He lives on the opposite end of C-Pod, but he was feeling good this morning and ran all the way over to my neighborhood. I said we should run together sometime.

"No way," he replied. "I couldn't keep up with a cross-country star."

I was never a cross-country star. And I am a far cry from the shape I was in during college. I told Prescott so.

"Well, maybe if you promise to go easy on me," Prescott said.

Prescott took the brunt of the blow from the scandal of '41. Being the Grand Pooh-bah, Master of Ceremonies, King Cobra, Maestro of Debauchery and Sin at the time *Vanity Fair* published its exposé, Prescott was subject to all manner of criticism and castigation. How could he have let it happen? they asked him. How could he have been so reckless? They practically put the full blame for Freddy Euler's death on his shoulders.

We agreed to run together sometime soon—if I didn't wind up in prison, I said jokingly, referring to the upcoming interrogation.

Then I showered in the communal bathroom and returned home. Cady was still asleep, and I didn't want to wake her. So I dressed in silence and snuck out to get a coffee at the Starbucks along the Sector 2 Promenade.

Everything in Pod City is close to everything else. It took me only about twenty minutes to walk to the Sector 2 Promenade. Most of the shops were still closed. But the Starbucks was alive with early-morning activity. Even on Mars, everybody needs coffee to get through the day. We actually grow our own coffee beans out in Sector 4, although we frequently run out. Which, as you can imagine, is the worst thing that could possibly happen to some people.

We run out of everything on Mars. Toilet paper, toothpaste, gasoline, soap. You name it, we've run out of it. Or we never had any of it in the first place. Thankfully, we get shuttles in every few months, bringing new supplies. And we can often improvise with what we've got up here. We have to if we want to survive.

I finished my coffee around 8:00 a.m. and had an hour to kill before my meeting with Inspector Dunst. The easiest way to kill time on Mars is to walk. You can walk the whole perimeter of Pod City in about an hour. So that's what I did. I walked from Sector 2 to Sector 3 to Sector 4 and back to Sector 2. I didn't run into anybody I knew the whole time, which was a relief. Ever since Adolf Dussel's death, people have been bothering me about the spent nuclear fuel pellet that killed him. Everyone knows I have access to nuclear waste, and they want to know: How did it get under Adolf Dussel's mattress?

Beats me.

I was exhausted by the time I showed up at the police headquarters in D-Block. Running and then walking—at my age? Ridiculous. And that's exactly what Inspector Dunst said to me when I told him how my morning had gone.

"That's too much activity for a fifty-year-old man," he said.

"I'm only forty-eight," I said.

"All the same," he said. "Shall we start the interview?"

He wanted to know where I had been on the day of Adolf Dussel's death. I told him I had been at home with my wife because we both had the day off. We had been planning to go to the beach when we heard the tragic news.

"We were already questioned extensively by the police," I said.

"Well, I want to hear what you know straight from your mouth," Inspector Dunst said.

He wanted to know if I had ever taken radioactive waste out of Dr. Dauer's physics lab. I told him that of course I have. I wear a special suit to handle the waste and put it in a special bag and deliver it directly to Frank Gutierrez at Danvers Cavern.

"Do you keep a log of all the nuclear waste you dispose of?"

I do. I am required to. The last time I had disposed of nuclear waste was two weeks ago when Dr. Dauer had finished experimenting with several spent nuclear fuel pellets.

"So you have access to spent nuclear fuel pellets, like the one found under Adolf Dussel's mattress?"

I do.

Then he wanted to know if I had any idea how the spent nuclear fuel pellet had found its way to Adolf Dussel's pod. I told him I had no idea how it had gotten there.

"May I see your disposal logs?"

"You'll have to talk to my boss, Yuji Ishida," I said.

"Does he have access to the physics lab?"

"No," I said. "But he collects my logs and files them away at the end of each day."

Inspector Dunst seemed satisfied with this answer. He told me he would request to see the logs and that I would be called in again if they needed to question me further.

"Any time," I said.

The interview took all of twenty minutes. I wasn't really a suspect, Inspector Dunst told me confidentially. He had a suspect. But he couldn't tell me who just yet. He would hold a press conference as soon as he had anything definitive.

"Until then, I should be checking under my mattress, right?" It was a joke.

"Frankly, yes," Inspector Dunst said. He wasn't joking.

The headline this morning in the *Martian Gazette* read NU-CLEAR WASTE HANDLERS UNDER INVESTIGATION. They are talking specifically about the twenty people who have access to nuclear waste. My name is listed among the handlers. I haven't been this famous since the scandal of '41. And this time, like then, it's because someone died.

Go figure.

Governor Harding is quoted as saying, "A tragedy. Terrible, terrible. We must fight for law and order. Justice is nigh!"

That's Harding's new campaign slogan: "Justice is nigh!"

He's already politicized Adolf Dussel's death. People are scared, and Harding wants everybody to know he's a real hard-ass on crime. This, of course, is a new strategy for Harding's campaign. Before Adolf Dussel's murder, there was no crime on Mars. The worst thing anybody would ever do was go over the water quota or improperly sort their waste.

Governor Harding is polling ahead of William Garfield, but it's close. Harding has been governor for four years. He's only a few years older than I am.

William Garfield—or Best Bet Bill, as he's calling himself for the campaign—is young, only thirty years old. He graduated from VU third in his class and was snatched up right away by the MDA, the Martian Department of Agriculture. There he managed to reduce food waste by 30 percent, which is a big deal on Mars. We can't afford to waste anything. Best Bet Bill is charismatic and intelligent; he's gained quite a following since he announced his gubernatorial bid in March. He is polling well among Democrats and numbskulls alike, and he's doing especially well with blue-collar workers because he's proposed significant labor reform and increasing the minimum wage.

I'm voting for him.

Cady is undecided.

I happen to loathe Frank Harding and his sycophantic sidekick, Lee Knowles. They really screwed me over in college. Cady says they were doing their due diligence, that Scepter and Gavel needed to be stopped, whatever the cost to my pride. She says I am lucky I wasn't expelled, that we weren't all expelled.

I say phooey. Freddy's death was a tragic accident. That's why we weren't expelled.

"And because the Harrington family hired the best lawyers in the country to defend you," Cady says.

That's true: Jake and Prescott's dad saved our asses. He stepped in and paid all our legal fees and got us representation and caused such a fuss that the trial became one of those long, drawn-out affairs where everybody starts to doubt their own good sense.

My father did not spend a single penny to help me. His words when he found out I was in trouble: "Sounds like you deserve to be expelled."

Mother was more forgiving. She and I used to talk on the phone a lot. She liked talking on the phone because there was no way she could kill me over the phone. When I was five years old, she installed phone lines in every room of our house so that she could get a hold of me without having to get too close. So we developed a habit of talking on the phone.

When she found out I was in trouble, Mother called to say that I shouldn't worry, that I could always transfer to her alma mater, Swarthmore. She knew the director of admissions there and could get me accepted in a pinch.

One thing was certain: Mother did not want me to come home. What a relief it must have been to have me out of the house after eighteen years. Not that Mother got much better after I'd gone. She still couldn't go out for fear of strangling someone with her bare hands. There were people everywhere in New York, and Mother couldn't stand to be near people. There was no end to the creative ways she came up with for killing people.

Delia Styles wrote me shortly after I got in trouble.

Dear Herbert,

I just finished reading the *Vanity Fair* piece. Your father went out and bought a copy when he heard.

What were you thinking? Didn't I teach you better than that? You're lucky your father doesn't cut you off completely.

My best advice is to keep your mouth shut. Don't admit to anything. Let the lawyers do all the talking. And only speak when absolutely necessary. They're liable to use anything you say against you. Growing up, we learned to keep our mouths shut in situations like yours.

Not that we ever got into any situations quite like yours.

You'll get out of it, I'm sure.

Love,
Delia

We got out of it, all right. But now I'm a janitor, and Frank Harding is governor of the Commonwealth of Mars. And Lee

Knowles is his number-one man.

If only Jake hadn't tipped Lee off that night. I remember the date because it came up over and over again during the trial: October 28, 2040. I wasn't there. Jake came home from dinner to find Lee bent over his computer, growling. He had locked himself out of his email account and couldn't remember his password.

Jake never missed a chance to one-up Lee, so Jake said something like "I know the best way to make a secure password that's really hard to crack but easy to remember. Wanna know what it is?"

"Sure," said Lee.

1. Pick your favorite band.
2. Replace all the vowels in the band name with numbers, i.e., *a* becomes 1, *e* becomes 2, *i* becomes 3, and so on.
3. Now put the first letter of the account name at the front of the password (lowercase).*
4. And put a period at the end.

*Adjust the first letter depending on the site.

Now this method may not strike anyone as easy at first glance, but it turns out to be a very handy trick. It might be the only truly brilliant thing Jake ever came up with. Let me explain further. Say your favorite band is Coldplay. And the site you are logging in to is Gmail. Follow the steps:

1. Coldplay
2. C4ldpl1y
3. gC4ldpl1y
4. gC4ldpl1y.

Then the password would be *gC4ldpl1y*. But if you're logging in to, say, your Wells Fargo account, then the password changes by one letter: *wC4ldpl1y*.

Here's the thing: Everyone knew Jake's favorite band was Radiohead. So Lee immediately knew Jake's Gmail password: *gR1d34h21d*.

But it wasn't Lee who put this knowledge to use. That would be Frank Harding.

CHAPTER 15

WE TOLD LEE we were going to a frat party on Halloween. We knew Lee hated parties, especially frat parties, so we hoped he wouldn't ask any questions. He didn't. He said he would be studying in the library all night.

We slipped out at 9:30 p.m. Everyone we passed was dressed up, the men as sailors, hobos, and cowboys, and the women as kittens, ladybugs, and cheerleaders. The night air was cool and still. Very still. It had rained earlier in the day, just a light rain that had left the pavement glistening.

On our way to the Hattie Howard Hunt Theater, we ran into a group of cloaked forms coming up the hill and thought for a minute that they might be Order members. But they walked right by us, talking and laughing loudly. We continued on.

The theater was formidable, a big brick building with white

columns down the sides. The main entrance was set back a little, just up a short set of brick steps. The two iron doors were closed shut. The building, which had no windows, very like the Tomb, looked like an eyeless face with one big gaping mouth.

We couldn't hear any sounds, couldn't see anybody else in the whole place; the theater sat quiet and alone.

"You reckon it's open?" Jake asked.

"I guess we'll have to see."

Up the stairs we went, right into the mouth of the beast. If the building had wanted to swallow us whole, right then would have been the time to do it. I approached the double doors and gave a tug on one of the wrought iron handles. Much to my surprise, the door swung open effortlessly, as if to say "Climb right in."

And climb right in we did. I entered first, followed closely behind by Jake. Jake's breathing was uneven and labored. "Stop that," I said when Jake gave a heaving sigh. "You need to get back into shape."

"Injury," Jake managed to say between breaths.

"We're in," I said. "What do we do now?"

Jake pulled out the red envelope containing our instructions. "It says to meet on the stage," Jake said.

Right. Then it hit me: They might ask each of us to sing something. Maybe that was the third challenge. I smiled to myself. I would knock their socks off, no contest. I sang like Frank Sinatra, or so Mother always said.

Tra-la-la.

We moved from the lobby into the main theater, treading lightly so as not to make a sound. All around us, dim lights ensconced in yellowing glass flickered like candles, flickered like the ceiling of the Light Bulb where I first met Cady. In fact, the color of the light here was the same color I remembered from the Light Bulb: pumpkin orange.

The stage lay before us, wide and beckoning. Mother would have liked this theater. She would have called it an opera house. That's what she called old, ornate theaters like this one. She wouldn't be able to stand onstage with me and sing a duet without worrying she might asphyxiate me with the curtain rigging. But no matter, she would have liked it anyway, exactly as it was now: empty.

But it wasn't empty, I soon realized. There were two dark forms standing on the stage, immersed in shadow.

One of the shapes came forward to the lip of the stage where the light was better. It was Melissa Veracruz. And her companion was Freddy Euler. They had made it to the theater before us.

"Hello," I said, whispering.

"Hi," said Freddy.

Melissa didn't say a word. Jake and I climbed onto the stage, and suddenly I had the urge to sing "Amazing Grace." I was sure the others sharing the stage with me would be impressed. Nobody had the faintest clue that I could sing like a swallow.

Tra-la-la.

"So what now?" Jake asked.

Melissa and Freddy looked at each other and then back to Jake.

"We don't know," Melissa said.

"How about we sing?" I said, trying to lighten the mood.

Melissa shot me a withering glance. I shut my mouth.

Then all at once the orangey lights in the playhouse went out, and a bright white light flicked on somewhere in the wings of the theater.

"Hello?" Jake said. "Who's there?"

Nobody answered.

Jake and Melissa moved toward the light.

"What are you doing?" I said. "They said to convene on the stage."

"Yeah," said Melissa. "And so we have. Now I think they want us to follow the light."

"Yeah," said Jake.

"Okay," said Freddy.

"Fine," said I.

Furniture and set pieces cluttered the backstage area. Here there was the facade of an orphanage, there a table piled high with wooden bowls and ladles. I shimmied past a ragged couch and around the facade of a tavern. Freddy followed close behind. Up ahead, the white light shined brightly from beyond the clutter. Melissa had already disappeared behind a black curtain and Jake was right behind her.

"What's down here?" I heard Jake say.

"Beats me," said Melissa.

Freddy and I caught up to the other two and saw they were standing at the top of a staircase leading down into the basement of the theater. The light we had been following shined brightly from below.

Having been in many plays before, I knew exactly what we would find down there. "That's the green room," I said. "And probably dressing rooms."

"Okay," said Jake. "I'll go first."

"Like hell you will," said Melissa. "I'm leading the way."

Melissa pushed past Jake and tromped down the wooden staircase. When she reached the bottom, she called up. "There's no one here."

We followed Melissa and descended into the basement. Orange bulbs glowed in wall sconces. The large room was peppered with couches and armchairs for actors awaiting their scenes. Just off the room were the dressing quarters, complete with mirrors, clothes racks, and makeup tables. People had signed their names all over the walls—a tradition I knew well in the theater.

The place was deserted.

The smell of the basement was the same smell you find in any old theater, the musty odor of stale makeup, moldy costumes, and rotting upholstery. The couches and armchairs looked a hundred years old. They must have been down in the basement of the theater for ages. I perched myself on the arm of a puke-colored sofa and said, "Somebody's gotta be down here."

Jake roamed the perimeter of the room, peeking into each dressing room and calling out, "Anybody there?"

"They obviously don't want to be seen, whoever they are," Melissa snapped. "This must be part of the challenge."

Freddy nodded. "They're messing with us."

The air here was still. There were no sounds except for the steady ins and outs of our own breathing. I fidgeted as we waited expectantly for the next cue.

Amazing grace! How sweet the sound
That saved a wretch like me.
I once was lost, but now am found,
Was blind but now I see.

"Stop that," Melissa said. I'd started to hum quietly to myself. Melissa looked like a bear trap ready to be sprung, a jack-in-the-box ready to pop!

All around the mulberry bush,
The monkey chased the weasel.
The monkey stopped to tie his shoes,
Pop! goes the weasel.

"I said shut up!" Melissa barked. I stopped humming. Jake looked at me like I was crazy.

Then there was a creaking sound, and a panel of the wooden wall opposite me swung open. I jumped to my feet. Freddy stepped back. Melissa stood stock-still, tense. And Jake made a little shrieking noise.

The panel of wall swayed on its hinges. Beyond it, there was nothing but darkness.

Melissa was the first to move. "Look," she said, pointing into the darkness.

Deep, deep down a dark tunnel, a small flame flickered brightly, no bigger than the flame of a candle.

"What do you think?" I said. "Do you think we're supposed to follow it?"

"In there?" Jake asked incredulously. "It's pitch black!"

Melissa activated the flashlight on her phone. "Somebody's down there," she said. "Come on." And she stepped into the tunnel. Freddy followed close behind. Then me. And finally, after some hesitation, Jake.

We had traveled no more than a few yards into the tunnel when the flame went out. Then the wooden panel slammed shut behind us. Jake squealed.

"What the—?" said Melissa.

> *'Twas grace that taught my heart to fear,*
> *And grace my fears relieved;*
> *How precious did that grace appear*
> *The hour I first believed!*

"Herbert!" Melissa hissed. "Stop humming!"

Jake called out from behind us. "I can't open it! The door, it's locked." He was referring, of course, to the wooden panel, the secret doorway, which would not budge.

We were trapped. And I said so.

"We're not trapped," said Melissa. "We just have to find another way out of here. That's all."

Melissa's cell phone illuminated her face, and I could see the dark circles under her eyes. It looked as if she hadn't slept in weeks, which turned out to be mostly true—I would later learn that Melissa suffered from chronic insomnia.

I followed Melissa's lead and took my cell phone out of my pocket. It lit up and cast a muted glow about the tunnel. Jake and Freddy did the same.

"Come on," Melissa said. "Whoever was holding that candle has got to be somewhere in here."

The walls of the tunnel were smooth concrete. The ceiling and floor were concrete, too. Copper pipes lined the walls, some of them emitting heat.

"Hattie Howard Hunt's secret tunnels," Freddy said. "I've read about these."

The secret tunnels, Freddy explained, were a network of underground corridors whose purpose was to allow Hattie Howard Hunt to move from house to house when she lived on the estate. She did not like to go outside for fear of being kidnapped by Soviet spies.

She and Mother would have had a lot to talk about.

"Let's go," Melissa said. "We've got to find our way out."

We used our cell phones to light the way. Melissa led, followed by Freddy, then me, then Jake. The path was clear except for the occasional puddle that had formed underneath a leaky pipe. Having no other way to go but forward, we splashed through the puddles, letting the water soak our shoes.

I wanted to sing "Danny Boy." Mother always said "Danny Boy" made her want to cry. Would Melissa want to cry if I started singing it now?

No. Definitely not.

I kept my mouth shut.

It was warm in the tunnels. We walked for what felt like a quarter of a mile before we came to a fork in the road. The tunnel branched off in two different directions. Both were completely dark. There was no indication of which way the person with the candle had gone.

"Hello!" Melissa called. "Hello?"

"I don't think anyone is going to answer you," I said. "I think this is it. This is the next challenge. We have to get out of here, and nobody is going to help us."

"Where do you think we come out?" Freddy asked.

"There are probably several ways out," I said reassuringly.

"We've just got to find one that's open," said Jake.

"Let's go left," said Melissa.

We continued down the long, dark corridor for a long time. At one point we came to another fork in the road, and we went left again. The darkness was disorienting, and after two more left turns, I was sure we were back at the first crossroads we had encountered.

"Doesn't this look familiar, guys?" I asked.

"It all looks the same," said Jake.

"Yeah," I said, "but doesn't this look particularly familiar? I think we're back where we started."

"Could be," said Melissa. "Let's go right at the next fork in the road."

We all agreed.

Melissa was a natural leader. Fearless. Not that she was easy to get along with—she wasn't. But she knew how to bend others to her will. I would later learn that she suffered from several congenital birth defects. For example, her right leg was an inch shorter than her left. She wore corrective shoes, one an inch taller than the other. That was how she had managed to become such a good runner: special shoes.

Melissa also had a condition known as congenital heart block. She had undergone surgery at five days old to have a pacemaker wired to her heart. Since then she'd had the pacemaker replaced twice. But she never let that slow her down. No way.

And what's more, Melissa had been born without an anus. I learned this from Cady many years later. Melissa never talked about it. She had undergone corrective surgery to create an anus where there wasn't one when she was a toddler. Prior to that, she had to have a colostomy bag that attached to her abdomen and intestines.

I'll let you guess what the bag was for.

She was given a real anus when she was two years old. Every so often, she had to perform anal dilations to ensure that the waste could pass through the orifice. An anal dilation is simply an exercise in which you stretch your anus out.

I know a few people who could probably benefit from anal dilations.

Lee Knowles comes to mind.

Despite all these complications, Melissa lived a relatively normal life. Better than normal, I'd say. She got top marks in everything she did. She was beloved by her teachers. And with her family connections, she was destined for greatness.

Too bad she joined the Order of the Scepter and Gavel.

Melissa and Cady are still friends; Cady also vouched for Melissa during the academic council hearings of 2041. I see Melissa every couple of months or so when my dune buggy needs repairing. True to form, Melissa is the best damn dune buggy repairperson on the planet, perhaps in the universe.

After we were put on academic probation for the scandal of '41, all gavelmen were required to take classes in dune buggy repair, plumbing, woodworking, electrical wiring, and so on and so forth—classes that would prepare us for our jobs as handymen and janitors and garbage collectors. That was our punishment. We were rerouted to the lowest track at VU, the track for students who got low marks in everything else.

That didn't stop Melissa from becoming valedictorian. She aced plumbing and woodworking and electrical wiring. Her instructors loved her. She never got anything less than an A+ in anything she ever did.

But I digress.

We started to sweat. The deeper we went into the tunnels, the more stifling the heat became. Even tromping through the puddles, our feet stayed warm: The water was tepid, having dripped out of the hot pipes.

I thought of Mother. Whenever she caught a cold, she soaked her feet in warm water. I thought this was an odd thing to do, but Mother said it soothed her. This she told me over the telephone, with me in my bedroom and her in hers. Mother would not leave her room when she was sick; she thought I would catch whatever she had and that I would subsequently die. Her sickness would kill me. That's how she thought things would go.

I don't know why Father never got her professional help. It seems she could have benefited from cognitive behavioral therapy—the only form of therapy known to reduce the symptoms of OCD. My therapist, Dr. Paula Cuevas, says the idea behind cognitive behavioral therapy is to retrain the brain to respond differently to different stimuli. OCD patients practice what is known as exposure and response prevention. In this form of therapy, the patient with OCD is exposed to a known trigger of obsessive thoughts and then prevented from completing any of the compulsive behaviors associated with the obsessive thoughts.

For example, had Mother sought treatment (which she did not), she would have been assigned to hold a knife (the known trigger). This would start her thinking all sorts of distressing things: what if she sliced my throat, what if she killed me, what if I was dead and she was a murderer, and so on (the obsessive thoughts). Then the therapist would encourage her to sit with the feeling of dread without checking to see if I was okay (the compulsive behaviors). In this scenario, I would probably be removed from the room. Then Mother would not know for certain if I was dead or alive. This would cause her great anguish. But she would not be allowed to check on me, no matter how miserable she felt.

Exposure and response prevention. Look it up.

After what felt like an hour roaming aimlessly through the tunnels, we saw a light ahead. Excited, we started off at a run toward the source of the light, thinking perhaps we had found a way out.

However, as we got closer we realized that the light was coming from a headlamp belonging to a man wearing a tool belt and an orange safety jacket. He was fiddling with a pipe, ostensibly fixing a leak, though I would never know for sure. As soon as he saw us coming, the man called out. "Hey! You're not supposed to be down here!"

We stopped immediately, turned on our heels, and fled back the way we had come. In the confusion and panic that followed, Melissa and I got separated from Jake and Freddy. I had thought they were right behind me, but they must have turned down a different tunnel, because when I looked back, they were gone.

Melissa, as I already mentioned, was a good runner. So we were clear of the man in the headlamp in no time at all. But somewhere along the way, Melissa had dropped her phone. We dared not go back to where the man was working. (His name was Olaf, by the way. I would meet him formally during a course in plumbing during sophomore year. He wouldn't recognize me, but I would certainly recognize him.) We didn't want to go back to where Olaf was working, so we left Melissa's cell phone for dead and continued on our way, using my cell phone as a flashlight.

Now that we had lost Jake and Freddy, things felt more precarious. What if we couldn't find a way out? Would we starve down in these depths? Part of me started to think that maybe we should go back to where Olaf was working and let him escort us out. Surely he would know where to go. I ran this by Melissa.

"Are you kidding?" she said. "And risk getting suspended? No way. I'd rather die down here."

I don't think she was exaggerating. Melissa had probably never been in any kind of trouble in all her life. I, on the other hand, had been suspended, once, in middle school. I had a friend in eighth grade named Rafa Nadal—after the Spanish tennis champion. My Rafa, however, did not play tennis. My Rafa did not play any kind of sport whatsoever. My Rafa had an older brother who was in some kind of neighborhood gang.

Rafa admired his older brother the way younger brothers do. And I wasn't surprised when Rafa showed up one day at school with an eight ball of cocaine. Of course we were both curious. Neither of us had ever experimented with drugs before. A sniff of cocaine at eight o'clock in the morning seemed like a good time to start. So we did it.

We were completely ridiculous for the rest of the morning—and so off the wall (we were eighth graders, mind you) that our history teacher, Mr. Phillips, who was a young guy, maybe twenty-eight, knew right away that we were high. He commanded Rafa to empty his pockets, which Rafa did without hesitation (which was stupid, he could have just said no, I don't think Mr. Phillips would have been allowed to search Rafa's pockets on his own) and pulled out the baggie with about half a gram of cocaine left.

"What is this?" asked Mr. Phillips.

"Cocaine," Rafa said. He had tears in his eyes.

"That's it, you two," Mr. Phillips said. "Let's go." He actually left class to escort us to the headmaster's office. The other students were all abuzz as he led us out the door and down the hall. In eighth grade, this is one of the most exciting things that can happen on any given day: One or more of your classmates can get into serious trouble. There's a sick pleasure in watching a peer getting marched out of the classroom for some unforgivable sin. All that public shame. Rafa and I might as well have been wearing scarlet letters on our uniforms.

We were young—we hadn't yet mastered the art of bending the truth in order to minimize collateral damage. The cocaine, Rafa confessed, had come from one of his older brother's friends. We had both snorted it that morning. Why we thought it pertinent to spill every detail, I do not know.

Of course, all of this got back to the authorities, and Rafa's brother's friend was arrested.

How's that for collateral damage?

That goes to show that you shouldn't deal cocaine to eighth graders. They squeal.

Rafa and I were suspended for five days, and that was about all anyone could do to us at that age. So we got off easy, really. And from then on the rest of the kids at school regarded Rafa and me with a mixture of awe and fear. We were the bad boys on campus.

Anyway, Melissa refused to go back to find Olaf because she didn't want to get in trouble. So we continued onward, weaving our way right and left and right and left so as to get as far from Olaf as possible.

Then my phone died. Using it as a flashlight had taken its toll. The battery life was up. We were in total darkness now. Not a single speck of light shone from anywhere.

"This is what it must feel like to be buried alive," I said.

"Herbert!" Melissa said from somewhere to my right. "Don't make this worse than it already is."

I did have the impression of being buried alive, however. And claustrophobia was starting to set in. I hummed:

Oh, Danny Boy, the pipes, the pipes are calling
From glen to glen, and down the mountain side,
The summer's gone, and all the roses falling,
It's you, it's you must go and I must bide.

This time Melissa didn't stop me. I think the constant hum of my voice was keeping us both centered. This was not the time to crack.

"What do we do?" I asked the darkness when I had finished humming.

"We keep walking," Melissa said from somewhere down the corridor. She was already moving away from me. "Use the walls as guides."

I put my hand against the smooth concrete wall and followed Melissa's voice. Now we had to keep talking to avoid getting separated.

"What's the deal with Cady's boyfriend?" I asked, feeling like I could say anything I wanted in this darkness.

"Why's that any of your business?" snapped Melissa.

"I just don't get it. He's finishing a PhD and will be teaching at a university next year, and Cady just began her freshman year of college. How's that supposed to work? Plus, Cady's getting sent up in a few years. This guy can't possibly be thinking they can make it work with one of them on Earth and the other on Mars."

"Paul is very smart," Melissa said. "I'm sure he's thought

about all that already."

"Maybe Paul has, but I don't think Cady knows what she's doing."

"What makes you so interested in Cady's affairs?"

The darkness was complete. I could say words into it and they would be swallowed up forever.

"I like her," I said into the blackness.

"Hmm," said Melissa. We walked on in silence for some time, listening closely to each other's footfalls. Then Melissa said, in her very special way, "She has a boyfriend, Herbert. You'd better forget about it. It won't work."

Again I thought of Mother. Mother could be just as candid, her delivery and tone very matter of fact. I remembered telling Mother I wanted to apply to Yale when I was a junior in high school.

"You don't have the grades," Mother had said flatly. "You'd better forget about it. It won't work."

I remembered thinking I could have broken the course record at league finals during my last season of cross-country at Dalton.

"If you could have, you would have." One of Mother's favorite expressions.

And I remembered being very little and asking Mother if I could sleep in the same bed as her.

"No," she said. "I might strangle you with the bedsheets."

Yes, Melissa reminded me, at times, of Mother.

We came to another crossroads. We could continue on

straight ahead, or we could turn either right or left. Being unable to see anything in any direction, we had to draw on our other senses to help us decide which way to turn. I listened. There were no sounds except for the rustling of our clothing and the ins and outs of our breathing.

Then I felt it: a soft wisp of cool air brushing against my skin, making the little hairs on my arms stand on end.

"Did you feel that?" I asked.

"What?" said Melissa.

"That breeze."

I licked my finger and raised it in the darkness, feeling in different directions for the source of the cool air.

"This way," I said, finally deciding that the breeze was coming from the rightmost tunnel.

As we walked along, the wisp of cool air became a gust that sent chills down my spine.

"You were right," Melissa said. "There is a breeze coming from up ahead."

We quickened our pace.

We came to several other crossroads, and each time, I employed the same trick, using my finger as a weather vane. The air got progressively cooler the farther along we went, until finally we rounded a corner and we could see light up ahead.

Cautious now, not wanting to run into Olaf or any other person down here, we slowed our pace and listened.

"That sounded like a car," I said.

"Yeah," said Melissa. "Come on."

We inched toward the light. Then we heard the rumble of another car. Then another.

"It's the street!" Melissa cried. "We must be underneath the street."

At last we reached the source of the light. Above us there was a square opening in the smooth concrete. And beyond that, the crescent moon in the night sky.

"That's it! A way out!"

The opening was roughly three feet above our heads; reaching up, we couldn't quite touch the ceiling.

"Give me a boost," Melissa said. She was slight, no more than 120 pounds, so I lifted her from the waist and she caught the lip of the opening.

"I got it," Melissa grunted. She struggled to pull herself up and over the lip, with me supporting her weight from below. Finally she got her chest clear of the opening and she wriggled out of the hole and into the night.

"Melissa?"

Her face reappeared in the opening.

"Grab my wrists," she said, reaching down to me. I did as she said. "Now try to walk up the wall using me as an anchor," she said.

I yanked on her arms and began my upward ascent. I was able to catch hold of the lip of the opening, and I dangled there, Melissa pulling on my wrists with all her might.

It's just one pull-up, I told myself, arms aching. And I struggled up and over the mouth of the opening, rolling onto the pavement beyond, exhausted.

We were on the sidewalk just in front of a laundromat that was closed for the night. There were cars zooming up and down the street at fifty miles per hour.

"We're on the Huntington Turnpike," Melissa said.

"Yeah," I said, looking around. There were no other people on the sidewalks in either direction. Just cars racing down the turnpike.

"What time do you think it is?" I asked.

Melissa shook her head. "I don't know, but I'm ready for bed. Let's go." She helped me up and together we started off down the turnpike in the direction of the dormitories.

"What about Jake and Freddy?" I asked, suddenly remembering them.

"They'll get out of there eventually," Melissa assured me. "If they haven't already."

"Yeah," I agreed. "But if there's no sign of them by morning, we've got to do something about it."

"They'll get out by morning," she said calmly. "I'm sure of it."

I needn't have worried. Jake was already in bed asleep when I got home. His soaking shoes were sitting outside the door when I arrived. I removed my shoes and placed them next to his. It was 2:00 a.m.

Lee stirred as I changed for bed.

"Who's there?" he said, blinking about blearily.

"It's just me," I said. "Go back to sleep."

"You stink," Lee said.

"Thanks," I said. "Now go back to sleep."

Lee turned over on his side and buried his face in his pillow.

But come ye back when summer's in the meadow,
Or when the valley's hushed and white with snow,
It's I'll be here in sunshine or in shadow,
Oh, Danny Boy, oh Danny Boy, I love you so!

"What?" asked Lee.

"Nothing."

CHAPTER 16

CADY TELLS ME there's going to be a talent show next week in order to raise money for William Garfield's gubernatorial campaign. She says if I like Best Bet Bill so much, I should volunteer to sing.

Maybe I will. Maybe I will.

The newest poll results came out today: Best Bet Bill eked out a narrow lead over Frank Harding. He's in the lead by two points. I'm celebrating by uncorking a bottle of Pinot Grigio tonight. It cost me four lousy credits, since wine comes into Pod City only once a year, and we still haven't begun production of our own wine yet.

That's not the only thing I'm celebrating. Turns out I've been eliminated as a suspect in the Adolf Dussel murder case. Inspector Dunst stopped by our pod this evening to deliver the news personally. They think they know where the spent nuclear fuel pellet that was discovered under Dussel's bed came from, and they have a suspect in custody.

Turns out that once they got a hold of all the logs (logging in the waste, logging it out, noting the weight of each load, time of entry, etc.), they were able to trace the spent nuclear fuel pellet back to its source. And this is what they found: During the last fuel replacement process, a nuclear fuel bundle weighing 639 kilograms was removed from the nuclear reactor. The bundle contained exactly 17,178,082 spent nuclear fuel pellets, each weighing 36.5 milligrams. Add just over a dozen kilograms for the mass of the canisters and you get precisely 639 kilos. The technicians at the nuclear plant removed a dozen nuclear fuel pellets for shipment to Dr. Dauer's lab. The logs show all twelve pellets making it to the lab and eventually making it to the disposal site. Now here's where the exact numbers become relevant.

Minus the twelve pellets shipped to the lab, the fuel bundle now weighed 638.999562 kilos. Both the technicians' log and the nuclear transportation specialists' log confirm this number. However, the weight of the fuel bundle recorded by both the transportation specialist and the disposal specialist at the time the bundle was dropped off at the disposal site was 638.9995255 kilos.

Notice anything?

Yes, there is a 36.5 milligram discrepancy in the two measurements, meaning that at some point during transport to the disposal site, a single nuclear fuel pellet was removed from the spent nuclear fuel bundle.

And what did we find under Adolf Dussel's mattress? Exactly one nuclear fuel pellet.

The devil is in the details.

Furthermore, only one nuclear transportation specialist was on duty the day the pellet went missing: a man named Arnie Sphinx.

So we have our suspect!

Inspector Dunst says the nuclear fuel pellet must have been under Adolf Dussel's mattress for at least forty-eight hours. And then, poof! There went Adolf Dussel.

All this to say: I am no longer a suspect in the murder of Adolf Dussel.

So tonight Cady and I are popping open a bottle of Pinot Grigio in celebration of this news and because William Garfield pulled ahead in the polls. Cady says she will be fine if Best Bet Bill wins. And she says she will be fine if Frank Harding wins. She remains undecided, so it's no skin off her back who I root for.

Go Best Bet Bill!

When Inspector Dunst was over earlier this evening, he confessed that he still didn't have a motive for the killer. Why would Arnie Sphinx want to kill anyone? As far as Dunst knows, Arnie Sphinx didn't even know Adolf Dussel.

Go figure.

And Arnie Sphinx isn't talking—not until he gets a lawyer, anyway. So the mystery continues.

Meanwhile, nobody's been able to get a message through to Earth for the past eight days thanks to the solar conjunction. The sun is still standing in the way of any signals we try to send to Houston. So Adolf Dussel's murder hasn't made headlines on Earth yet.

It's all anyone can talk about up here.

Yuji Ishida, my boss, spent half the morning probing me for information about the case. He knows that Inspector Dunst interviewed me and thinks I know more than I do. Yuji knows as much as anybody. Inspector Dunst interviewed him, too, in order to collect the logs. And besides, the *Martian Gazette* has already reported on everything I know.

Now we're all waiting for Arnie Sphinx's testimony.

It won't be long before he gets a lawyer. Litigators are standing in line to represent him; this is the first murder case to be tried on Mars, after all. It's the best gig a lawyer can ask for up here.

We say *up here* when we're referring to Mars. *Down there* means Earth. For whatever silly reason, Mars is up and Earth is down, no matter where they are in their orbits.

I'm gunning for Clive Cohen to take over the case. Clive lived down the hall from me at VU. He was not a gavelman. His mile time was nine minutes and twenty-two seconds. I don't know Clive well, but I like what I do know of him. And word on the street is that he is the best damn lawyer on the planet.

Do I want to see Arnie Sphinx go free?

Well, I certainly don't want him to get locked up for something he didn't do. As Inspector Dunst pointed out, Arnie had no motive to kill Adolf Dussel. So there has got to be more to the case, and I have a feeling Clive Cohen will be able to suss it out.

The prosecutor will be Winston Roach, the district attorney, appointed by Governor Harding himself. Roach was one of the first students to graduate from Vanderough University, so he was one of the first people to make Pod City his home. He's been enforcing the law on Mars for almost four decades. Think of that: forty years. He had his own private practice until Governor Harding took over and made him DA. He's widely known to be the richest man on Mars—family money. He managed to secure three of Ling Ling Ng's luxury pods for living quarters, which is unheard of here. But Winston Roach is a big donor to VU, and our founder, Samuel Owens, isn't above playing favorites.

I respect Roach, but I don't think anybody up here should be allowed to occupy three pods, let alone three *luxury* pods. One of the things that's most notable about life on Mars is that nobody gets more than their fair share. Sure, there are people with more or less money up here, and sure, some pods are nicer than others. But when it comes to resources, there's not much a person can do to be better off than another person. Okay, so Roach probably has wine with every meal and coffee every morning, but he's still just a number like the rest of us. In fact, I know his number, since he's one of the founders of

Pod City: ID number 000005. That makes him the fifth resident of Mars. But that's misleading, since the first wave of colonizers numbered roughly seventy-five people. The reason Roach is number five is because he had the fifth-best marks among students graduating his year.

All seventy-five of the original settlers are known as founders or First Geners. I'm an Eleventh Gener because I was part of the eleventh graduating class at VU. But anyone with an ID number between 000076 and 001001 is known as a pioneer. My ID number is 000928 so I'm a pioneer.

The next nine thousand people are called builders. Our population has now passed the ten thousand mark; I don't know what we're calling people with ID numbers greater than 010000. I'm sure we'll think of something.

The most recent group of settlers to arrive are 37th Geners. I'm officially old.

Cady: "You're only as old as you feel."

Thank you, Cady.

CHAPTER 17

BEFORE I REGALE YOU with the story of our final initiation rite on the night of Friday, November 16, 2040, I would like to share my thoughts on the results of the 2040 presidential election. I also need to discuss the events of Saturday, November 10, 2040—the day of Cady Pinkleton's nineteenth birthday.

I won't beat around the bush: Republican Garrett Dougherty was elected president of the United States on Tuesday, November 6, 2040. His promise to crack down on Islamic extremism, coupled with his pro-gun, pro-life stances, guaranteed him a narrow lead over Tamara Holden, who still, in 2040, was too progressive for the majority of the country.

Mental health discussions were too taboo for the masses. That things could go wrong in someone's brain and that it might take outside intervention from professionals to fix those things—that would be akin to saying the American Dream was a farce.

What, you may ask, is the American Dream?

It is the notion that every person, no matter who they are or where they come from, can pull themselves up by their own bootstraps. Can overcome life's obstacles with the sheer power of their will. It is the notion that we are all equal in that way: We all have the same capacity to work hard and *overcome*.

Bullshit.

Thank god now in 2070 we don't think that way anymore. Now we recognize the American Dream for what it really was: a fantasy. Thank god now in 2070 we recognize that some people need more help than others to stay afloat. Tamara Holden was ahead of her time. She knew back in 2040 that not all brains are the same. There are disorders of the brain that put some people at a disadvantage in life. Like OCD, for example, which made my mother's life particularly difficult. Or depression. Or schizophrenia. To think that people, by the sheer power of their will, can overcome these disorders is ludicrous.

If someone has an infection, you give them antibiotics, don't you?

If someone has psychotic episodes, you give them anti-psychotics. It's that simple.

That's why everyone on Mars is assigned a psychiatrist. It is now widely accepted that people cannot possibly survive on a cold, empty planet far from everyone they ever knew without some kind of professional help.

Tamara Holden's message in 2040—that most of the world's ills, from homelessness to radicalization, could be ameliorated by providing proper mental health care—was radical for its time. It meant some people needed more help than others, and it suggested that the best way to provide that help was to pay for it with taxes.

And that was the naughty word: taxes. If you have to raise taxes, then you must be doing something wrong. If you have to subsidize someone else's healthcare, then you're just enabling bad behavior. Right?

Wrong!

So, so very wrong.

Now there is some consensus on the best way to improve a society. And that is to help people who don't have bootstraps by giving them bootstraps. In other words, we recognize that not everybody has the same luck, and therefore we have to *give* a little extra sometimes to keep people from falling through the cracks.

Simple.

But back in 2040, things weren't that simple. A lot of numbskulls still believed that the only way to teach someone to swim was by throwing them in the deep end of the pool to see if they could stay afloat. If they drowned, it was no one's fault but their own.

Numbskulls are twisted.

Tamara Holden conceded the election before midnight. Garrett Dougherty gave his victory speech. In it, he thanked Tamara Holden for putting up such a good fight.

"But the people have spoken," he added. "And they want someone who will lead this country with good, solid conservative values."

Blah, blah, blah.

Jake and his numbskull friends were ecstatic. Ursula Beal was crestfallen. She cried quietly to herself as Tamara Holden gave her concession speech. Then she clenched her jaw all through Dougherty's victory address.

Even Ling Ling had an opinion on the election.

"It's not so good," he said to me. His English had improved in recent months.

"No," I said. "It's not so good."

"What are you talking about, Herb?" Jake cried. "This is great! Down with the welfare state!"

Ursula got up without saying one word and left the apartment. We wouldn't see her again until after Thanksgiving. And then she would contact us only to tell us that she had been diagnosed with leukemia.

In the meantime, Jake went around gloating to anyone who would listen. He had *known* Dougherty was going to win. He had called it. Now the country was going to get on the right track. Now we wouldn't be wasting our money on social welfare programs that didn't work. Education that didn't work. Healthcare that didn't work.

Insufferable.

I needed a break from Jake after that. So it came as a nice surprise when I was invited to Cady Pinkleton's birthday party, and Jake was not. The invitation popped up on my phone the day after the election. The party was scheduled for November 10. It was going to be a themed affair: a cocktail party in formal attire. Who would provide cocktails to a bunch of nineteen-year-olds? I would find out later that Cady had stolen her older sister's ID before she left for college and was using it regularly to buy booze for friends.

Cady's older sister, Claire, is a dental hygienist in Seattle. She is married with three children. We hear from her every now and then. The most recent update: Claire's oldest just finished his MBA at the Haas School of Business at UC Berkeley. Cady sent him a nice note of congratulations just before the solar conjunction.

That week I went shopping for a present for Cady. I decided on a Tiffany T-clip ballpoint pen—silver. It was only about $300. I had my earnings from the zoo, so it wasn't all that unreasonable. On the day of the party, I dressed to the nines, putting on my nicest suit and tie. I hoped Cady would see that I was a true class act. As good as any doctoral candidate.

From Instagram, I could see that Paul was not going to make the party. He was at a wedding in Lake Tahoe that week. So this was my one chance to swoop in and get the girl.

The invitation said the party would take place in Cady's suite, which I assumed looked a lot like my own suite: one big common room with two bedrooms branching off the sides. I didn't know any of Cady's roommates, but I assumed Melissa Veracruz would be there, since she and Cady were friends.

At about 7:00 p.m. I headed down the hill from Owens Hall and crossed Carmelo Square to Xavier Hall, where Cady lived. I climbed the stairs, and with each step my heart pounded harder and harder in my chest. My stomach was in knots. I believed I could win Cady away from Paul if only she got to know me. She would see what a wonderful guy I was and would decide that she didn't want to do long-distance any-more, and she would leave Paul to be with me.

That was my fantasy.

Just as I was about to knock on the door to Cady's suite, it swung open, and there was Melissa Veracruz blocking the way. I could hear the sniffles of someone crying behind her.

"What are you doing here?" Melissa growled.

"I'm here for Cady's birthday party," I said, confused.

"Didn't you get the notification on your phone?" she hissed.

I shook my head and pulled my phone from my pocket. There was a message from Cady, sent an hour before, saying that the party was off.

"I didn't see this until just now," I said. "What happened?"

Melissa, who was guarding the doorway like a junkyard hound, eyed me suspiciously. "It's none of your business," she said.

"Who are you talking to?" Cady called from inside, her voice choked with sobs.

"It's Herbert Palminteri," Melissa replied.

"Oh," said Cady. "Let him in."

Melissa reluctantly opened the door to let me pass. "I was just going to get Cady something to eat from the dining hall," Melissa said to me. "Do you want anything?"

"No, thank you," I said.

Then Melissa was gone.

Cady was sitting in a desk chair with her face in her hands. She looked up briefly when I came in, and I could see the streaks of tears running down her face. Nobody else appeared to be home. It was just me and Cady. My heart jumped into my throat.

I looked around. All the furniture had been pushed to the sides of the room to clear the way for a makeshift dance floor. A desk was laden with booze: vermouth, whiskey, beer, wine, gin, vodka, rum. And mixers: Coke, Pepsi, orange juice, Sprite, ginger ale, carbonated water. There were slices of lemons and limes and an array of clear plastic cups.

"Want a drink?" Cady offered, sniffling.

"What's wrong?" I asked, ignoring her offer.

"Oh, Herbert," she said. "It's so awful."

"What happened?"

Cady wiped her big green eyes and pushed the red hair back from her face. "Paul's dead," she said flatly.

My heart skipped a beat. Could it be true?

"What? No way."

"Yes," Cady said. "He had some sort of accident while waterskiing."

"What kind of accident?"

"They think he died of carbon monoxide poisoning," she said. "From the tailpipe of the motorboat."

Paul. Handsome, dashing, wonderful Paul. Dead. I had never been so thrilled in all my life. I fought the urge to cheer.

"I'm so sorry," I said. "Let me make you a drink."

Cady didn't object, so I set my gift on the makeshift bar and poured two gin and tonics. One for Cady. One for me.

"I didn't get your message until just now," I said.

"It's okay," Cady said. "I'm glad for your company."

My heart sang! Tra-la-la!

Cady wore a slim green cocktail dress that brought out the green in her eyes. A pair of yellow heels lay discarded on the floor beside her.

I sat in the chair opposite Cady. I sipped my gin and tonic for a while in silence. Cady stared into the clear liquid as if hypnotized. Finally she spoke. "It feels like I've lost a limb."

"I can only imagine," I said.

"I keep thinking, 'I need to call Paul and tell him about this.'"

I nodded.

"But he's really gone," she said.

There was the sound of a key in the door, and in burst three girls I had never seen before. They rushed to Cady's side at once, smothering her in hugs.

"Oh, Cady," said one of the girls. "I'm so sorry."

I gathered these were her roommates. They paid me no attention. It was as if I were transparent. The three girls surrounded Cady so that I could no longer see her. The moment was lost. My alone time with Cady had come to an end.

"I'll be getting out of your way," I said, standing to leave.

Only then did the three girls seem to realize I was there. They turned and stared at me in my suit and tie.

"He didn't get the message?" one of the girls asked.

"No," said Cady. "It's all right. He's been keeping me company while Melissa gets me something to eat."

"Nice to meet you all," I said. "Cady, I'm so sorry." I moved toward the door. Cady leapt up and threw her arms around me. I felt my whole body tremble. She smelled like strawberry lip gloss.

"Thank you, Herbert," she said, letting go. Then she returned to the chair she had been sitting in, and the three roommates surrounded her again, blocking her from sight.

I slipped out quietly, leaving the present for Cady on the desk with the booze.

As I descended the stairs of the building, I ran into Melissa again. This time she was holding a bag of to-go boxes from the dining hall. I thought I smelled french fries and pickles.

"How is she?" Melissa asked curtly when she saw me.

"As well as can be expected," I said.

"Hmm." Melissa pushed by me and didn't say another word.

Neither of us knew then—couldn't have known—that Cady was far from well. She was pregnant with Paul O'Malley's child.

CHAPTER 18

I GOT AN EMAIL TODAY over the Martian intranet. Mickey G. is getting married and he wants me to offici- ate the ceremony. Why me? Well, I introduced Mickey to Georgina back in 2054. Georgina works in the astrobiology lab in A-Block, studying extremophiles. She wants to test whether anything can possibly survive Mars's cold, barren environment on its own.

She has yet to come up with any conclusive results.

Georgina is quite a bit younger than me, so we weren't at VU at the same time. I only met her when she started working in the lab and I was ordered to clean up after her. But as soon as I met her, I thought of Mickey G. For one thing, they both hailed from Anchorage, Alaska, which is a very unusual place to be from. I immediately assumed they knew each other in Anchorage, since I assumed everyone in Alaska knew everyone else. I was wrong. The population of Anchorage is 300,000, which is a lot bigger than you'd expect. Mickey G. and Georgina had never crossed paths before I introduced them in 2054.

For another thing, they were both gymnasts. Mickey used to compete on the pommel horse, parallel bars, and high bar, while Georgina competed on the balance beam. Since Mickey is twelve years older than Georgina, he had already left for Mars by the time Georgina joined the team at VU. But they had practiced at the same gym with the same team, just a decade apart.

So when I met Georgina, I immediately thought to introduce her to Mickey. Mickey had recently broken up with a woman from the cafeteria, Mary, who had torn his heart to pieces. Mary cheated on Mickey several times with several different men and women. Mickey had only just called it quits with Mary when I told him I'd met a gymnast from Alaska.

At first Mickey was hesitant to meet Georgina. He was still caught up in the feelings he had for Mary the cafeteria worker. And he didn't think an astrobiologist would be interested in dating a handyman. But I reminded him that Cady was a botanist, and she didn't mind dating a janitor.

"You guys started dating *before* you became a janitor," he said.

I shrugged.

Cady and I took Mickey and Georgina to dinner at the Bon Soir, a nightclub down on the Sector 2 Promenade—the only nightclub on Mars. It cost us a pretty penny—about six credits apiece—but we wanted to give love a chance.

Mickey and Georgina took to each other like white on rice. And they've been together ever since—sixteen years. Now they're finally getting married, and I've been asked to officiate the wedding.

Go figure.

Cady has been asked to be a bridesmaid.

"Of course we'll do it," she says. "What else do we have going on?"

The thing is, the wedding is in two weeks. It took them sixteen years to decide to get married, and now they want to pull it off in two weeks?

Crazy gymnasts.

"You can't stand in the way of true love," says Cady.

G stands for Galinski. We call him Mickey G. because there were two other Mickeys in Scepter and Gavel: Mickey Braverman and Mickey Donahue.

Incidentally, both the other Mickeys are dead now. So there's really no need to go on calling him Mickey G. anymore. Mickey Braverman died of a heart attack in 2052, before Georgina even arrived on Mars. Mickey Donahue developed a brain tumor and died last year.

Mickey Donahue started behaving oddly long before he was diagnosed with brain cancer. For one thing, he started chain smoking at the age of forty-seven when he had never touched a cigarette before in his life. When he turned forty-eight, Mickey became obsessed with astrology. He had a side hustle telling fortunes on the Sector 2 Promenade—one credit to have your palm read, two credits to have your astral chart drawn up.

We all thought these were quirky hobbies to develop late in life, but we wrote them off as symptoms of a midlife crisis. We had no idea they were symptoms of something far more sinister.

When Mickey Donahue turned forty-nine, the real problems began. He stopped showing up for work, and then one day the Martian patrol found him trekking through the red wilderness in a space suit, headed god knows where. His only explanation: His dog had run away.

Mickey D. didn't have a dog.

There are only twelve dogs in Pod City. I know each and every one of them. A dog is an expensive pet to keep on a planet where food and water are rationed so carefully. All the dogs on Mars are intended for scientific study. Whenever we get a new dog up here, you can enter a raffle to foster the dog—if you have enough money to take care of it, that is. But technically the dog belongs to the government and can be "borrowed" at any time for any manner of experimentation. The dogs are monitored throughout their lifetimes to study the effects of Martian gravity on bone density, musculature, brain development, etc., etc., etc.

Anyway, Mickey D. never owned a dog. He certainly

couldn't afford to be a caretaker for one on an electrician's salary. Not even with the extra money brought in from fortune telling. But at the end of his life, all Mickey D. cared about was that damn nonexistent dog. He called it Chuck, said it was a golden shepherd, loved it better than he had ever loved anything.

After the Martian patrol brought Mickey D. in from the red wilderness, his therapist decided he needed a medical evaluation ASAP. That's when they found the tumor. It had already metastasized. Mickey Donahue was dead within the year.

Then there was one: Mickey Galinski.

And now he's getting married in two weeks to Georgina Farley, and I'm going to officiate, or so says Cady. In his email to me, Mickey G. said the ceremony is going to be small, only about two dozen people. They'll be married in the Exotic Garden, a very popular wedding site. If I agree to help out, then he'll send me a script to read at the ceremony. He promises it'll be easy. All I have to do is follow the script.

"You can do that, can't you?" says Cady.

Hmm.

CHAPTER 19

THANKSGIVING was fast approaching. They gave us the whole week off at VU, and I was planning to head home to New York for the holiday. But Scepter and Gavel had other plans for me.

Just before midnight on November 16, 2040, only hours before I was supposed to catch the 5:00 a.m. train to New York City, I was awakened by a loud bang. Lee was asleep in the bed across from mine. We both sat up at the sound.

"What the—?"

Several hooded figures flooded the room. They grabbed me by the shoulders and dragged me out of bed. Lee, who was white as a sheet, started screaming. "Help! Help! Home invader! Help!"

I knew this was another of the Order's initiation rites, so I didn't struggle. The largest of the hooded figures chucked me over his shoulder. Lee raced to my aid—uncharacteristically, yes—and started hammering on the hooded figure's back with his fists. "Let him go!" Lee cried.

"Knock it off!" said a voice I vaguely recognized, and another hooded figure, this one tall and spindly, shoved Lee back into bed and pinned him there while the others carried me into the common room.

Now Jake appeared from the opposite bedroom, also in the clutches of the hooded figures. Our eyes met, and Jake grinned. He was obviously thrilled to be on his way to becoming a member of the secret order. The hooded figures carried us into the hall and down the stairs. Neither of us put up a fight. We knew the Order members were going to do what they were going to do to us, one way or another.

Jake was shirtless, wearing only white briefs. I was in a pair of SpongeBob boxers and an undershirt. The hooded figures dragged us out into the courtyard. The air was chilly. Cold gusts of wind gnawed at our bare hands and feet.

The hooded figures carried us down the hill, across Carmelo Square, and into the heart of campus. Small clusters of drunk students roamed the campus, either going to or coming from parties. Nobody said anything as Jake and I went by in the hands of our cloaked kidnappers. They must have known that this was some sort of initiation rite. The sight of two boys in their underclothes being dragged across campus by half a dozen cloaked persons wasn't too unusual for a college campus and certainly did not warrant any alarm.

When we reached the Tomb, a dozen more cloaked figures streamed out the front door and helped haul us into the big common room. There, they set us on our feet. The room was dimly lit. Several candles burned on the side tables and shelves. The furniture had all been cleared; in the middle of the floor sat four roughly hewn plywood coffins, open and empty, their lids lying inert beside them.

"What are those for?" Jake asked.

"You'll see," said that same familiar voice.

At that moment, the door to the Tomb burst open again and several more hooded figures streamed in, carrying Freddy Euler and Melissa Veracruz. There was a commotion as Freddy and Melissa were set back on their feet. Then the hooded figures fanned out into the room, leaving the four of us standing there before the four empty coffins.

The familiar voice spoke again. "Take off your clothes."

I looked around at the others. We were already in our undergarments, so we didn't know if they meant for us to strip down to our birthday suits. We stood unmoving, unsure of what to do.

"He said to take off your clothes," said a woman's voice.

Hesitantly, we began to undress.

"All the way," the familiar voice said, pointing at Jake, who hadn't removed his underwear.

Cursing to himself, Jake peeled off his briefs. All four of us stood there naked and trembling. We each had a hand over our genitals, and Melissa had thrown her other arm across her breasts.

"Now step inside," said the voice, pointing at the four empty coffins.

We did as we were told. We stood in the coffins for a few moments, wondering what to do next. Then the woman's voice said, "Lie down!"

The coffins were snug, as if they'd been custom-made to fit our exact dimensions. The others disappeared from view as I lowered my head onto the cold, hard wood. I could see only the forms of several hooded figures hovering above me. One of the hooded figures produced a jar, and in the jar was an enormous spider. It was a big brown thing, about six inches across, with eight crab-like legs and eight beady eyes.

I heard Jake squeal from the coffin beside me.

The hooded figure set the jar down near my feet and un-screwed the lid.

"No!" I said. But before I could scramble up and out of the wooden box, the entire world went dark. The coffin reverber-ated as they hammered the lid into place. Then everything went still. The wood felt rough against my bare skin. I lis-tened. I could just make out the sound of the spider's legs drumming against the glass jar.

I screamed, "Please! Let me out!"

The Order members said nothing. All was silent on the other side of the plywood lid.

Then I felt a lurch as the coffin was lifted into the air. The jar tipped over, rolled the length of my leg, and came to rest against my hip.

I held my breath. The coffin continued to pitch this way and that—it felt as though I was being carried down stairs. The glass jar rolled back toward my feet.

Then I felt them: long spindly legs wiggling against my bare skin. I shivered and tried to wriggle the spider off me. The spider climbed up my side and onto my sternum. In the confines of the wooden box, the spider felt huge—at least the size of a small dog. I swiped at it with my hands, trying to brush it off me. All the while, the coffin dipped and swayed as I was carried god knows where.

The spider had found its way to my neck and was tentatively tapping my throat and chin with its feelers. I screamed. "Let me out!" No one answered.

I brought my hand up to my face and brushed the spider aside. I felt a stinging sensation as the spider bit my finger. My hand began to throb.

"Fuck!"

I used my arm to squish the spider's body against the wall of the coffin. After several jabs with my elbow, the spider ceased to move.

I clutched my throbbing hand to my chest. Tears welled in my eyes. The remains of the spider slipped between my shoulder blades, tickling my back.

It had to be done, I thought, feeling guilty for killing the poor creature. The Order had given me no choice.

Then I felt the coffin being lowered to the ground. They set me down with a thud. I could hear the sounds of the other three coffins being set on the floor. The Order members had taken us somewhere deep inside the Tomb.

Then the familiar voice spoke again: "The spider symbolizes patience and cunning. As the spider weaves its intricate web, so too do we weave the story of our lives. We are in charge of our destinies. Joining the Order of the Scepter and Gavel is the first choice you will make in a long line of choices that will lead you to greatness."

"So it shall be!" came a chorus of voices.

"The spider also represents death," said the voice. "To master the spider is to master death."

"So it shall be!"

"Kill the spider, and you shall rise from the coffin in defiance of death."

"So it shall be!"

"Knock three times when the spider is dead."

Still feeling the legs of the crushed spider poking at my spine, I rapped on the wooden lid of the coffin. I heard the frantic rapping of the others nearby.

There came a loud creaking sound as the lids were pried off the coffins and tossed aside.

"Stand in defiance of death!" said the familiar voice.

We stood. At least twenty hooded figures surrounded us, each holding a flaming candle. Otherwise, there was no light whatsoever. I waited for my eyes to adjust. Then I saw that we were in a basement of some sort. The walls were made of solid granite blocks. The floor was concrete. A grate in the floor allowed for some sort of drainage or ventilation, I did not know which. The room was empty save for four large barrels; they rested along the wall, just visible behind the hooded figures.

I trembled. The air tasted stale.

"Come forward," said the familiar voice. He stood directly in front of us, flanked on both sides by identical hooded figures.

We stepped out of our coffins. My hand was throbbing from the spider bite. All of us stood naked before the congregation.

"Now you shall be cleansed of all your past misdoings."

A half dozen Order members descended on the large barrels and lifted them. They carried what looked like a considerable weight over to where we stood. As they came, liquid sloshed over the sides of the barrels.

The figures lifted the barrels over our heads and dumped what turned out to be ice water onto our naked bodies. I screamed. Melissa and Jake cursed. Freddy gave a little yelp. The water flowed over us, onto the concrete, and down the drain.

"Welcome to the sacred Order of the Scepter and Gavel."

Cheers broke out among the congregation. The cloaked persons began pulling off their hoods, finally showing themselves. Several members rushed forward with dry robes. The four of us slipped into them eagerly.

Prescott Harrington stood before us. To his right stood the young woman who had spoken earlier. To his left stood Surge. They extended their hands in congratulations and proceeded to introduce us to the rest of the congregation.

The woman's name was Lynn Boyles. She was second-in-command, lieutenant, and deputy chief. Surge was third in the pecking order, vice lieutenant, and scribe. Yolanda Perez was treasurer. There was also a boy called Howie Van Bruggen who was the technology officer. He promised to meet with us later in the evening to get us "into the system."

Several Order members took us by the shoulders and led us into an adjacent room—the wine cellar. Bottles upon bottles lined the walls, floor to ceiling. Prescott pointed to a few choice selections, and Surge hurried to retrieve them.

Then they led us up a winding set of stone steps into a grandiose dining hall, where a feast had been laid out upon a long, polished table.

"Eat!" cried Prescott Harrington.

I was overwhelmed. Every few seconds, a new person popped up to congratulate me. My cheeks were sore from all the smiling. And my hand still throbbed from the spider bite, never mind that everyone was shaking it so vigorously.

After a few glasses of wine, the pain in my hand subsided. I found myself seated at the far end of the table between Mickey G. and Freddy Euler. Bowls of peas and mashed potatoes floated around the table. A tray of roast turkey passed by. I helped myself to a drumstick. There were candied yams and cranberry sauce. I scooped a large helping of green bean casserole onto my plate, followed by a heaping helping of stuffing. Then came the pumpkin pie topped with homemade whipped cream.

Despite the late hour—it had to be two or three in the morning—my appetite was ferocious. I helped myself to a second slice of pie. I was wide awake when I felt a hand on my shoulder, and I turned to find Howie Van Bruggen standing behind me, smiling.

"You ready to get logged on?" he asked.

"Sure," I said, not exactly sure what he was talking about.

Howie led me out of the dining room and up a flight of stairs. We passed several closed doors along the way, and I wondered what could possibly inhabit all these rooms. Finally, we stopped in front of a door at the end of the long hall. Howie pushed the door open, and we entered what appeared to be a tech office. There were several computers scattered about the room, two large servers, a wireless router, and two large Xerox machines. Wires climbed the walls like vines. A constant buzzing sound came from the fans inside the servers.

"We have a full suite of the latest technology," Howie said. "The Tomb has its own wireless network. And you can use these guys to print or copy anything you need." He pointed to the two Xerox machines. "Do you have a laptop?"

"Yeah," I said. "It's in my dorm."

"Great," Howie said. "Why don't you bring it in sometime after Thanksgiving break and I'll get it connected to the network."

I thought of my train to New York. It was set to depart in a few hours. I gave up all hope of catching it. I'd have to take a later train if I still wanted to go home for the holiday.

"Okay," said Howie. "Why don't you sit down here and I'll show you how to access the Order's directory and messaging system?"

I sat in front of a large monitor, hands poised over a keyboard. Howie stood over me, watching carefully as I followed his instructions.

"Go to Scepter and Gavel dot com," Howie instructed.

I typed the web address into the browser. A nondescript page appeared, all gray except for two little white boxes asking for my username and password.

"Okay," said Howie, "I've already got you in the system." I typed my full name into the little box and, at Howie's prompting, typed in *PaS$w0rd123* for the password.

The page reloaded, and suddenly there was a whole suite of options.

"You'll want to change your password to something only you know," Howie said. He directed me to my account profile. There I was able to reset my password to something a little less conspicuous. Then Howie showed me how to complete my profile, listing things like graduation year, gender, email address, phone number, etc., etc., etc.

"This is so anyone in the Order can message you over our secure network," Howie explained.

I clicked on "Messaging" and found myself on a page with an empty inbox.

"In order to protect the secrets of the Order, we communicate solely through the internal network."

"Cool."

"You're all set. You can log in from any computer. Just be sure to keep your password to yourself. Never show an outsider how to get in. Otherwise, it could jeopardize the entire secret society."

Never were words truer.

CHAPTER 20

ARNIE SPHINX has hired Clive Cohen to be his attorney. Arnie is the nuclear transportation specialist who is suspected of stealing the spent nuclear fuel pellet that killed Adolf Dussel, remember? And Clive Cohen is the best damn defense attorney on the planet.

Good news: Arnie didn't do it. At least that's his story. He can still be tried as an accessory to murder, though, because he's not entirely innocent either.

Arnie's story is this:

Just over two weeks ago, Arnie received a note delivered directly to his pod. The note was from an anonymous person promising Arnie two hundred credits for a single spent nuclear fuel pellet. Whoever wrote the note knew good and well that Arnie had access to nuclear waste. They also knew the schedule for the replacement of fuel rods in the nuclear reactor because somehow they knew Arnie would be transporting waste the very next day. And two hundred credits is a lot of money. So Arnie, who isn't that bright, decided this would be an easy way to make some extra dough.

The note specified a time and place to drop off the nuclear fuel pellet: the next evening at eleven o'clock in the dumpster behind the Brazilian Steakhouse in Sector 2. Arnie—who has access to all sorts of nuclear waste disposal equipment—removed the offending pellet mid-transport and zipped it up in a special bag for safe delivery. He dropped the bag in the dumpster behind the Brazilian Steakhouse that evening at the suggested time. The next day two hundred credits in copper showed up on his doorstep.

Arnie claims not to have known what the nuclear fuel pellet was going to be used for. He has surrendered the note with the instructions as evidence. The message is typed and has no signature. However, Inspector Dunst has found two sets of fingerprints on the note. He has confirmed that one set of fingerprints belongs to Arnie Sphinx. The second set of fingerprints, we assume, belongs to the murderer.

Unfortunately, Pod City does not keep records of its residents' fingerprints on file. But headquarters back on Earth does. We were all fingerprinted before we enrolled at Vanderough University. So once the solar conjunction has passed, Inspector Dunst will send the fingerprints down to Earth for analysis, and hopefully, we'll have our killer.

The solar conjunction ends in four days.

Four days in which the murderer is on the loose. Four days in which Arnie Sphinx stays locked up in a jail cell. Four days in which the only thing on anybody's mind is this.

One thing is certain: Whoever killed Adolf Dussel isn't getting away. There isn't anywhere to get away to. Nobody is allowed to leave on the next transport unless the mystery is solved. So we're all trapped here on Mars, and one way or another they're going to find the culprit.

* * *

Tonight is the big fundraiser for William Garfield's campaign. I signed up to sing in the talent show. I'll be performing "My Way," lyrics by Paul Anka, music by Claude François and Jacques Revaux. Many people don't know this, but "My Way" started out as a French song called "Comme d'habitude," which translates roughly to "per usual." The original lyrics of the song have nothing in common with the lyrics of "My Way," but both are quite beautiful.

Am I nervous? Sure, I'm nervous. I haven't sung for an audience in twenty-some-odd years. My voice is a bit gravelly now, more like Frank Sinatra's than it ever was in my youth. But all I gotta do is get up there and let the sound come out. I'm really a good singer, so it should be easy.

The last time I can remember singing for an audience was that Thanksgiving after I was inducted into Scepter and Gavel. I missed my train to New York the morning following my induction—Saturday—and because it was so close to the holiday, I didn't catch another train until Sunday afternoon.

I hadn't been home to see my folks in nearly three months, which was the longest I had ever been away from home before. Father insisted that I visit for the holiday because my grandmother and two uncles would be in town, and Father thought it important that I see them while they were in New York since I hadn't seen any of them in quite a few years.

My grandmother lived out in California in a small municipality called Knights Landing, population 1,046. My father and his two brothers grew up in Knights Landing. We never visited because, Father said, "Small towns melt your brain." So if we wanted to see my grandmother, she would have to come to New York City, which she didn't much like to do. She always said it was too crowded.

One of my uncles—Uncle Todd—lived in San Francisco, working as an accountant for a restaurant group that operated a series of Vietnamese restaurants in the Bay Area. Since Uncle Todd often had to travel to New York for business, I saw more of him growing up than anyone else in my dad's family. My other uncle—Uncle Abe—lived in Austin, Texas, where he worked as a data analyst for Whole Foods Market, a subsidiary of Amazon. I don't have to tell you what Whole Foods does, or what Amazon does, for that matter. Everyone on Earth already knows that.

Everyone on Mars should know what Amazon does, too.

Samuel Owens has a contract with Amazon's outer space division to provide supplies to Pod City every few months. So even up here we get Amazon deliveries.

Go figure.

Anyway, Father insisted I come home to New York City for Thanksgiving. So—after missing the train Saturday morning—I caught the only available train Sunday afternoon and hightailed it to NYC. Soon enough I was sitting on my old bed in my old room, suitcase at my feet, in our penthouse apartment on Broadway and 93rd with Delia staring at me from the doorway, shaking her head, and saying, "You're late. Yessiree. Late. Late. Late."

Father was furious that I had missed my train. My grandmother had already arrived and had spent the whole of Saturday sitting around, waiting for me to show up. I was her pride and joy, or so she always said, and Father certainly didn't want to be stuck entertaining Grandma all on his own.

Why all on his own? Well, Delia didn't entertain, per se. That wasn't her job. And Mother was locked up in her room again. This time she thought she was going to poison my grandmother with Drano.

Uncle Todd showed up shortly after I arrived. He was a large, burly man with a lot of facial hair and a big round belly. As soon as I saw him, he scooped me up in his arms and gave me an enormous bear hug. His wife was there, too, and their children, Alex and Stacy.

Uncle Abe arrived the following day. Uncle Abe was unmarried. Said he would never get married. Said he liked being on his own too much to saddle himself with a wife. People have their reasons, and I don't blame them.

It was a full house. Delia had her work cut out for her, what with cooking for nine people and cleaning up after everyone, too. We managed to get a few minutes alone, Delia and I, and that's when she told me she had breast cancer. It came as quite a shock. Delia had always seemed invincible to me. She assured me everything was going to be okay. They had caught it early. And Father was paying for her treatment.

The news was a blow to me. Delia might die. I'd never known anyone who had died before. Except Paul O'Malley. But he didn't really count. Delia was like a mother to me. Contemplating her death left me shaken and upset. Little did I know that Delia would outlive both my mother and my father, and Uncle Todd, and Uncle Abe, and even young Ursula Beal, who was just then learning from her doctor in Bridgeport that she had blood cancer.

Delia's still kicking today.

Go figure.

Mother made an appearance on Thanksgiving Day, tolerating her OCD long enough to sit down with everyone for dinner and to play a few ditties on the piano. Of course, I was begged to sing for the family, and sing I did.

Tra-la-la!

If I remember correctly, I sang three songs. The first song, requested by Uncle Todd, was an old standard popularized by

Tony Bennett, "I Left My Heart in San Francisco." The next song, "People" was from the Broadway hit *Funny Girl*. And I concluded with a rendition of "My Way," which I will be singing tonight at the campaign event for Best Bet Bill.

My grandmother was delighted. She had grown up with the real Frank Sinatra, had even seen him sing at Caesars Palace live in Las Vegas in 1977. Unfortunately, I never got to see Frank Sinatra perform live. He died in 1998, twenty-four years before I was born. But on my eleventh birthday, after hearing about my success in *The Will Rogers Follies*, my grandmother gifted me an old turntable along with her collection of Frank Sinatra records. So I grew up with the sound of Sinatra crooning in my ears, crackling and hissing on the old record player.

My cousins, Alex and Stacy, had never even heard of Frank Sinatra before that Thanksgiving—had been raised on trashy pop music and Billboard number ones. This displeased my grandmother greatly. She used the same expression my father used all the time: "The young don't know a damn thing about anything."

Alex and Stacy only laughed and spun around in their chairs. They were twelve and ten years old, respectively.

As Aristotle said, "The young are permanently in a state resembling intoxication."

To my mother's great relief, everybody went back to their respective homes the next day—Uncle Todd and his family to

San Francisco, Uncle Abe to Texas, and grandma to little old Knights Landing.

"What a to-do!" Mother said when everybody was gone. "I don't need to see another relation as long as I live." She meant it. Mother hardly ever saw anybody from her own family, even though they all lived right there in New York.

She often said, "Family is a frightful malady. It spreads like malaria. And the only cure is death."

I could tell Mother wanted me out as well. So I caught the train back to Bridgeport that afternoon and spent the rest of my weekend in bed streaming *Battlestar Galactica* and reflecting on my recent induction into Scepter and Gavel.

Remembering the online messaging system Howie Van Bruggen had shown me, I logged on to ScepterAndGavel.com to see what was going on with the Order. I discovered that Prescott Harrington had recently sent out a notification reminding everyone that the next meeting would be the following Friday at 7:00 p.m. in the Tomb.

The purpose of the meeting, Prescott wrote, would be to discuss that year's April Fools' prank. And then, to my surprise, Prescott added, *We have a very good idea for this year, courtesy of one of our newest members, Herbert Hoover Palminteri.*

CHAPTER 21

I **HAD NO IDEA** what Prescott was talking about. Until that moment, I'd never heard anything about an April Fools' prank. So I pulled Jake aside on Sunday to ask about the cryptic message from his brother.

"I'm as clueless as you are," Jake said. "Prescott never tells me anything."

So I would have to wait until Friday to find out what great idea I had inspired.

Ursula Beal had been MIA since the election earlier that month. The excitement of being tapped for Scepter and Gavel had distracted Jake from his heartache. But it caught up to him over the holiday. Jake returned to VU crestfallen.

"Ursula," he said to me. "I love that girl."

"Call her," I suggested. Jake had been hesitant to reach out to Ursula after the blowup on election night.

"I can't call her," he said.

He needn't have bothered. On the Wednesday after Thanksgiving break, Ursula showed up at our door. She was as white as a ghost.

"We'll give you guys some space," I said, motioning for Lee and Ling Ling to join me in the hall.

"No, Herb," Ursula said. "Stay. You all need to hear what I have to say."

"You don't have to say anything," Jake said. "It was my fault. All my fault."

"I have leukemia," Ursula said.

We looked around at one another. College students didn't get cancer. Cancer was for grown-ups, like Delia.

"It is quite advanced," Ursula said. "And aggressive."

Nobody said anything.

"I'm not going to survive," she said.

Jake burst into tears and threw his arms around Ursula. I looked at Lee, who clearly didn't know any better what to say than I did. Ling Ling just nodded gravely.

Ursula, who had been so composed delivering the information, collapsed onto the floor crying.

"Why are you even here?" Jake asked. "You should be getting treatment."

"It's too late," Ursula sobbed. "And I couldn't bear to sit around all day waiting to die. So I convinced my parents to let me come back to school, at least until I can't handle it anymore."

Jake was on the floor, cradling Ursula in his arms. Lee and I stood motionless on one side of the room. Ling Ling stood on the other, shaking his head.

"It's not so good," Ling Ling said quietly.

Jake cried. "It's terrible!"

"I'm so sorry," I said. I motioned to Lee and Ling Ling. "We'll give you guys some privacy."

I picked up my book bag and headed for the door. Lee and Ling Ling followed me out into the hall. Once the door had closed behind us, Lee mouthed, "Oh my god!"

"I know," I whispered. "Awful."

"It's not so good," Ling Ling said again.

"We should let them have the room for a while," I said.

"Yeah," said Lee. "Let's go to the library."

This was the first time in a while that Lee had behaved civilly toward me.

"Okay."

The three of us headed down the stairs and out into the brisk November air. A light snow had fallen, and we had to watch our steps to keep from slipping on the icy pavement. The library was a five-minute walk from Owens Hall. We covered the ground between the two buildings in silence. We found a table at the library and sat quietly, studying for an hour or so. Then I shifted in my seat. I was beginning to get antsy, so I excused myself and went for a stroll along the winding passages of the vast library.

I was just passing the circulation desk when I saw Cady heading for the exit. I chased after her.

"Cady!" I called when we were both outside. "Cady!"

She turned to me. Her cheeks were flushed and her breath came out in thick, vaporous clouds. She was wearing a beanie and a fluffy down jacket.

"Herbert," she said. "Hello."

The last time I had seen Cady had been on the day of her birthday when Paul had died. She had been a total wreck. But now she looked calm—peaceful, even.

"How have you been, Cady?" I asked. "I mean, how are you doing these days?"

"I'm okay," she said with a faint smile. There was a sadness in her eyes. "I'm glad we ran into each other. I've been meaning to thank you for sitting with me the other week. You were very sweet."

"Of course," I said. I felt a flutter in my chest.

"We should get together again soon," Cady said. "Under less unfortunate circumstances."

"Yes," I agreed.

"What are you doing Friday night?" she asked. "My room-mates are taking me out for a belated birthday dinner. Would you like to join us?"

I tingled all over. I could feel the blood rising in my cheeks. I tried to play it cool. "That'd be great!" Then I remembered my obligation to attend the next meeting of Scepter and Gavel on Friday night. "Oh shoot. I can't. I have a . . ." I stopped.

Cady looked at me inquisitively. I went on. "I have a meeting."

"What sort of meeting?" Cady asked. This was very like Cady: never content with a partial explanation and wanting to know all the details.

"Oh, just a team meeting. For cross-country," I lied.

"On a Friday night?" she asked.

"It's a sort of party," I said, thinking on my feet.

"Oh," she said. She seemed satisfied. "Well then, some other time. Perhaps after the winter holiday."

My heart sank into my stomach. We were just about to enter our exam period. Then we would have two weeks off for break. That meant I wouldn't get to see Cady again until after the new year.

"Whenever is most convenient for you," I managed to say.

Cady smiled again, a sad, serene smile. "I'll let you know," she said.

And then she tromped off into the snow.

CHAPTER 22

DEATH WAS WAITING around every corner that fall. First, Paul O'Malley died unexpectedly. Then Delia told me she was in treatment for breast cancer. And then Ursula. It was a lot to process, and I felt sure that if I could just get through my exams all right, I would be able to sort it all out over the winter break.

Then I got another message reminding me to arrive two hours early for the next meeting of Scepter and Gavel. New recruits were in charge of making dinner for the twenty-odd members of the society. Ursula, of course, wanted to know where Jake and I were off to on a Friday night when we could be spending time with her. We were in Jake and Ling Ling's bedroom chatting about something or other.

Lee, who was standing just inside the doorframe, explained, "They're in a secret society."

"Is that true?" Ursula asked. The news seemed to temporarily revive her. The color rushed back into her face. She sat upright in the bed where she had been lying.

I said nothing and looked to Jake to see what he would say.

"If I were in a secret society, babe, do you think I'd be allowed to tell you?"

"But I'm your girlfriend!" Ursula protested. She was now on the edge of the bed. Her eyes were flashing brightly from me to Jake to Lee.

"Sorry, babe," Jake said. "No can do."

"But I'm dying!" Ursula said.

We all got very quiet. I think Ursula had sort of meant it to be funny. But it wasn't funny.

"Fine then," Ursula said, noting our discomfort. "Don't tell me. I'll just stay in tonight and watch *The Kardashians*."

The Kardashians was Ursula's guilty pleasure. Various shows about the family had been running for thirty-three years and featured three generations of Kardashians. They're still on the air to this day, even though most of the original cast members are dead. There are always more Kardashians.

"Family spreads like malaria," Mother always said.

So we left Ursula and headed to the Tomb.

When we arrived, we found a dozen or so gavelmen lounging in the common room.

"Kitchen's that way," one of the older gavelmen said.

Jake and I proceeded to the back of the building, where

199

there was a sprawling kitchen that looked like it'd seen better days. Melissa Veracruz and Freddy Euler were in the kitchen already, getting dinner started.

"What's on tonight's menu?" Jake asked, sniffing the air.

Melissa looked up at him from where she was busy flouring the chicken. "What does it look like?" she said. Then she gestured toward the other ingredients on the crowded island countertop.

"Chicken marsala, scalloped potatoes, and asparagus," Freddy elaborated.

"I call the asparagus," Jake said. "I'll fuck up anything too complicated."

"Freddy's fixing the potatoes," Melissa said. "Herbert, why don't you help me with the chicken. You do know how to work a range?"

"Duh," I said.

Melissa passed over a plate of raw chicken breasts coated in flour and seasoning. "Start by frying these."

"Jake, you can steam the asparagus over here," I said, making room on the massive range. "And it looks like you guys already got the oven preheating."

"We were on time," Melissa said curtly.

At the end of two hours, we had managed to prepare a feast to feed an army, and we were oil-stained and sweaty from the effort. The gavelmen had already gathered around the enormous dining table; they looked on hungrily as we brought in dish after dish.

"Dig in!" Prescott called from the head of the table. And within minutes the serving trays were virtually empty.

"Delicious," said Surge, patting his bulging belly.

"Good job, newbs," said Howie Van Bruggen.

The four of us new recruits seated ourselves at the table last. It was slim pickings once the others had taken their fill, but I didn't have much of an appetite anyway. The oil from the frying pan felt like it was in my blood. I contented myself with a glass of pinot noir, and before I knew it, I was drunk. I wasn't the only one. A good number of gavelmen were lushes like me. By the time dinner was done, at least seven of us had started up a chorus of "No Woman, No Cry."

Then Prescott took out a large wooden gavel and hammered it on the table. The whole room seemed to shake.

"Order! Order!" he cried.

When everyone settled down, Prescott commenced the meeting by stating the date and time. Surge, who was seated right beside Prescott, copied these down in a big leather-bound book.

"This will be our last formal meeting before exams and the holiday," Prescott said. "And as is our tradition at this time every year, we will use this meeting to discuss ideas for the annual April Fools' prank. We will vote on the best prank when we return for the spring semester."

"I second that!" cried another gavelman from down the table.

Everyone nodded their assent.

A hand shot straight up. It was Mickey Donahue. "I propose we lock all the bikes on campus to the bike racks using our own locks. You know, so people can't use their bikes."

"We have a motion to lock up all the bikes on campus," Prescott said.

"I second that!" cried Mickey G.

"Surge, please note for the record that the motion to lock up all the bikes on campus will go to vote in January."

Another hand went up. Prescott nodded. "Yes, Laura?"

"I propose we set all the clocks on campus back one hour. That way everybody will be late to everything and there will be general mayhem."

"I second that," said another gavelman.

"Surge, please note that the motion to set the clocks back one hour will go to vote in January."

The room broke out in excited chatter. "Order!" Prescott cried. "Order!" There was silence. Then, when it appeared nobody else was going to speak, Prescott said, "This year, our very own Herbert Palminteri has given me an idea. Something I think you'll all like."

I felt my face flush at the mention of my name. All heads turned toward me.

Prescott went on. "Herbert works at the zoo in Beardsley Park just across the street, don't you, Herb?"

I nodded.

"And he knows how to get around the zoo, don't you,

Herb?"

"Yes," I said, sobering up. "I'm pretty familiar with the place."

"And he has access to people with keys to the zoo, right, Herb?"

I thought of the caretakers who sat around the break room most days, drinking coffee and telling stories. They carried sets of keys that unlocked all sorts of doors in the park.

"Yes," I said hesitantly.

Prescott's eyes gleamed. "Well then," he said. "I propose we set the animals free!"

CHAPTER 23

PRESCOTT'S MOTION was seconded and then seconded again. The congregation burst into excited conversation. I felt my stomach turn over. What was Prescott thinking? Letting all those animals loose in Bridgeport. It would be mayhem.

"Do you think you could get us those keys?" Lynn Boyles asked, calling across the table. The whole room went silent again, and all eyes focused on me.

"Um," I said.

"Of course he can!" cried Prescott. "He got that cross off Geraldo Gelatti."

"*I* got the cross off Geraldo Gelatti!" Melissa interjected.

"Well then," Prescott said, smiling at Melissa. "You can help Herbert acquire those keys before our next meeting. Then we'll have our vote."

"Oh god," I muttered under my breath. How the hell were we supposed to steal a set of keys without the whole zoo going nuts? Surely, if they discovered a set of keys missing, they would change the locks. There was no way they would risk letting the animals loose.

"Meeting adjourned," Prescott said, hammering the gavel on the table.

I stood in a daze and began clearing the table. New recruits were also in charge of cleaning up that evening. I met Jake, Melissa, and Freddy in the kitchen.

"What the hell!" I said. "What are they thinking?"

"What?" Jake said, shrugging. "It sounds fun."

"Don't you think it's a little crazy?" I said. "He wants to set the animals loose in Bridgeport."

"It's crazy," said Melissa. "But I think we can pull it off!"

"Not you, too!"

Freddy patted my shoulder. "Don't worry, Herbert. We'll help."

I didn't say another word to them the rest of the evening. I hoped that when put to a vote, the motion to set the animals free would lose. I liked the idea of setting back the clocks. That was easy and harmless. But with the way the other gav-elmen were talking after dinner, I was pretty sure the other motions had been forgotten. Nobody spoke of anything else but setting the animals free.

The next day was my last shift at the zoo before exams and

winter break. I promised Jake, Freddy, and Melissa that I would scout out the situation, see what I could do about getting those keys. On my ten-minute break, I headed through a door marked employees only and wound my way through the corridors to the break room.

When I entered, several employees looked up from where they were sitting around little square tables, sipping coffee and chatting idly. Some of these people were janitors. Some worked for guest relations, like me. But the bulk of the people in that room were animal caretakers. And they were the ones with all the keys.

Most of the caretakers wore their keys on large rings attached to their hips. A few, however, had set their keys on the tables, along with water bottles, coffee mugs, and snacks. I took a seat next to one of these caretakers. His name tag read Tom.

Tom was eating a bagel and sipping his coffee. His keys rested on the table, just a few feet from where I sat. I could reach out and touch them if I wanted. But how would I manage to get the keys without Tom noticing? And what would happen when he *did* notice they were gone? I had to have a plan.

Then Tom got up, walked over to the bathroom door, and disappeared inside. His keys lay beside an empty coffee mug and a half-eaten bagel.

I froze. Should I take the keys now? How would that go? Just grab them and walk out? But then what would happen when Tom couldn't find them? Would he report them missing? Would they rekey the entire zoo? I had no idea. But there they were, ripe for the taking.

Before I could decide what to do, I heard a toilet flush and Tom reappeared from the bathroom. He seated himself beside me and nibbled some more on his bagel. I sat through the remainder of my break, waiting for another opportunity to arise and cursing myself for not having the guts to grab the keys when I had the chance.

When my ten minutes were up, I took one last look at Tom's keys and then tore myself away from the break room.

I told Jake how things went when I got home later that afternoon. He railed on me for not taking the keys when I had the chance. I explained that if the keys went missing, there was a possibility they would rekey the entire zoo. That sobered Jake up a bit.

"Why don't we steal the keys, make copies, and put them back by the end of the day?" Jake suggested. "Surely that'll keep them from rekeying the place."

"Who's gonna make copies for us?"

"I know a guy," Jake said, smiling.

We had to believe the opportunity would present itself again after the winter break. I still had to take my exams, and then I was spending the two-week holiday with my parents at our cabin in Upstate New York. A Palminteri family tradition. Like many of our friends, we always got out of Dodge before the city went into militant Christmas mode.

We would have to try again for the keys in January.

* * *

I spent winter break at the Lodge—as Mother called it—in Upstate New York. The Lodge was a six-bedroom and five-bath monstrosity in the Catskills, near a small ski resort town called Alpine Slopes. Father purchased the Lodge shortly after Google bought GeneTech, and we spent nearly every winter there, waiting out the frantic Christmas season with fellow rich Manhattanites. In high school, my parents used to let me invite a friend up with me, and we would spend our days on the slopes. But I hadn't thought to ask anybody that year. My mind had been on so many other things. So I ended up spending the two weeks alone with Mother and Father in a remote mountain village with nothing to do but ski and read.

Father used to ski when he was younger. But by the time I went off to VU, his back was so bad he couldn't tolerate being in boots all day. Mother, as you can guess, did not ski. She hid out in her bedroom all day, watching the Home Shopping Network. We would always arrive home to New York City after New Year's Day to find a pile of packages six feet high stacked up in the doorman's office, the spoils of Mother's phone-in shopping sprees.

Thankfully, the cabin in the Catskills had decent Wi-Fi and I could stay in touch with my fellow gavelmen through the messaging system on ScepterAndGavel.com. I spent those first few days at the Lodge clicking through every page of the society's website, trying to learn as much as I possibly could about the Order of the Scepter and Gavel. The crown jewel of the website was a confidential directory that listed every gavelman going back to 2030 when the society was founded, along with their current contact information. It didn't matter how renowned or famous the former gavelman was, com-numbers, addresses, etc. were available for all to see. I learned that the governor of Mars at the time, Pedro Ferreira, was a former gavelman and could be reached at his private MMail address whenever a fellow gavelman needed a favor.

MMail stands for Martian Mail.

During the trial of 2041—after Freddy Euler's death—we leaned heavily on the existing network of former gavelmen to help keep us out of prison and enrolled at VU. The Order would personally appeal to Governor Ferreira for asylum on Mars after graduation from VU, even if it meant we would amount to nothing more than janitors and trash collectors.

What do you know? It worked. Yay for us.

Since our fellow countrymen saw Pod City as a hostile place—a pioneer town of sorts—they were glad to see us sent up, never to return. Back then, Pod City really *was* a pioneer town. It certainly wasn't the vacation destination it is now. I use the term *vacation destination* loosely, since Mars is still a pretty hostile place for citizens and visitors alike. Imagine taking exactly one two-minute shower with exactly one dollop of soap every other day.

It isn't easy.

ScepterAndGavel.com was wiped clean after the trial, and the entire society was dissolved. If you want to get ahold of a former gavelman now, you have to go about it the old-fashioned way, using the public Martian directory, which usually doesn't list anybody's private MMail or com-number or address. Most gavelmen have lost touch with one another, effectively crippling the elite network we relied so heavily on to get us out of trouble back in '41.

But that winter, I had direct access to some very high-profile Martians thanks to the gavelman directory. If I had wanted, I could have reached out to Linda Falk, the famous Martian engineer and First Gener who was responsible for the original Martian pod design. In fact, I planned to do exactly that when it came time to look for a job on Mars. I had just been inducted into Scepter and Gavel as a lowly freshman, so I didn't have the courage to get in touch with the likes of Linda Falk at the time. But I hoped I could work up the courage by senior year.

Not to be. Not to be.

That winter, when I wasn't surfing the web, I was out on the slopes by myself or napping in front of the television. Mother came out of her room precisely six times during the whole of those two weeks. Father pretended to like me long enough to get through a couple of dinners together. Otherwise, he kept to himself as well, taking long drives around the Catskills alone.

Of course Delia was a constant presence, fussing about the house as always. She was probably the only person in the world who cared whether I was there at all. And she could tell something was on my mind.

"You've been distracted, Herbert," she said about a week into the vacation. "Did something happen at school?"

Yes, something had happened. Two things, actually. One: I had been tapped to orchestrate a dangerous April Fools' prank for a notorious secret society. Two: I had fallen for a girl mourning the tragic loss of her near-perfect boyfriend. The future was looking particularly grim.

"Nah," I lied. "Just tired."

On our last day at the Lodge, New Year's Day, I received a direct message from Melissa addressed to me, Jake, and Freddy. In it Melissa mapped out a scheme to nab the zookeeper's keys without getting caught. The content of this message, which we assumed no one else would ever see, would later be published in *Vanity Fair* and used as evidence for both the prosecution and the defense. It clearly showed premeditation in setting the animals free, but it also proved that Freddy Euler was as willing a participant as anyone else. Specifically his reply to Melissa's DM, which read *Awesome! I'm ready.*

Famous last words.

CHAPTER 24

CADY AND I just got home from the fundraiser for Best Bet Bill, where I brought down the house with my rendition of "My Way." The crowd went wild. I ended up singing two encores, "I've Got the World on a String" and "The Best Is Yet to Come."

I sang.

The audience cheered.

Cady cried with joy.

Best Bet Bill came up after the show to shake my hand. Nice guy. Cady liked him, too. I think he managed to win her over. Finally. I honestly can't believe Cady was even considering voting for Sleazebag Harding. So what if the last four years on Mars have been prosperous? So what if he is a great orator? So what if he donates half his income to charity? He screwed me and the rest of the gavelmen with his stupid *Van-*

ity Fair article. Good writer, yes. But an asshole all the same.

Cady switched on her tablet the minute we walked in the door and clicked through to the *Martian Gazette*. She's a crime junkie, and she's obsessed with the Adolf Dussel murder case. Arnie Sphinx is in the clear, she tells me. He may be charged as an accessory to murder, but he is definitely not the prime suspect anymore. After sifting through security videos, Inspector Dunst found CCTV footage of Arnie depositing the bag with the spent nuclear fuel pellet behind the dumpster in Sector 2 as predicted. And guess what? They also found CCTV footage of someone arriving a few hours later to retrieve the spent nuclear fuel pellet.

Prime suspect number two!

"He looks like a Grim Reaper," Cady says, watching the grainy security video that has been posted to the *Gazette* website.

"Let me see that," I say.

Cady shows me her tablet. The suspect is wearing a hooded cloak and gloves. Their face is covered entirely with black mesh. I have a sudden flashback. The cloak. The hood. The masked face. It's the uniform of the Order of the Scepter and Gavel, exactly as I remember it from all those years ago! It's the cloak and hood we used to wear when we were up to no good!

* * *

I was awarded my cloak and hood at the first meeting of the

new year. My initials—HHP—were sewn discreetly inside the cape where no one could see them. Black embroidery on black fabric—practically invisible. We were there to vote on the April Fools' Day prank. It didn't matter that I hadn't yet nabbed the zookeeper's keys. Jake had told his big brother all about Melissa's plan, and Prescott felt we had plenty of time to make it happen. Three months, to be precise.

So the vote went ahead as scheduled, and it was unanimous: In the wee hours of April 1, 2041, we were going to loose the animals of Beardsley Zoo upon the people of Bridgeport.

CCTV footage from the zoo would later be used by the prosecution to convict us in the trial of '41. In the video—played for the jury—nearly two dozen hooded figures could be seen swarming the zoo in the dark of night. Although our faces were never visible thanks to the mesh masks, it didn't take long for investigators to connect the black cloaks and hoods with Scepter and Gavel.

Thank god the roster of its members was a closely guarded secret, right?

Wrong.

Now, looking at the grainy footage of the hooded figure on Cady's tablet, I get a sick feeling in my gut. Are the gavelmen up to something? All these years after the scandal of '41?

"What is it?" Cady asks.

"I have to call Inspector Dunst."

* * *

It was the first week of February in the year 2041, and we still hadn't pinched the keys to the animal cages. The caretaker, Tom, who did not attach his keys to his hip like other zookeepers, took his ten-minute break at the same time every Saturday. So every Saturday, during my four-hour shift, I asked Geoffrey to cover for me while I took my ten-minute break simultaneously with Tom. And every Saturday, Melissa bought admission to the zoo and hung around the monkey cages, waiting for me to bring her the keys. And every Saturday, Freddy and Jake would idle in the parking lot just outside the zoo entrance, waiting to whisk the keys off to Jake's guy down at the docks.

Four Saturdays in a row. And never once had Tom or any other caretaker left their keys unattended. We were starting to think it would never happen. But that all changed on the fifth Saturday. I sat at a table in the break room, playing on my phone while Tom the caretaker methodically worked through his ceremonial coffee and bagel.

My phone buzzed. I looked down to find a message from Cady, whom I hadn't heard from since before the break. She wanted to get dinner—that very night. I fumbled with the phone, trying to make my response sound enthusiastic yet casual. Excited but not too eager. I was so busy typing and retyping my reply that I didn't see Tom get up from the table and disappear into the bathroom.

I had settled on "Sure, that'd be nice" and sent the text to Cady when I realized Tom was gone. But the keys were still there, just sitting all alone on the table. There had to be at least twenty keys on the ring, each one labeled in Sharpie with a three-letter code: MKY, BSN, TGR, WLF, LNX, and so on. I leapt up and swept the keys into a small paper sack that I used to carry my snack. Tom emerged from the bathroom just as I exited the room.

Melissa was talking softly to Musk the howler monkey, who had come right up to the edge of the cage and was staring at Melissa with those humanoid eyes, when I burst out of the admin building, trying hard to look casual. Melissa looked me over and shrugged as if to say "Too bad. We'll try again next week." But then I rattled the lunch sack, and the jingling sound of the keys made Melissa jump. She snatched the bag out of my hands and ran for the exit.

"I'll be back before your shift ends!" she called.

You'd better be, I thought. If Tom didn't have those keys back in his hands by the end of the day, they'd rekey the entire zoo overnight.

I returned to the carousel with a knotted stomach.

"You're late!" Geoffrey barked. He was wearing a Gucci baseball cap and aviator sunglasses, the latest spoils of his raid on the cash register.

I took up my place at the entrance to the carousel and, because there was nobody in the queue, checked my phone quickly to see if Cady had responded yet.

Nothing.

The anxiety was crushing. Waiting for Cady to respond. Waiting for Melissa to return with the keys. It would not be easy to copy that many. At least two minutes per key. And then they had to keep track of them. As Jake's guy forged duplicates, Freddy, Jake, and Melissa would have to transfer the code from each key onto its copy—MKY, BSN, TGR, WLF, LNX, and so on—in Sharpie so we'd know which key opened which cage. It was a monumental task, but if anybody could make it happen, it was Melissa. She'd have them in an assembly line—copying, labeling, and reattaching the keys to the ring.

At least that's how I imagined it.

It was just after two in the afternoon. Two hours until my shift ended. I hoped that would be enough time.

My pocket buzzed.

I glanced at Geoffrey. He was leaning over the ticket counter, totally immersed in some game on his phone. The bill of his baseball cap covered his eyes. I quickly pulled my phone from my pocket and read the message:

Cady Pinkleton: *How about Jerry's at 7pm?*

Me: *Sure. Meet you there?*

Another text buzzed through.

Geoffrey: *Get off your phone and help the fucking customer!*

I looked up and found a woman standing in the queue with two small children.

"Sorry." I thrust my cell phone into my pocket and took her tickets.

Once all three were seated comfortably on the carousel, I pulled the lever.

Whee!

My pocket buzzed again. But Geoffrey was still watching me like a hawk. Was it Cady confirming? Or Jake or Melissa trying to reach me?

As soon as Geoffrey was back in the world of *Angry Birds* or whatever game he was playing, I stole a glance at my phone.

Cady Pinkleton: *You mind if I bring a friend?*

My heart dropped into my stomach. So this wasn't a date?

Me: *Sure. No problem.*

Another buzz.

Geoffrey: *You gonna let them go around all day on that thing?*

I looked up to find the woman on the carousel frowning at me. I'd clearly let the ride go on too long. One of her children was crying.

"Sorry!"

I released the lever, and the carousel gradually came to a stop. The woman lifted her children from their steeds and set them on terra firma, all the while glaring at me as if I'd run her cat over with a car.

So the kiddies got a few extra minutes on the carousel? What's wrong with that?

Whee!

As four o'clock approached, I started to sweat. Then Tom the zookeeper swung by to ask me and Geoffrey if we'd seen a set of keys lying around.

I shrugged and shook my head and pretended to know nothing about it.

"What do they look like?" I asked.

"They look like keys, what else?"

Four o'clock came and went. I lingered around the carousel, making small talk with Geoffrey as he locked up the ticket booth. They weren't letting guests into the park anymore. Now it was just the cleaning staff ushering visitors to the exit. I kept my eyes trained on the entrance, and when Melissa finally appeared outside the turnstiles, I cut my conversation with Geoffrey short and bolted toward the gate.

"I just gotta give something to my friend," Melissa was saying to the kid who worked the turnstiles. "He operates the carousel. He's literally *right there*." She pointed and then saw me approaching.

"Sorry, miss," the kid was saying. "Zoo's closed."

"It's okay, Brian," I said to the kid. I reached over the turnstile, and Melissa handed me the paper sack with the jangling keys.

"Snack," I lied.

Brian frowned.

I bolted for the admin building. I had to return the keys

before Tom left for the day. Just as I was entering the main building, I collided with Tom, who had a frantic look on his face.

"Are these your keys?" I asked, yanking them out of the paper sack.

"Oh! Where'd you get 'em?"

"They were on the ground back there." I pointed vaguely toward the carousel. "You must have dropped them or something."

"What a relief!" Tom snatched the keys from my hands and examined them carefully.

"All there?" I asked.

"Looks like it," he said. "Thank you."

"No problem." I turned quickly and ran for the exit. Melissa was waiting for me outside.

"So?" she asked.

"I think we pulled it off!"

"Jesus, that guy was a jerk!"

"Who?"

Melissa cast a sideways glance at the kid guarding the turnstiles.

"Brian?" I asked. "He's like fifteen."

"Whatever. Come on, Freddy and Jake are in the car."

We crossed the parking lot to where Freddy and Jake sat in a beat-up Volkswagen Jetta. Freddy was at the wheel. Jake dangled a shiny new set of keys out the passenger-side window.

"There were like fifty of them," Jake said.

"Twenty-eight," Melissa corrected.

"Did you make sure to label them?" I asked, grabbing the keys from Jake and examining them for myself. Yes, they had labeled them: MKY, BSN, TGR, WLF, LNX, and so on.

"What's L-N-X?" Jake asked.

"Lynx, dipshit." Melissa had a knack for putting Jake in his place.

"Let's go. Now." I climbed into the back seat with Melissa, and Freddy screeched out of the parking lot.

Whee!

CHAPTER 25

"**S**HE LOOKS like a killer."

Cady is scrutinizing a blurry photo in the *Martian Gazette*. She holds her tablet up for me to see. Under the headline FINGERPRINTS MATCHED TO YOUNG MUNICIPAL EMPLOYEE is a picture of Polly Platt, a young, blonde office administrator from the governor's office.

The solar conjunction ended yesterday, and Inspector Dunst was finally able to get a message through to Earth. There were two sets of fingerprints on the letter to Arnie Sphinx. We already knew one set of prints belonged to Arnie. It didn't take long to get an analysis from Houston on the other prints. Turns out they belonged to Polly Platt—Adolf Dussel's ex-fiancée!

"Of course she killed him," Cady says. "She had the motive."

But there are some things that don't add up.

First of all, friends close to the couple claim that Polly Platt broke things off with Adolf Dussel and not the other way around. Adolf Dussel was devasted. So why would Polly Platt feel the need to kill him? Polly herself swears she ended the relationship, wanted it to end, was glad it was over. She isn't the spurned lover the press wants to make her out to be.

Why did she end the relationship? the press asked.

"Because I didn't love Dolfie anymore."

She calls him Dolfie.

Second, Polly claims her paw prints are all over the letter because she's responsible for restocking the printer paper in the municipal offices. Anyone could have used the communal printer in city hall to print the letter, and Polly's fingerprints would have been on it. The communal printer is connected to the workstations in the neighboring public library. Any citizen of Pod City can log on to the library computers and print up to four pages a month for no fee.

Paper is scarce here on Mars.

Polly is quoted in the *Gazette*: "I'm not stupid. If I were a killer, I would have worn gloves."

"Looks pretty dumb to me," says Cady.

But did she do it?

"Of course she did it," Cady says. "Look at that smug little face."

Cady has an aversion to blondes.

That didn't stop Cady from bringing her bleach-blonde suitemate, Francine, to dinner with us that Saturday in February of 2041. Turns out, Cady was trying to set me up with Francine. Francine was one of the girls who had stormed in on me and Cady the day Paul died, the day of Cady's not-to-be birthday party. Apparently, Francine had gotten a look at me and wanted to meet. I should have known. Cady was still mourning the death of Paul O'Malley, and she'll tell you now that she wasn't even thinking about dating at the time.

"You weren't even on my radar in that way," Cady says.

Thanks.

So the dinner was a bust. Francine spent the evening ogling me over spaghetti. I spent the evening ogling Cady over gnocchi. And Cady spent the evening staring into a bowl of minestrone soup, hardly talking, longing for Paul.

I wasn't even on her radar!

After a few more of these awkward dinners, all in the span of a week or so, Francine got the hint. I kept accepting Cady's invitations because I wanted to see Cady. And Cady kept inviting me because Francine was too scared to go out with me on her own. She happened to be a devout something-or-other, so she didn't believe she should be alone with a man before marriage.

Francine is now a nun. On Mars.

Yeah, they still try to get you up here.

Francine's mile time is thirteen minutes flat.

When Francine got the hint, Cady stopped asking me to

dinner. This had to be toward the middle of February. I remember because I spent Valentine's Day alone in the dorm with Ling Ling, hoping Cady would call, even if that meant another evening with Francine ogling me from across the table. But Cady did not call. I passed the evening playing *Mario Kart* on Ling Ling's Nintendo. Lee was probably in the library. And Jake was making a grand show of his affection for Ursula on a dinner cruise in the Long Island Sound.

Ursula's leukemia had advanced; she wouldn't last the spring.

I checked ScepterAndGavel.com before turning in for the night. There were two messages in my inbox. The first was an invitation to a meeting of the Order of the Scepter and Gavel for the following evening. It was time to hand over the zookeeper's keys to Prescott Harrington, the Grand Pooh-bah, Master of Ceremonies, King Cobra, Maestro of Debauchery and Sin.

The second message was from Melissa: *Don't worry, guys. I'll bring the keys.*

I wasn't worried. Melissa never fucked up.

* * *

The Tomb had two entrances: the main entrance used for ceremonial rites and a secret back entrance used for the day-to-day comings and goings of its members. After our initiation in November, we were instructed to use only the back entrance so that nobody wandering around campus late at night (our meetings were held almost exclusively at night) would identify us. We were still newbs, so we didn't get our own keys to the Tomb. We had to earn that privilege with at least one year of demonstrated loyalty. Instead, we were always at the mercy of older members, who would admit us only after we gave the secret password, which changed day to day, and which could be found on the website every morning.

"Funambulism," Melissa said when a voice behind the door asked for the code word.

We had arrived together—Jake, Freddy, Melissa, and I. The narrow oaken door swung open. It was Surge, the massive sophomore, who seemed to always serve as bouncer.

"You got them?" Surge asked.

Melissa dangled the zookeeper's keys noisily in front of Surge's bulbous nose.

Without a word, Surge let us pass. The Tomb was huge and mazelike, so Surge led us through the darkened hallways to the big common room that served as the main gathering place of the Order.

The room erupted in applause as soon as we entered.

"Well done, well done!" Prescott Harrington stood at the front of the room with a glass of champagne raised in honor of our arrival. "Get our new recruits something to drink."

Lynn Boyles, the lieutenant and second-in-command, doled out champagne flutes, followed closely behind by Howie Van Bruggen, who poured each of us a generous draught of sparkling Dom Pérignon.

"Very expensive," Jake whispered, sniffing the champagne.

"To our new recruits!" Prescott cried.

"Cheers!"

There were at least two dozen people gathered in the common room. I had only just begun to learn their names: Yolanda, Frederick, Mickey G., Mickey B., Mickey D., Samantha, Nisha, Akari, and so on and so forth. I never did learn all their names. We were only in the club six months before it was sentenced to oblivion by a Connecticut state judge.

We milled about for a while, sipping champagne and making small talk. Prescott sidled up to Melissa. "So what's the deal with the keys?"

Melissa placed the ring of keys in Prescott's hands. "There are twenty-eight. Each opens a different habitat, plus a few admin buildings and the front gate. They're labeled."

Prescott nodded and flipped through the set of keys. "What's S-L-T stand for?"

"How the hell should I know?" Melissa turned away and started up a conversation with Freddy Euler. Clearly, Melissa felt her job was done.

Prescott blinked.

"Sloth," I said. "It stands for sloth."

"So each of these keys is for a different animal?"

"Yep," I said. "But I honestly have no idea how easy it is to set them free. It's not like a birdcage where you just open up a door and the bird flies out. The animal habitats are complex. I'm not even allowed in most of the staging areas where the animals are kept overnight."

Prescott nodded. Then he signaled to Lynn. She peeled off from a small group of girls and disappeared with Prescott into an adjoining room.

It looked like my job was done, too.

After about half an hour of sipping champagne and chatting with my new friends, Prescott reemerged and called the room to attention. Lynn walked to the middle of the room and set a cast-iron cauldron down on an upholstered stool.

"Each key opens a different habitat," Prescott announced.

Lynn shook the cauldron and it rattled noisily. "There are twenty-three habitats in all, so twenty-three keys in the cauldron."

"There are twenty-seven of us," Prescott said. "So Lynn, Yolanda, Howie, and I will be on the lookout. The rest of you will pick a key. Whatever key you pick, that's the habitat you're responsible for opening on April Fools' Day."

"Line up," said Lynn. "And draw your key at random."

The room erupted in excited whispers. Freddy Euler was ahead of me in line. When he drew his key, he read the label out loud.

"B-S-N. What's B-S-N?"

"Bison," I said.

Freddy looked pleased.

I drew the key labeled TGR. That was Jinx, the old, arthritic tiger.

Was I pleased?

Hell no!

CHAPTER 26

DO I FEEL RESPONSIBLE for Freddy Euler's death? Sometimes. But he did have a relatively easy assignment. Bison aren't usually too aggressive . . . Usually.

I, on the other hand, had to get up close and personal with a tiger, so it could have just as easily been me that night.

So . . . I don't know. In the end the judge ruled that Freddy's death was his own fault, since nobody made him do anything he didn't want to do.

Cady isn't much help, though. "He wouldn't be dead if you had just refused to steal those keys," she says. "It's at least partly your fault."

Okay. Sue me.

Freddy's parents did sue me, and Father settled the case for a couple million dollars. They could've gotten more if they'd hired someone to fight harder for them. The Eulers deserved Father's money more than Father's mistress, Martha Mary Mae Krall, and my half brother, Wesley.

Speaking of the Kralls, a transmission came from Delia today. She wrote:

Dear Baby Boy,

Ms. Krall may be losing her mind. The other day I found her wearing a lampshade on her head. I told Wesley straightaway, and he came by as soon as he could to check on her. But by then she was her old self again. I don't want her to lose her mind because then I'll be totally alone in this big house.

My arthritis is bad. At this rate I'm gonna need someone to take care of me! Maybe Ms. Krall and I can lose our minds together.

Some days I think about you living your life on Mars and wish I could come for a visit. You were brave to leave your family, knowing you'd probably never see them again.

Love,
Delia

My reply:

Dear Delia,

You were brave to leave your family, too, knowing you'd probably never see them again.

We do what we have to do to survive, I guess.

Yours,
Herbert

PS: Ask Wesley to buy you a round-trip ticket to Mars. He's got the money. Cady and I would be glad to have you.

In other news, Inspector Dunst has hired an amateur hacker to find out exactly who logged in to the municipal network a couple of weeks ago to print that message to Arnie Sphinx. He's been keeping me updated ever since I tipped him off about the Scepter and Gavel cloak and hood. Polly Platt may be the prime suspect at the moment, if only because the inspector doesn't have any other leads. But Dunst thinks he'll be able to find out exactly who printed that letter, and he suspects it could be a former member of the Order, hence the robes.

"Whatever happened to *your* cloak and hood?" Cady asks.

"I left them under my bed in Owens Hall when I moved in with you."

* * *

Yes, Cady and I moved in together. But that was later, after all hell broke loose. After Freddy.

On the heels of that lonely Valentine's Day in 2041, I decided to be more direct with Cady. What can I say? I'd fallen for the girl.

It was a Wednesday. I remember because I had signed up for a freshman seminar that met at noon on Wednesdays called Beam Me Up, Scotty: Martian Telecommunications Explained. I was hardly listening to the instructor because I was worrying over Cady. She had stopped inviting me to dinner with Francine, and I was in serious withdrawal. Every time my phone buzzed, I got an adrenaline rush thinking it could be her.

It never was.

The lecture that day was about the first Martian satellite that had enabled wireless communication in the early days of Martian colonization. I wondered whether the Earth-bound satellites were doing their job and relaying Cady's messages to my phone. Maybe she had texted and it hadn't gone through.

I became obsessed with this possibility, and I decided to go see Cady directly to make sure I wasn't missing some essential communication. After class, I marched over to Xavier Hall and banged on the door to Cady's suite. Francine opened it.

"She's in her room," Francine said flatly, stepping aside to let me pass.

Boy, had she gotten the hint.

I knocked softly on Cady's door.

"Come in."

I opened the door to find Cady lying in bed with the covers up to her chin. A blast of heat hit me as I entered the room. Cady had cranked up the thermostat to its maximum setting. Sure, it was chilly outside. It was February in Connecticut, after all. But Cady's room felt like the inside of an oven on Thanksgiving Day.

"Are you okay?" I asked.

Cady shivered. "I'm fine. Just cold is all."

"You look like you might have a fever."

"No," she said, sitting up slowly. "Just the chills."

"Is that why I haven't heard from you in a few days?" I asked.

"No." Cady sat cross-legged on her bed, still wrapped in her blanket. "It's just that Francine thinks you don't like her very much."

"She's nice." I shifted awkwardly on my feet. "But I actually like you."

Cady frowned. From the other room Francine shouted, "Told you!"

I closed the door so that Francine wouldn't hear the rest of our conversation.

"That's what I was worried about," said Cady. "Herbert, you're a great guy. But you know Paul died not too long ago. I'm not ready to date someone else."

"We don't have to date," I said quickly, sensing that my chance with Cady was about to slip away. "We can just hang out, as friends."

Cady sighed. "I have a lot going on right now."

"Can I help?" I asked.

"No." Cady tugged the blanket tighter around her shoulders. "But maybe when I'm feeling a little better, we can get froyo or something."

"I'd like that."

It felt like a pity prize.

"Thanks for checking in on me." Cady readjusted the blanket. "I'll call when I'm feeling better."

I went home thinking it was over. She wasn't going to call. But then I got a text the first week of March.

Cady Pinkleton: *Froyo?*

That was the start of it. I won't bore you with the details of how we came to be a couple. It happened the way it happens for most couples: Cady and I simply got used to each other. Soon Cady was hanging around all day at Owens Hall with Lee, Jake, Ursula, Ling Ling, and me, or else I was hanging around all day at Xavier Hall with Cady and her roommates: Francine, Porsche, and Meg.

I didn't tell Cady I was in the Order of the Scepter and Gavel, and Cady didn't tell me she was twenty weeks pregnant with Paul O'Malley's child.

You'd think I'd be able to tell at twenty weeks. But Cady wasn't really showing yet. At least not to an untrained eye. I was only nineteen years old, so I was an untrained eye if ever there was one.

The Order started having more frequent meetings in March to plan for the April Fools' Day prank. I scheduled my dates with Cady accordingly. Cady was never the wiser.

Prescott relied heavily on me to help strategize. First, he asked me to do some reconnaissance. Find out what security was like. Was there an alarm? Did they have a security guard?

Turns out security was lax. It wasn't much of a zoo, after all. There were cameras trained on all the enclosures, but there were no alarms. The park always closed at 4:00 p.m. Cleaning staff and animal handlers usually stayed on the premises until 8:00 p.m. Then security locked everything up for the night, leaving one man to look after the park until 4:00 a.m. when the handlers returned to feed the animals and clean out the cages.

I managed to find out the night watchman's schedule by asking around a bit. The night watchman was a fellow by the name of Ford. He spent most of the night stationed in a windowless room in the admin building, monitoring live feeds from all over the zoo. However, he was required to do a loop around the zoo every two hours, on the hour, during which time nobody would be watching the security footage.

If we snuck in at midnight while Ford was doing his loop, then we'd have about twenty minutes to unleash the beasts. We just had to stay out of Ford's way, and it'd all be over by the time he got back to the admin building.

That meant we would have to work fast. In mid-March, I took a pile of maps from the visitor center and distributed them among the gavelmen. We studied the maps carefully, planning our routes with precision. Every gavelman visited the zoo at least once to get the lay of the land. It was serious work, but we were young and dedicated.

Cady says she still can't believe we pulled it off.

"With casualties," I remind her.

"You were lucky there weren't more," she says.

It was also lucky we had some of the best lawyers in the country defending us in court after the fact. Jake's dad was a lifesaver. Money can buy almost anything, but especially freedom.

We were young, so of course we felt immortal and didn't think anyone would die. But looking back, I can see how stupid we were. There were so many ways we could have died. It may not be any consolation to Freddy's parents, but it certainly made a difference to the judge that the only person who died was complicit in the prank.

Hah. It sounds funny calling it a prank. Prank-gone-terribly-awry.

I couldn't believe we were allowed to stay on at VU after that. Like I said, the American public really thought the best punishment was to exile us to a distant planet. So in the end we were sent up to Mars, every one of us. It almost didn't happen. But we were sent up because nobody on Earth wanted to see our faces ever again.

Cady almost screwed up her shot at Mars too. If she had chosen to have Paul's baby, she would have been assigned to mission control or some other administrative position on Earth after graduation. Cady had secured herself a spot on one of the transports to Mars by enrolling at VU. But she couldn't bring along another person. Even if that person was a toddler. The population on Mars is strictly regulated. That's why we have no children today. We never won the lottery.

"Fuck 'em," says Cady.

* * *

On March 17, 2041, I invited Cady to Wilde House's big Saint Paddy's Day party. I hadn't been to Wilde House since the back-to-school party where I first met Prescott Harrington. Prescott told Jake we could each bring a date, so Ursula came along, too. Lee and Ling Ling weren't invited.

Ursula lasted all of thirty minutes before she and Jake headed back to Owens Hall. She was fading fast. Soon she'd have to make a permanent move to the hospital.

Cady and I stayed on. But I noticed that Cady wasn't drinking.

"Want me to get you something from the bar?" I asked. The music was so loud that she didn't hear me.

"WANT ME TO GET YOU SOMETHING FROM THE BAR?" I shouted.

"NO THANKS!" she shouted back. "NOT FEELING IT TONIGHT!"

I shrugged. That could have been the end of the discussion.

I wasn't going to push it. But Cady wasn't herself after that. She went silent, and a pall settled over the fun. So I pulled her into a vacant bedroom and sat her down on a mattress piled high with coats.

"What's up?" I asked.

"Nothing. Let's just go back to the party."

"Did I say something to upset you?"

"No, Herbert. Just drop it."

"I can take you home if you want."

Cady ran her hands through her hair. She was radiant. Frowning but radiant.

"Herbert . . ."

"Let me take you back to your dorm."

"Herbert, I'm pregnant."

I had no illusions that the child might be mine. Cady and I had not slept together. Not in that way.

"Is it Paul's?" I asked.

Cady nodded, and a tear ran down her cheek.

"Does that mean you're not going to be sent up?" I asked.

Cady sniffed. "Going to Mars is my dream."

I think we both knew what we had to do next.

"How many weeks are you?" I asked.

"Just over twenty."

I pulled out my phone and searched "Planned Parenthoods near me."

CHAPTER 27

I **JUST PICKED UP** an extra shift cleaning rooms at the Westin Resort over in Sector 2. I'm still full time down at the lab, but now I work at the hotel on my days off. Cady is in a mood. We were planning to go to Joshua Beach on our next mutual break. But now that I'm working nonstop, we're not going anywhere for a while.

The gig is temporary, I keep telling her. The hotel housekeeping staff is on strike for better wages. They've unionized, and apparently, strikes are happening all over North America, too.

Solidarity.

Yuji Ishida came to me in a panic a few days ago. The big boss at the top of the janitorial food chain had entrusted Yuji with finding temporary staffing for the hotel effective immediately. He begged me to take a shift or two.

Sure, why not? Housekeeping at the hotel pays better than cleaning the labs. Plus they get to wear those spiffy uniforms. And no mopping up radioactive waste. It's a cushy gig, and although Cady is pissed that we won't have any time together until the strike is over, I promised her we would use the money from the extra shifts to dine out at the Brazilian Steakhouse. I don't remember the last time either of us ate meat. Meat is highly restricted on Mars. Something about keeping the biosphere balanced, blah, blah, blah.

Come to think of it, I don't remember the last time either of us ate dinner somewhere other than the C-Pod mess hall.

Cady is sulking, but it's not like she has all the time in the world right now either. Governor Harding plans to make his acceptance speech from the Exotic Garden in a few weeks, so she's been putting in extra hours to help set up the governor's pavilion. Yes, Governor Harding thinks he's going to win reelection. Polls show him leading Best Bet Bill by eight points.

What happened? Best Bet Bill held the lead briefly about a week ago. But then he was caught on tape saying something not-so-nice about Governor Harding's wife. He said, "She's one ugly son of a gun." That's how Best Bet Bill talks. He says things like "son of a gun."

Virginia Harding is actually quite beautiful. Best Bet Bill claims he was talking about her personality. I believe it. Nobody would mistake Virginia Harding for an ugly person. Ugly in spirit, yes. But nice to look at.

So it wasn't really the worst thing he could have said. Best Bet Bill still gets my vote.

Cady's back on the fence. She says insulting a woman's appearance is a nonstarter.

"He's talking about her personality," I say.

"He used the word 'ugly,'" Cady argues.

"She's a mean, mean woman," I say. I should know. When we first moved to Mars, I cleaned toilets over at city hall. Frank Harding was just a lowly city councilperson at the time. It was his first term. He was still riding high from breaking the story of Scepter and Gavel in '41. Don't forget that Frank was only a few years ahead of me in school.

Virginia is older. Age unknown. But she was already on Mars when I started at Vanderough University. The first time I saw her, she whisked right by me into the councilpersons' offices as if I were invisible. I was polishing the glass doors that led into the front office. Seeing her coming from a mile away (who could miss her?), I swung the door wide open to let her through.

Whisk! And not a word of thanks.

Then she whisked right up to the desk of the administrative assistant and said, "I'm here for Councilman Harding. We are to have lunch."

The administrative assistant, a meek young thing from my year, clicked a few times on her computer and then said, "I'm sorry. I seem to have double-booked the councilman. He's in a meeting with the city planner as we speak."

"You what?" Virginia asked as if someone just told her they had run over her dog.

"I'm sorry, Mrs. . . . ?"

"Harding," she spat. "You don't even recognize the councilman's wife?"

"Of course! Mrs. Harding. I can be a little harebrained sometimes. Forgive me. You work over at the legal offices of Owens, Zhang, and Harding."

"I don't just *work over at the legal offices*." Her face flushed. She was as red as a bowl of punch. "My name is on the door."

"My mistake," said the young woman. "How could I be so . . . ?"

"Stupid?"

The young woman looked as though she'd been slapped. But she carried on the best she could given the circumstances. "Yes, stupid. How could I be so stupid? If you'd like to wait, the councilman has some free time later this afternoon."

"You are harebrained," said Virginia. "I can't just wait around for my husband all day. I work, too."

"Yes," said the girl, clearly frazzled. "At Owens, Zhang, and Harding."

Virginia shot the girl one last contemptuous look and whisked out of the office, slamming the glass door hard in my face as she exited.

The next day, the young administrative assistant was gone.

That's just one story I can tell you about mean old Virginia

Harding. I saw a lot of her the year I worked over at city hall.

"We're not electing *Virginia* Harding for Governor," Cady says. "So I don't see why it makes any difference."

"But you *are* electing Virginia Harding," I say. "Frank is putty in her hands."

"Well, I'm still on the fence."

Cady is also on the fence about who killed Adolf Dussel. She felt sure it was Polly Platt from the governor's office until the *Martian Gazette* reported they had a new suspect. Apparently, Inspector Dunst has identified the man responsible for printing the letter to Arnie Sphinx. He will be holding a short press conference at noon to elaborate.

Notice that the report identified the suspect as a *man*. Male.

At Cady's request, I contacted Inspector Dunst at his MMail account to see if he could tell us anything before the press conference. I got no reply whatsoever. I'm trying not to take it personally.

"Send him another email," says Cady.

She and I are having breakfast together before we both head out to our respective jobs. I'm at the hotel today. Cady is clearing space in the Exotic Garden for the governor's pavilion.

"Just check the news at noon," I say.

* * *

Cady was too far along in her pregnancy to schedule an abortion in Connecticut, so we decided to take the train up to New York City the last week of March to have the procedure done at a Planned Parenthood in the East Village. The law in New York State at the time allowed a person to get an abortion up until twenty-four weeks after the start of their last period, no questions asked. We were cutting it close. Thankfully, the Planned Parenthood had an opening that week. Cady was nineteen and had good insurance through VU, so she didn't need to say anything about it to her parents. The copay was twenty dollars.

My parents were up at the Lodge for the week. They had taken Delia with them. So Cady and I could stay a few nights in the penthouse apartment on the Upper West Side without fear of discovery. The doormen knew me well and wouldn't bother to check with my parents before letting me in. Buildings like ours pride themselves on discretion.

Sally Wyatt, the famous actress, used to live in my building.

And Joon-ho Choi, the Olympic gymnast with six gold medals.

And one of the Kardashians, although I never knew which one.

The day we arrived in New York City, Cady went in to have her cervix dilated. I stayed in the waiting room and read a profile of Samuel Owens in *Forbes*. Apparently, he, too, had an apartment on the Upper West Side, but the article didn't specify the address. The article kept me busy for all of twenty minutes. Then I pulled out my laptop and started on some chemistry homework, knowing I was going to have a lot of work to make up when we got back to Bridgeport.

It was about an hour before Cady emerged, her face set like stone.

"So . . . ?" I asked.

"So I come back tomorrow for the surgery. They'll monitor me for a couple hours, and then I have to take it easy for a few weeks."

"Are you scared?"

Cady's face remained impassive, statuesque. "No."

"Okay."

We stopped by the local drugstore to stock up on sanitary pads and ibuprofen. Then we went back to the apartment on the Upper West Side and watched a few hours of mindless television in my father's den. It was about eight o'clock that evening when we finally left the apartment, ready for something to eat. There was a nice Italian restaurant down the block, and I still had some money left over from my most recent paycheck from the zoo, so I treated Cady to a lavish dinner, knowing she would have to fast for at least eight hours leading up to her appointment.

Cady wanted to sleep alone that night. We had bedrooms to spare in the apartment, so I put her up in a room I had always called the Pink Palace due to the fact that everything in it, from the curtains to the carpet, was cotton candy pink.

"Are these photo albums?" Cady removed an aging tome

from the bookcase beside the flamingo bed.

"My mother likes to have hard copies of all our family photos," I explained.

Cady's face had been stone cold all evening. But as soon as she flipped open the photo album, a smile spread across her face.

"Cute!"

I looked over her shoulder. It was a photo of five-year-old me walking around the apartment wearing nothing but Mickey Mouse ears.

I blushed. "Do you need anything else before I leave?"

She didn't respond. She was immersed in the family album. I left her sitting on the edge of the bed.

Turns out Cady stole that photo of me with the Mickey Mouse ears. I know because we have it with us on Mars. She thinks it's just about the cutest thing she's ever seen, and she pulls it out for show-and-tell every time we have someone over to our pod. I used to be mortified. But now I'm numb to it. Go ahead and show my wee-wee to the guy changing our air filter. That's not at all awkward.

We took a taxi to the clinic the next morning. When Cady emerged from the doctor's office a few hours later, still groggy from the sedative, I lent her my shoulder, and together we made our way to the street where a cab was waiting to whisk us back to the apartment. I left Cady sleeping in the Pink Palace and ran out to the pharmacy to fill her prescription for doxycycline.

Cady slept all day, appearing only once to nibble on some soda crackers. She slept solidly through the night. I looked in on her a few times before turning in myself. When I awoke the following morning, Cady was sitting on the edge of my bed, fiddling with a toy truck that had been sitting on my nightstand since I was eight years old.

"Good morning," I said, yawning. "How do you feel?"

"Lousy." Cady rolled the toy truck along the edge of the bed, like a child would do.

"Did you take your antibiotics?" I asked.

"Yes." The truck rolled up my sleeve and along the length of my arm.

"You want me to fix you some breakfast?"

Cady nodded, and together we plodded down the hallway to the kitchen, where I poured her a bowl of Honey Nut Cheerios.

"Thank you, Herbert." Cady sat poised over her cereal, staring at me with those big green eyes.

"It's just cereal," I said.

"Thank you for supporting me through this whole thing. It means a lot to me."

I blushed. Later that afternoon, we took the train back to Bridgeport. That was Wednesday, March 27—five days before all hell would break loose.

CHAPTER 28

I **GOT CADY'S TEXT** while I was scrubbing the toilet in an executive suite at the Westin Resort.

Cady: *It was Jake!!!*

Me: *What was?*

Cady: *Your old roommate! He's the one who printed that letter!*

Me: *To Arnie Sphinx?*

Cady: *Yes! They traced it back to his login.*

Me: *That doesn't make sense. How is he connected to Adolf Dussel?*

Cady: *I don't know, but the police have him in custody.*

Me: *WTF? What about Polly Platt?*

Cady: *They're still looking into her. Read the news, will you?*

So now I'm sitting on the toilet in executive suite 409,

scrolling through the front page of the *Martian Gazette*. There's a mug shot of Jake Harrington, looking haggard and sleep deprived. I haven't seen Jake in years. He's grown a mustache like the one his brother had in college. He looks like a murderer with that stupid mustache, but I just don't believe he could have done it.

We're not close anymore, me and Jake. He's a plumber, so you'd think I'd run into him a lot given that I often have to report a clogged toilet or a leaky sink. But there are like a hundred plumbers on Mars, so the odds aren't good. Last time I saw him, actually, was at Joshua Beach, maybe four years ago. We caught up while Cady napped on the embankment. Jake's not married. At least he wasn't then.

"Living the dream," he said.

The article in the *Gazette* was published just after the big press conference at noon. Apparently, the hacker Inspector Dunst hired was able to trace the print job back to Jake's account. They also searched Jake's pod and found his old cloak and hood from Scepter and Gavel, which is identical to the cloak and hood the person in the CCTV video was wearing when they picked up the spent nuclear fuel pellet. So it's pretty damning evidence.

The article makes a big deal about Jake's prior arrest back in '41. They basically blame him for Freddy Euler's death, even though Jake was nowhere near Freddy when he died. But it makes better copy to paint Jake as a serial murderer. It's pretty fucked up.

So now Jake is in a holding cell down at the station awaiting trial. Who knows when the trial will be. They have yet to establish a motive for the killing.

Jake's bail is set for four hundred credits. Too much money for me to do anything about it. I can only hope Jake has some friends or maybe a girlfriend who will fork over the cash.

Living the dream, indeed.

The *Gazette* paints a pretty grim picture of that night in 2041 when Freddy died. Thankfully, the reporter doesn't mention me or any other former gavelmen. She heaps all the blame onto Jake, which is ludicrous since Jake didn't even manage to free any animals that night. Jake was assigned the two-toed sloth, and he did manage to open the enclosure with his key. But when officials took stock of the damage the following morning, they found the two-toed sloth hanging exactly where Jake had left it. I guess it didn't have any reason to explore beyond the confines of its cage. Everything a sloth could ever want was right there.

Living the dream.

That happened with lots of the animals. Gavelmen opened their enclosures, but the animals refused to budge. In the end, that turned out to be a very good thing. Less mayhem meant an easier job for our lawyers. Things could have been a lot worse, considering.

But I don't want to get ahead of myself.

I stayed a few more nights with Cady in her dormitory. She didn't seem to be having any complications from the surgery. The expected bleeding, but nothing serious. Then, on the night of March 31, 2041, I made some excuse about having to attend an overnight star party for my astrophysics class. Everybody who goes to Vanderough University has to take the most basic sequence of astrophysics courses. Graduates are headed into space, after all.

Cady didn't mind me leaving. Frankly, I think she was getting a little tired of me hovering over her like a fussy nurse. Cady has always been very independent.

The members of the Order met in the Tomb at ten o'clock that night. When I arrived, Prescott offered me a margarita on the rocks. That was the drink of choice for the evening. Several gavelmen looked like they'd been drinking since noon. I couldn't help but feel a little queasy. Alcohol and wild animals don't mix. I knew it then, and I know it now. But we were already in too deep. Prescott could see the worry on my face. He patted my back and said I'd done good. I would go far in Martian society. If we pulled this off, our prank would become the stuff of legends.

He was right about that last part. He couldn't have guessed I'd end up cleaning toilets for a living. But you can't put the blame squarely on Prescott. We were all complicit. As the prosecutor would say to me when I took the witness stand in May, "Nothing was preventing you from turning around and going home that night—is that true, Mr. Palminteri?"

Turns out peer pressure isn't a valid defense in a court of law.

Knowing I would be dealing with the most dangerous animal in the zoo—an Amur tiger—I decided to pour my margarita down the kitchen drain. I wanted to have all my wits about me in case arthritic old Jinx turned out to be more formidable than she looked.

She did. She was.

We kept our robes in the Tomb, in a big wooden chest in one of the empty bedrooms on the second floor. Around eleven o'clock, Lynn Boyles ordered us to suit up: cloak, hood, and mask. We knew we would be caught on the security cameras, so a disguise was essential if we didn't want our identities to be known. I dug through the chest and located my robes using the nearly invisible monogram embroidered on the inside of the cape. I hadn't yet had an occasion to wear the robes. The black mesh that concealed our faces was transparent from the inside. We wore black gloves and black shoes, careful to hide anything that could be used later to identify us.

We were a macabre sight: twenty-seven Grim Reapers standing in a circle in a windowless room. Silence settled over the Tomb.

"Whatever you do, don't hang around the zoo once your job is done." Prescott stood atop a chair. "Just get out of there as quickly as you can."

"But don't come back here," Lynn warned. "We don't want anyone tracing this back to us. Go home and don't congregate again until we know we're in the clear. If you have to communicate, do so over our secure website."

Lynn was all about the details.

"Hide if you see the night watchman," Prescott added. "Don't let him see you."

"And if he does see you," Lynn said, "run."

"Right." Prescott nodded.

"What if the police show up?" somebody asked.

"If you hear sirens, then abort the mission and get out of there as fast as you can. There will be two exits. A service road runs behind the zoo. Howie will be monitoring the back gate."

One of the Grim Reapers—I assumed it was Howie—held up a shiny brass key, bigger than the others.

"Yolanda will be monitoring the front gate," Prescott continued.

"They'll go on ahead," Lynn said, "and let us know when the coast is clear."

"Can we go now?" said the Grim Reaper with the shiny key. It *was* Howie.

Prescott nodded. Then Howie and Yolanda broke from the circle and disappeared out the back.

"When I get the signal from Howie, you'll head out in pairs. Don't cluster together. I'll assign each pair either the back gate or the main entrance. The gates will open at midnight."

I glanced at the towering grandfather clock in the corner.

It was now eleven thirty-five.

"Once inside, you're on your own."

"And remember," said Lynn, "we'll only have about twenty minutes before the night watchman returns to his post. Anything you do after then, he'll see on the security cameras."

"Grab a partner while we wait for the signal."

"How about it?" said a voice in my ear. "Wanna be partners?"

Freddy.

"Sure," I said.

About ten minutes ticked away in silence, then Prescott's phone buzzed.

"Line up with your partner," said Lynn.

Prescott monitored the exit. As pairs of gavelmen approached, he assigned them a gate. Freddy and I got the front gate, which was good for me since the tiger enclosure was closer to the front gate. Freddy had it a bit harder. The bison paddock was at the far end of the zoo near the service road. He would have to traverse the entire length of the zoo.

I suppose if Freddy and I had been assigned the back gate, things might have gone differently for Freddy, and he might still be alive today. In a decision that had no meaning, no greater purpose, Prescott sealed the fate of Freddy Euler that night when he said to us, "Front gate."

But we didn't know any of that then. It was an arbitrary directive that would have dire consequences.

Freddy and I slipped out the back of the Tomb and set off

for Beardsley Park. All around us, other pairs of gavelmen were gliding through the shadows like ghosts, branching off in different directions. I had done this commute many times before, and I definitely knew the quickest way to the zoo. I motioned for Freddy to follow me.

There was a misty fog over Beardsley Park, which gave us cover as we weaved through the trees. We didn't encounter anyone on the path. Students didn't usually venture into the park after dark. There may have been a few unhoused people sleeping in the shadows, but they didn't make themselves known. Anyone who saw us dressed as we were did not dare approach.

Finally the trees broke away to reveal the empty parking lot and, beyond that, the main entrance to the zoo. I grabbed Freddy by the arm and held him back. The gate was still closed. It must not have been quite midnight. We waited in the shadows until a cloaked form appeared from behind a bush. It approached the gate, fumbled around with the lock, and then slid the gate open.

"Now!" I hissed.

Freddy and I broke from the trees and ran straight for the main entrance.

CHAPTER 29

HAIR IN THE TOILETS, hair in the sinks, hair in the showers, hair in the linens. Hair. Probably the number-one contaminator in any hotel room. Still a lot better than slopping up chemical waste in the labs.

I've been working nonstop. Two days at the hotel. Seven days in the labs. Only yesterday did I finally get a chance to visit Jake down at the station. After some prodding, Yuji agreed to let me clock out early. Visiting hours at the station end at five, and Yuji didn't let me off until four, so I had to jog all the way down to the D-Block holding cells just to get fifteen minutes with Jake.

Jake didn't know I was coming. How could he? I had no way of contacting him in jail. So when I appeared on the opposite side of the plexiglass wall, Jake's eyes lit up. He promptly grabbed the telephone receiver and started talking straight into my ear.

"Herbert! Man, you gotta tell them. Tell them I didn't do it!"

"Calm down, Jake," I said. "Even if I vouched for you, there's no way they'd let you out of here without some kind of proof of your innocence."

"But I didn't kill that guy! Hell, I hardly knew him!"

"I believe you," I said. "Do you have a lawyer?"

"The court appointed some guy to my case. He's only been down here to see me once."

"You couldn't afford somebody better?"

"Are you kidding? On my salary?"

"What about your dad?"

"He hasn't responded to my transmissions."

"Arnie Sphinx was able to afford Clive Cohen."

"Rub it in my face, why don't you?"

"Sorry, I just—"

"Herb, I didn't do it! I was set up. You think I'd knock off some random guy? And for what? What's in it for me?"

"I hear you," I said. "But they can prove that the letter was printed from your account."

"Somebody must've hacked it."

"Does anybody else have your password? A girlfriend maybe?"

"I wish. You think I can get a girlfriend at my age? Look at me!" Jake gestured toward his face, which was haggard and wrinkled from a life of hard living.

"I have to ask," I said. "I mean, after what happened back in school . . ."

"Fuck!"

"What?"

"Lee!"

"Lee Knowles?"

"Yeah, he could've guessed my password."

"Are you still using the same trick from college?"

"I'm such a dumbass." Jake slammed his head against the plexiglass panel. "Idiot!"

I shook my head. Jake was still using the same password trick, where he uses the first letter of the website followed by the name of his favorite band with the vowels replaced by numbers, and a period at the end. Even I remember his stupid trick.

"Don't tell me your favorite band is still Radiohead?"

"Fuck."

"What were you thinking, Jake?"

Jake lit up. "So it was Lee! Lee set me up. That little conniving bastard!"

"Slow down, Jake. Lee is the last person I can think of who might murder someone."

"I wouldn't put it past him," said Jake. "He ratted us out back in college."

"But *why* would Lee want Adolf Dussel dead?" I asked. "We have to think of a motive before we start throwing around accusations."

"They don't have a motive for me, but they locked me up!"

"But Lee? A murderer?"

"Think about it. That Adolf guy died from radiation poisoning! That's smart. If Lee were to kill someone, he'd be smart about it."

"Okay, okay." I sighed heavily. "You'll have to explain all this to your lawyer. In the meantime, I'll reach out to Inspector Dunst, let him know. Maybe he'll pursue it."

"Fuck!" Jake slammed his head against the plexiglass again. "How many times can one guy screw himself in a lifetime?" Jake's forehead was turning a dark shade of purple.

"How many times are you going to use the same stupid password?"

From somewhere, a robotic voice blared. "Five minutes until visiting hours are over!"

"It's Lee," Jake said. "It has to be."

"I'll look into it. I promise."

As I walked back to C-Pod, I tried to imagine a reason Lee Knowles would want to kill Adolf Dussel, but I drew a complete blank. Lee was a snitch, sure. But a killer?

When I got home, I explained everything to Cady.

"What a bonehead." She meant Jake. "He didn't learn from the first time?"

"Apparently not."

"All these years later and you guys are still paying for that night at the zoo."

* * *

Jake had paired up with Mickey G. that night and had gone in the back entrance of the zoo. I sometimes wonder if Freddy would still be alive today if he had paired up with Jake or Melissa—anyone else—instead of pairing up with me. Not that I think I caused Freddy's accident. That was Howie Van Bruggen. But the difference between life and death really is just a matter of timing. And if Freddy had gone in the back gate, he would have freed the bison sooner and would have been out of harm's way by the time Howie did what he did. Probably.

As it was, Freddy and I entered through the front gate. We hopped the turnstiles and immediately turned right. Freddy followed me past the carousel and up the short path that led to the tiger enclosure. We were nearly there when a bright light swept the path ahead of us.

"The night watchman!" I hissed.

Freddy and I turned and raced back toward the carousel. There were two other gavelmen coming up the path. I motioned for them to turn around.

The other gavelmen turned and disappeared into a cluster of bamboo. I pulled Freddy toward the carousel. We leapt onto the platform and squeezed past the wooden horses. There was a storage area in the middle of the carousel that held rakes and brooms and other cleaning supplies. I removed a wooden panel from the scenic facade, ushered Freddy into the cramped space, and jumped in behind him.

"Are there spiders in here?" Freddy whimpered. He was worried about spiders. Twenty minutes from a gruesome death and he was talking to me about arachnids.

"No." Maybe there were spiders, but I didn't want to scare him.

"How long do we have to stay in here?" Freddy asked.

"To be safe? Five minutes." One minute too long. If only I had known.

"You think he'll be gone by then?"

"Sure," I said.

"Okay." Freddy shifted his weight uncomfortably.

"You've got the bison?" It was more of a statement than a question, but I didn't really know what else to say to Freddy.

"Yeah," he said. "I feel lucky. I mean, you have to deal with a tiger."

"She's a pretty old tiger," I said. "I doubt she'll give me any trouble." I wasn't as sure as I sounded. But Freddy was clearly nervous, and I wanted to calm him down.

"You think we'll get caught?" Freddy asked.

"I don't think so." In reality, I was wondering how we wouldn't get caught. Security cameras everywhere. A gaggle of hooded figures on the security footage. Surely they'd trace the robes back to Scepter and Gavel. Maybe they wouldn't be able to prove anything. I didn't know. It was too late to worry about that now.

"Yeah," said Freddy. "My mom will kill me if she finds out."

Prophetic.

"Do you know what Melissa has?" I asked to fill the time.

"I think she's freeing some prairie dogs."

"That should be easy."

"She hates rodents." Freddy lifted his mask briefly and scratched the peach fuzz on his upper lip where beads of sweat were forming. "I told her I'd trade with her if she wanted, but she just said she had to suck it up and be a man."

Another fork in the road to Freddy's untimely death.

"She's tough," I said. "I can't imagine she'll have any trouble."

Freddy and I sat in silence for a minute longer. Then I slid the wooden panel back and peeked out into the darkness. There was no sign of the night watchman.

"Okay," I said. "Let's go."

We reached the tiger enclosure in less than a minute. Jinx was nowhere to be seen.

"Keep going," I hissed to Freddy. "Up that path!"

Freddy nodded and darted away. Once Freddy had disappeared around a corner, I traced the perimeter of the enclosure, peering through the thick glass at the dark, grassy hills and shallow ponds. Most of the rocky landscape lay in shadow, but it didn't matter. I knew Jinx wasn't in the habitat. She would be sleeping in the holding area, locked in her pen. I'd scouted the habitat a couple of times during daylight hours, and I'd found an inconspicuous door in a concrete wall that I thought might lead back to the tiger holding cells. When I reached the door, I tried my key in the lock.

It worked. The door swung inward. The space inside was crowded with two large aluminum tanks, part of a freshwater filtration system, I guessed. I propped the door open with an empty bucket. There were a few wrangling tools scattered about: a tranquilizer gun and a long pole with a lasso at the end.

It occurred to me that I might need the tranquilizer gun, but I didn't know how to work it. I studied the lasso. The pole was maybe six feet long, and I didn't plan on getting that close to Jinx if I could help it. So I left the tools lying where they were and crossed the small space to another door that opened easily from the inside. I propped this door open, as I had done the first, and stepped into a concrete yard. A ramp led down to the service road. The yard was fenced in. Chain-link, thirty feet high with rings of barbed wire at the top. I tried my key in the gate leading to the service road, thinking Jinx would make her escape that way. But the key didn't fit.

Opposite the loading dock stood another concrete building with a large garage door on vertical tracks. I was getting close now—I knew it. I tried my key in the lock, and the latch lifted. For all I knew, Jinx was on the other side of the door, waiting to pounce. So I lifted the sliding door just an inch and peered into the darkness beyond. I couldn't see a thing, so I lifted the door another inch. Thankfully, a motion-activated lamp flickered on in the space beyond. The room contained six cages, five of which were empty. In the one occupied cage, I saw

Jinx. She was lying on her side, looking at me with one half-opened eye, like she couldn't care less that I had intruded into her space in the middle of the night.

Her enclosure was small, just big enough for her to stretch out on the concrete floor. I slid the garage door fully open and stepped into the dimly lit area. Jinx's tail wagged lazily, like she was happy to see me.

"Hey, girl," I said. She looked so sweet right then, almost domesticated. "How're you doing?"

Jinx stretched and yawned like a cat in the sun and then sat on her haunches, eyeing me patiently. What was that look? Indifference? Recognition? I had the passing notion that Jinx knew me from all the times I'd walked by her enclosure. And maybe she did. But that didn't make her any less of a tiger.

I approached the cage slowly. Jinx flicked her tail.

"Good girl," I said. "I'm just gonna open your pen. You can leave if you want. Or you can stay." I hoped she would stay.

Jinx's ears twitched. She was more alert now. I could tell. The key fit neatly into the lock. I turned it quietly, and the catch drew back, freeing the gate. When I stepped away, the gate swayed loosely on its hinges. But Jinx remained stock-still, watching me with those yellow eyes. I didn't want to make any sudden moves, so I backed out of the holding area in slow motion, leaving the garage door open. When I was finally in the yard, I turned my back on the tiger and hurried into the first building, inching around the bucket that held the door open. I couldn't see Jinx from here, so I took my time, crossing the room on tiptoes. Just as I reached the first door, a shadow passed over the room.

I glanced over my shoulder. There was Jinx, crouching in the yard, teeth bared, ready to pounce. She snarled once, muscles taut and twitching. I screamed and jumped through the doorway just as she leapt at me, claws extending in midair. I swung the door behind me, and it smacked the giant cat in the face and bounced open again.

I was already running up the path toward the bison paddock. Jinx followed me with her eyes, then began to trot in my direction. The trot turned into a gallop. She was following me and gaining speed with every step.

I was in a full sprint now, but Jinx was quickly closing the distance between us. That would have been the end of me if three white-tailed deer hadn't sprung out of a copse and darted up another path. Jinx saw the deer and changed directions. The deer were sprinting one way, the tiger right behind them, and I was sprinting the other way, searching the darkness for any sign of my fellow gavelmen.

"Fuck, fuck, fuck, fuck!" What had I done? A tiger loose in Bridgeport? Fuck.

All I wanted to do was get out of there. I nearly wiped out trying to dodge what turned out to be a pygmy goat emerging from the bushes. Most of the animals in the zoo were harmless. But the tiger. The fucking tiger.

I jogged up the winding path toward the bison paddock,

hoping to find Howie Van Bruggen standing guard at the back gate. There were wild howls coming from the primate center now. Maybe someone had managed to set the monkeys free, or perhaps the tiger was upon them. I didn't want to stick around to find out. The wide, grassy bison habitat finally came into view. A cloaked figure—it could only be Freddy—was fumbling with the lock on the gate.

"Leave it," I called to Freddy. "Let's go!"

Freddy spun around, saw me running toward him, and then turned his attention back to the gate. I was maybe a hundred feet downwind of Freddy when the gate slid open with a deafening clang. The bison, which looked like giant black boulders in the foggy meadow, stirred when the gate opened, stomping their feet and snorting.

Right where I stood, the service road branched off the main road, leading through some tall trees to the rear exit. In front of me, Freddy stood triumphant on the wide prairie path. To my right, Howie was waving gavelmen through the gate. When Howie saw me at the end of the road, he let out a shrill whistle to get my attention. The shriek of the whistle was so loud that it spooked the bison, and as one giant mass, they began to rumble toward the open gate—toward Freddy.

"Look out!" I screamed.

Freddy registered the throng of muscle and hair stampeding toward him and ran toward me. The bison followed Freddy down the road. I made a sharp right and sprinted down the service road toward the exit. I looked back in time to see

Freddy emerge in the gap between the trees. He leapt off the main road just as the bison stampeded past. I let out a long hiss of air, like a balloon deflating.

Freddy stooped over to catch his breath and waved once in my direction. I waved back. Then a huge form burst through the trees, head lowered and horns frontward. The giant ball of hair pummeled right into Freddy, scooping him up with its horns and tossing him over its back.

Freddy's body lay motionless on the ground. I screamed. Howie Van Bruggen, who had seen the whole thing, came sprinting down the path. By the time we reached Freddy, he was already dead. I felt for a pulse, found none. No rise and fall of the chest. No twitching motions. Just stillness and dead weight.

Sirens blared in the distance. Someone had called the police.

"Go," Howie said. "Get out of here!"

I didn't know what Howie was going to do, but he was two years older than me, and that means a lot in college. So I did as he said and left Freddy's crumpled body lying in the mud.

Turns out Howie didn't do anything except drag Freddy's body onto the main road so the authorities would find him quicker. Howie later explained that he didn't want the animals to get to the body first.

I made my way back through Beardsley Park alone. I stripped out of my robes behind Xavier Hall, which stood on the edge of the campus, and bundled them under one arm. I didn't want Lee or Ling Ling to see me in my cloak and hood. They would probably be asleep when I got home. But just in case.

I vomited twice as I crossed campus, once in Carmelo Square and again in front of Owens Hall. Passersby probably thought I was drunk, had had too much at a party. Late-night barfing on a college campus is nothing special.

Really, I couldn't get the image of Freddy's mangled body out of my head. I thought I might turn my stomach inside out, I was heaving so hard.

When there was nothing left to throw up, I crept up the stairs to our suite. The lights were out inside. When I opened the door to my and Lee's shared room, Lee was fast asleep. I stuffed my robes deep under my bed, and I swore I would never wear them again.

I've kept that promise.

CHAPTER 30

MICKEY GALINSKI and Georgina Farley are now husband and wife, pronounced so by yours truly yesterday in the Exotic Garden under a setting sun. I had to take off early from work to be at the ceremony on time. So did Cady. Cady was in the bridal party, so she had to be in all the formal wedding photos, too, which were taken after the ceremony all over the Exotic Garden.

While Cady was posing for pictures, I hung out under the big tent with the other guests and ordered myself several drinks from the open bar. Honestly, I was still baked from earlier in the day when I'd shared a joint with a kid who works the front desk at the Westin. His name is Albert Ni. Funny guy. Always has a doobie to smoke on his lunch break. Sometimes we smoke it together. That plus the open bar really did me in. Cady is pissed. She worries I'll get fired for smoking on the job.

You really have to do something stupid to get fired up here. The Martian community is small. They need all hands on deck.

Maybe I can get some weed from Albert to bring home to Cady. She'd like that.

Albert is not yet twenty-four years old, just up from Earth, but we really hit it off. He's got some of the best stories, since he's the one who takes the reservations and checks the guests in and deals with their complaints. Diplomats, celebrities, famous dignitaries. They all stay at the Westin Resort when they come to Mars. And they all go through Albert. He tells me a Kardashian came to visit for a few days. Ended up spending the whole week locked in her bathroom with food poisoning. Get this: It wasn't even from something she ate on Mars. She got food poisoning from a juice bar on her transport ship.

Go figure.

Anyway, I was baked and drunk by the time dinner was served, and Cady was trying to keep me from falling asleep in my soup. She got me up and dancing a little later, and that helped. I boogied the pot and alcohol out of my system.

I'm not a good dancer. Like, can't-even-stay-on-beat bad. But by the end of the night I was feeling well enough to get up with the band and sing a rendition of "Love and Marriage," an old Sinatra hit. Then I sang "Makin' Whoopee." Then Cady pulled me off the stage with one of those big canes you see in vaudeville acts.

JK. JK.

Mickey G. seemed happy. Georgina, too. Incidentally, they're staying at the Westin Resort for their honeymoon. You can't really honeymoon on Mars since there's nowhere to go. But the Westin has a spa, a gym, tennis courts, a pool, a hot tub, and the Brazilian Steakhouse. So it's a nice getaway even if it isn't "away."

In other news, Delia Styles wrote me to say she's on her way to Mars for a three-month sojourn. I was joking when I told her to ask Wesley to buy her a round-trip ticket to the red planet. But it turns out she actually asked, and Wesley felt he owed it to her, for all her years of service.

So Delia is on her way to Mars now. She won't be staying with us; we don't have enough room in our tiny pod to play host. Wesley agreed to put her up in the Westin Resort for three months. Honestly, I don't know what she'll do here for three months. It's the first time Cady and I have ever had a visitor, and I don't know how I feel about it. Thankfully, Delia isn't the kind of person who needs someone to show her around the whole time she's visiting. She'll be happy just sitting by the pool or taking a spa day. But it's weird. Part of the reason I moved to Mars was to get away from all the people I knew on Earth.

Delia won't arrive for another six months or so. The bulk of her vacation will be aboard the cruise ship that will bring her here. A space cruise is a great way to get to Mars if you can afford one. Wesley can afford one. Space cruises have a lot more to do than we have in Pod City. Endless buffets, live performances, bingo nights, casinos. The list goes on and on. Hopefully, she won't be too disappointed when she arrives on our humble planet.

"I'll get her a monthly pass to the Exotic Garden," Cady says. "You can spend days exploring the garden."

"I don't know if she should be out alone with a murderer on the loose," I say.

"Herbert, the police said they weren't looking into anyone else. They feel fairly confident Jake is the murderer."

"He isn't," I say.

"You still think it's Lee Knowles? You're just angry about what happened all those years ago."

Hell yeah, I'm still angry. Lee squealed on us all those years ago. But that's not the reason I think Lee murdered Adolf Dussel. I just don't think Jake did it, and Lee is the only other person who would have used Jake's password to set him up.

I did write to Inspector Dunst about it. He said the connection was tenuous at best and that without any other evidence, he couldn't pursue it further.

Not good for Jake.

By the way, Lee is on track to becoming lieutenant governor of the Commonwealth of Mars. Frank Harding just selected Lee as his running mate. Surprise, surprise. The election is only two weeks away, and Governor Harding stands the best chance to win. Best Bet Bill is trailing Harding in the polls by eleven points. It's all but over for Bill.

Lee always was an ambitious prick, and he's been Harding's chief of staff and campaign manager for years. So it shouldn't shock anybody that he's now on the ticket. Another reason why Inspector Dunst doesn't want to open an investigation into Lee right now. It could unduly influence the election.

If Lee is a murderer, I'd like to know it before he ends up as our lieutenant governor. But that's not how politics work.

* * *

Lee knew something was up the morning of April Fools' Day when I couldn't get out of bed because I was sick over Freddy Euler's death. I told Lee it was the flu. But Lee's no dummy. As soon as news of the jailbreak broke, he started asking questions: *Where were you last night? Don't you work at the zoo? Are you planning to go in this weekend for your shift?* On and on.

The security footage wasn't made public right away, so Lee didn't have the robes to go on yet. But he suspected me. And Jake. Jake was a little too excited that morning. He had not yet heard about Freddy's death. When they announced it on the news, Jake became as ill as I was, and that made Lee even more suspicious.

"Let me take your temperature," Lee said.

"No fucking way," said Jake.

I couldn't bear to be around the others. So while Jake, Lee, and Ling Ling watched live updates on the television in the common room, I stayed in bed and followed the reporting on my phone.

The zookeepers, with the help of Bridgeport Animal Control, were busy tracking down their escaped charges. They found the six bison grazing not too far away in Beardsley Park. The one bison still had Freddy's blood on its horns. Also among the grazers in Beardsley Park were a miniature horse, a herd of llamas, three pronghorns, three San Clemente Island goats, three African pygmy goats, a herd of Dexter cattle, and a herd of sheep. These were the easiest to corral.

They found only two white-tailed deer. The half-eaten remains of the third were found near the primate center in the zoo.

Also found in the zoo were the two-toed sloth that had never left its cage, a giant anteater, six North American porcupines, eleven guinea hogs, six red-rumped agoutis, eleven prairie dogs, and a river otter. Four prairie dogs and two river otters were never recovered, nor were any of the fourteen domestic rabbits.

Hop, hop!

One of the red pandas was found in a nearby backyard. The other managed to get as far as Seaside Park before it was picked up by animal control. All seven peccaries wound up getting trapped in a drained public pool.

In their search, the zookeepers picked up a bobcat on the

Fairchild Wheeler Golf Course. It wasn't the bobcat they were looking for, though. Bobcats are native to Connecticut, so the zoo ended up giving up on the missing bobcat altogether, assuming it would fare okay in the wild.

The Canada lynx was located nearly four months later, in—would you believe it—Canada.

Twenty-three vampire bats had to be exterminated a month later when they were found to have started a colony under a bridge straddling the Pequonnock River.

The Mexican wolves teamed up with the red wolf and maned wolf and ate several neighborhood cats before they were cornered and tranquilized.

A leopard was found roaming the streets of downtown, and a Brazilian ocelot was shot dead by a farmer tending a community garden.

A friendly gray fox ended up in the local animal shelter because someone mistook him for a dog.

The primates were hardest to track down. Seven monkeys of various types raided a farmers' market on the East Side before being ensnared by a professional dog-walker. Five pygmy marmosets entered Xavier Hall through an open window and sent the occupants running. They trashed the whole third floor, including Cady's suite. And finally, five golden lion tamarins invaded a preschool to the surprise and joy of many three- and four-year-old children.

And what, you may ask, became of Jinx, famed Amur tiger? Jinx wasn't located on that first day, which meant most of the city had to go into lockdown. When she was found, she was preening on a private sailboat in the Long Island Sound. An eccentric sailor had lured Jinx onto his boat with a raw ribeye steak, and there they both stayed until the family on a neighboring yacht reported them to the authorities.

Jinx could be friendly after all.

Sometime around noon that day, Cady called to ask if she could come over to my dorm while animal control tried to capture the marmosets that were loose in her building. I told her that Jake and I were sick, so she went to the library instead. I felt terrible lying to her. I thought if she knew the truth, that I had been behind the freeing of the animals, she would never talk to me again. I didn't know she would end up testifying as a character witness on my behalf in the trial. I'll never be able to repay her for that.

As I sat in my room alone, feeling like a murderer, I logged on to ScepterAndGavel.com. There were already multiple threads from my fellow gavelmen, most expressing shock at Freddy's death. Only Howie Van Bruggen and I had witnessed it that night, so everyone was trying to get the story straight.

Mickey Braverman [10:03 a.m.]: *Anybody know what happened to Freddy?*

Prescott Harrington [10:05 a.m.]: *What do you mean?*

Mickey Braverman [10:11 a.m.]: *You haven't seen the news? He's dead.*

Prescott Harrington [10:12 a.m.]: *What?! Shit! What hap-*

pened?

Mickey Braverman [10:24 a.m.]: *That's what I'm trying to find out.*

Prescott Harrington [10:25 a.m.]: *Anyone know anything?*

Howie Van Bruggen [10:47 a.m.]: *He was gored by a bison. I saw it with my own eyes. Threw him like ten feet into the air.*

Prescott Harrington [10:49 a.m.]: *Fuck.*

Yolanda Perez [11:02 a.m.]: *Should we turn ourselves in?*

Prescott Harrington [11:07 a.m.]: *Hell no! We didn't kill Freddy. Sounds like a freak accident.*

Yolanda Perez [11:08 a.m.]: *But, I mean, we have information about his death. Howie's a witness.*

Howie Van Bruggen [11:12 a.m.]: *I don't want to talk to the police. There's nothing anyone could have done. One of the new kids saw it, too. Herbert. If he wants to go to the police, I can't stop him.*

Prescott Harrington [11:16 a.m.]: *Herbert? What do you say?*

Prescott Harrington [12:05 p.m.]: *Hey, Jake? Can you talk to Herbert about what he saw?*

Jake Harrington [12:17 p.m.]: *Yeah, he's been locked in his room all day. I'll go check on him.*

There was a knock on my door.

"Come in," I said.

Jake entered, frowning. "Have you seen the message board?"

"Yeah."

"What do you want to do?"

"Howie's right. Nobody could have done anything for Freddy. I don't want to go to the police."

Jake nodded. "You gonna write them back, or should I?"

"I'm not up to it," I said.

Jake approached my bedside, patted my shoulder. "It's not your fault."

"I know." But I *did* feel like it was my fault.

"I'll message the group." Jake left the room, closed the door behind him. Then I heard him shouting in the common room. "What the fuck are you doing on my computer?" Then the slamming of another door.

Lee poked his head in a few minutes later. "What's going on with you and Jake?"

"What do you mean?"

"I just looked at Jake's laptop. He was on the Scepter and Gavel website."

"I don't know what you're talking about."

Lee's eyes narrowed. "Did you guys kill Freddy Euler?"

"What? No!" I shouted. "Let it go, Lee."

Lee scowled and closed the door, leaving me in silence.

I returned my attention to the message board.

Jake Harrington [12:28 p.m.]: *Herbert says he doesn't want to go to the police.*

Prescott Harrington [12:30 p.m.]: *That settles it. Everyone sit tight. It'll blow over eventually.*

Not to be. Not to be.

Lee was onto us. I knew it, but I didn't think Lee had the nerve to go to the authorities. And he didn't, really. Instead, he took what he knew to Frank Harding, the editor of the school newspaper. Lee gave Frank the website address of the Order and Jake's login information, which Jake had stupidly disclosed when he told Lee about his password trick, and Frank wrote an exposé that was picked up by *Vanity Fair* a month later.

Thus began the friendship between Lee Knowles and Frank Harding, a friendship that endures to this day. Now it looks like Lee will become Frank's lieutenant governor and I'll still be a lowly janitor in A-Block.

CHAPTER 31

"**W**HOA, THAT WAS YOU?**"** Albert Ni was sufficiently impressed when I told him today about the zoo prank. He had asked how I ended up cleaning rooms for the hotel, and I gave him an abbreviated version of the story. He quickly caught on. He says Vanderough University tour guides still talk about the scandal when they lead prospective students around the campus.

I'm famous.

"*In*famous," Albert said.

Yes, infamous.

I was able to score some pot to take home to Cady today. It was expensive, even at Albert's "VIP rate." Two credits for one joint. But Cady loves a good doobie. She isn't home yet. I came home early today because I wasn't feeling so good.

Something I ate. Cady is still at work, but I texted her a picture of the little rolled-up joint. I haven't heard back.

Interestingly, as I was leaving the hotel through the front lobby this afternoon, who should I see but Lee Knowles. I kept my head down so he wouldn't recognize me, but I'm sure it was him. He walked right up to the check-in counter and started talking to Albert. I'd have stuck around to learn more, but I was so nauseous that I had to double-time it onto the Sector 2 Promenade so I could barf in a public trash can.

I think it was the fish from last night's dinner.

We farm fish here on Mars. Out in Sector 3. It's not an easy thing to do on a planet with very little water, but we manage somehow. Every drop of water is recycled and reused, so the fish farm doesn't draw too heavily on the water supply. But fish meat is expensive. One credit per ounce. I bought three ounces as a reward for all my hard work. Cady doesn't like fish. She says it makes her skin crawl. So I got her some of her favorite coffee beans, imported from Earth. Five credits. We usually can't afford these little luxuries—but the extra cash from the hotel gig is paying off.

Since Cady isn't home yet, I'm assuming she did not get food poisoning, which leads me to believe it was, in fact, the fish.

I wish I could have found out what Lee was doing at the hotel today. If I'm well enough to go into work tomorrow, I'll be sure to ask Albert about it.

The investigation into Adolf Dussel's death is ongoing, but

it looks like Inspector Dunst is just trying to shore up the case against Jake. Reports say Dunst has even ruled out Polly Platt as a possible coconspirator.

I'm still a bit suspicious of Lee. But only because of what he did to us all those years ago. There is no reason I can think of that Lee would want to kill Adolf Dussel. Plus, the suspect was wearing Scepter and Gavel robes, and Inspector Dunst found identical robes in Jake's pod. So that strengthens the case against Jake.

Maybe Jake did kill Adolf Dussel. Turns out multiple calls from Adolf Dussel's office line can be traced to Jake's phone in the three days leading up to the murder. Jake claims Adolf was just getting on his case about completing the Martian Census. But the calls link the two in a way that Jake didn't bother to mention to me on my visit.

What does that mean for Jake?

I'm drawing my finger across my throat in a slicing motion. That is to say, it doesn't look good.

Cady keeps telling me I should go down to the jail and talk to Jake again, see if I can gather any more info. But, honestly, if Jake really is the murderer, I don't want to get mixed up in his defense. I've had enough scandal to last me a lifetime. Jake's not taking me down with him this time.

Even Delia has heard the news of Adolf Dussel's murder. It made big headlines on Earth, apparently. She wrote me from her cruise ship yesterday to ask me about it.

Dear Herbert,

Don't tell me you're mixed up in this business about a murder on Mars. I read that you were interviewed by the police. Something about working with toxic waste. Are you in trouble?

I also recognized that other boy's name: Jake Harrington. He's the one who got you into all that mess back in school, isn't he?

You need to stay away from him. Keep your head down. Do your work. Mind your own business, that's what I say.

I'm doing well. The cruise ship is magnificent. It's called the *Neptune*. There's every kind of food available at all times of the day. There are lots of games and shows. This is certainly the most fun I've had in all my long life. I don't have to clean or cook for anybody. Everything is done for me.

I won $100 on the penny slots yesterday. That was a pretty prize. There is a crystal candlestick for sale in the gift shop that I've got my eye on. Would look pretty next to your mama's old clock on the mantel. I'm sure Ms. Krall wouldn't mind. She probably wouldn't even notice, seeing as she's not been all there for some time now.

Wesley hired a caregiver to stay with Ms. Krall day and night while I'm away, but I worry the caregiver won't do things the way Ms. Krall likes. I left detailed instructions, just in case, telling how to fold the laundry and stock the pantry. Makes me feel guilty leaving her all alone with a stranger. But Wesley said to me, "Delia, you haven't had a day off in all your life. It's time that I make up for that." So here I am, on a trip to Mars.

I hope Cady is doing well. You're lucky to have married such a nice girl, and I am hoping to spend some more time with her when I arrive.

Stay out of trouble.

All my love,
Delia

I'll let Cady write her back. Delia and Cady only interacted a few times before we were sent up, but they became fast friends. They took to each other instantly. The first time they were introduced was later that April in 2041, before shit hit the fan. Cady had a follow-up appointment at Planned Parenthood the week of our spring break, which also happened to be around Easter. Cady was supposed to go home for Easter. Easter is a big deal in her family. But she canceled on them last minute, claiming she would be doing Easter with her boyfriend (me) in New York.

Her family was Catholic, so she couldn't tell them she'd had an abortion and was dating an atheist.

My family doesn't celebrate Easter, but when I told Mother I would be bringing a girl home for the break, she decided to prepare a big Easter dinner anyway. By "prepare," my mother meant Delia would prepare the dinner.

Mother always took Delia for granted.

Cady and I left for the city on a Monday. I had not been to the zoo since the accident; it had been closed for two weeks because of the ongoing investigation into the jailbreak and Freddy's death. I would have called out sick from work anyway. I could barely keep it together around Cady or anybody else. Cady wondered if I should get tested for mono since I was sleeping all the time and throwing up all my food. I lost something like fifteen pounds.

I simply went along with the mono excuse because it was so much better than the truth.

Track season was in full swing, and I was supposed to be competing in the mile and two-mile that spring. But I told the coach I had mono and would have to sit out the rest of the season. He was not happy and demanded a doctor's note. I promised I would get one to him soon.

Not to be.

Up until April 1, 2041, I had made it to track practice every morning, reliable as a metronome. But after Freddy Euler's death, I wasn't up to it. I wasn't up to anything. Even my grades were falling because I was skipping class. Father would be furious, but thankfully, report cards wouldn't come out until June, and by then I'd be backpacking in Europe with Jake.

Or so I thought.

Jake and I wanted to get away. Get out of the country. We

were scared of getting caught. Security footage from the night of the prank was released to the public, and it clearly showed people in cloaks and hoods descending on the zoo like a plague of locusts. Plus, authorities had found Freddy's body, still dressed in his cloak and hood. So they were looking into all the student groups on campus with which Freddy had any affiliation. Nobody knew Freddy was a member of Scepter and Gavel except other gavelmen. But the secret society was on the authorities' radar, and that freaked a lot of us out. Thankfully, there wasn't any public record of the society. And Prescott had been sure to scrub headquarters of any evidence in case the police came knocking. We all agreed not to convene again that year in case the authorities were staking out the Tomb.

Even with those precautions in place, I wanted to get out of the country. In my naivete, I really thought that if I was in Europe, I wouldn't get caught.

Silly me.

Jake and I hoped to fly to Spain the day final exams ended. Unless Ursula was still alive. Jake and Ursula were still a thing, and Ursula had been admitted into hospice care at Bridgeport Hospital. She wasn't expected to make it through exams. Jake visited her every day, but it had gotten to the point where she could hardly register his presence. Her parents were there, too. Ursula was from Bridgeport, so the whole family was around.

I asked Jake how he would feel, leaving for Europe if Ursula was still alive.

"If by some miracle she is still alive, I'll stay."

Alive or dead, there was no way I was staying in the US after final exams. I told Cady about my summer plans on the train to New York City. Cady was not happy.

"You're going to gallivant around the world while your girlfriend is stuck picking weeds in Connecticut?"

Cady had just been hired as a summer intern at the Vanderough University Botanical Gardens.

"I didn't think—"

"What?!" Cady growled. "You didn't think your girlfriend would care if you abandoned her for three months?"

"Yeah."

"If you've still got mono in a month, I don't think you should go."

"I'm improving, aren't I?"

"You still sleep half the day."

"Yes, but I'm not throwing up as much."

"Listen," Cady said flatly. "You do what you want. Just don't be surprised if I've taken up with a hot botanist by the time you get back."

A joke. Was it a joke? I changed the subject.

"My mother is a little . . . strange," I said. "She has OCD."

"Like needing to clean all the time?"

"No, actually it's another form of OCD. She thinks she's going to kill people. Stab them with a knife, smother them with a pillow, throw them out the penthouse window. That kind of thing."

"Is she dangerous?" Cady was squinting at me as if she thought I might be pulling her leg.

"No," I said. "Harmless as a kitten. She'd never do anything to hurt anyone. She just gets weird around people, especially new people, since she has these worries about causing them harm."

"So, how can I help?" Cady asked.

"Just be understanding. Mother probably won't come out of her bedroom much while you're there. Don't take it personally."

"What's your dad like?" Cady asked.

"Father is ... difficult. But he's usually polite with my friends, especially if they're smart. He'll like that you're studying to be a botanist on Mars. But he may not stick around the house much either. He's not very sociable."

"So it's going to be just you and me most of the time?"

"And Delia," I said. "She's our live-in help. She'll be around."

"Maybe I shouldn't be meeting your parents just yet. It *is* early ..."

"No, please. My mother is preparing a huge feast in your honor. You have to be there."

The first thing we did after we pulled into Grand Central Terminal was catch a cab down to the East Village. The doctor at Planned Parenthood said Cady ticked off all the boxes. She was in good health and everything had gone smoothly. She could continue on birth control if she wanted, and she could expect her period again in a few weeks' time. The only thing she had to watch for was any irregularity in her next few periods. Otherwise, she didn't have to follow up with Planned Parenthood again.

The people in the clinic assumed I was the "father" of the embryo. They kept talking to me like I had some say in the matter.

Even if I had been the father of the embryo, I don't think I should have gotten any say in the matter. Her body is her body.

It was late Monday when we finally left the clinic, maybe five o'clock. But I wanted to linger a bit before introducing Cady to my parents. My parents weren't expecting us until later anyway.

"Want to get some coffee?"

"You're sure your parents won't mind?" Cady chewed on her knuckle nervously.

"They're not those kinds of parents," I said.

"Do you have a place in mind?"

"Starbucks?"

"We're in New York City, and all you can come up with is Starbucks?"

I shrugged. New York City wasn't a novelty to me like it was to Cady. So I let her drag me into some hole-in-the-wall café called NY's Finest Coffee and Donuts. The first thing I noticed was that "NY's finest" seemed to refer to the New York City Police Department, because the walls were covered with photographs of officers in blue uniforms posing with do-nuts and coffee. The man at the checkout counter had a face like a weathered baseball mitt.

"You kids from the college?" he asked.

I assumed he meant NYU, which was just down the street.

"No," I said. "We go to Vanderough."

"Ah," he said. "Martians."

"Yeah," I said.

I could already tell that Cady regretted pulling us into this place. She hovered at my shoulder, unsure of how to respond. The man was eyeing us like we were lepers. Clearly, he didn't want anything to do with two young whippersnappers from out of town.

"So what are two Martians doing in New York?"

"I grew up here," I said. "We're visiting my parents for Easter."

"Come on, Herbert," Cady whispered. "I'm not hungry anymore."

"No," I said. I didn't want to let this guy win. "You said you wanted coffee. Go ahead and order."

Cady looked at me like I was out of my mind.

"I'll have a latte and a chocolate old-fashioned," I said, pointing to a crusty donut behind the counter.

The man took his time making my latte. Cady ordered a small coffee with milk. The guy pretended not to hear her. He handed me a donut and the latte, and I had to repeat Cady's order. After some grumbling, he poured Cady a small coffee.

"Milk is on the counter." He indicated a jug at the end of the bar.

"Thanks." I paid with cash. "Let's eat here." There were a table and chairs stuffed in the corner of the shop. I wanted to irk the guy by lingering, so I sat down in one of the chairs.

"Are you serious?" Cady hissed. "I'd rather leave."

"No way," I said. "I want to enjoy my donut."

The man scowled at us from across the counter. He took up a remote control and flicked on the television that hung on the wall. Then he pumped up the volume so that I could barely hear anything Cady was saying.

"I don't think it's safe to be here," Cady whispered. "Let's go."

"Hold on." The local news was on, and a woman was interviewing the Bridgeport police chief.

"The boy's family wants answers," she said. "They say he would never voluntarily break into a zoo. His mother thinks it was some sort of hazing ritual for a fraternity or something."

Cady sipped her coffee and watched the news. "Tragedy," she said. "You know Melissa Veracruz, the girl who lives down the hall from me? She was best friends with that boy. He was at her birthday party, remember?"

"Really? I didn't notice," I lied. It was the first time since the incident that Cady had mentioned knowing Freddy at all. Suddenly I didn't feel like eating.

"Yeah," Cady said. "Melissa is devastated. Hasn't come out of her room since it happened."

"Want the rest of my donut?" I pushed the half-eaten old-fashioned across the table. Just the sight of it made me want to throw up.

"You don't want it?"

"I'm feeling nauseous," I said.

"It's probably the mono," Cady said. "You really should see a doctor."

"I just need some sleep." I licked the chocolate off my fingers. "Come on. Let's head over to my parents' house."

Delia was in the kitchen doing dishes when we arrived.

"Your mother and father have turned in for the night," she said. It was only seven o'clock.

"Delia, this is my girlfriend, Cady."

Delia nodded politely to Cady as she dried a pot with a dish towel. "You're very pretty."

Cady blushed. "Thank you."

"I prepared a guest room for you." Delia placed the pot on the drying rack. "We call it the Pink Palace." Then she turned to me. "And you'll be sleeping in your own bedroom."

I sighed. It wasn't Delia who cared whether or not Cady and I slept in the same room. It was Father. He liked to pretend he cared about things like that. I'm pretty sure it didn't matter to him if Cady and I shared a bed; he just wanted to piss me off.

"Are you hungry?" Delia asked. "I put aside a couple of plates for you."

"Yes, please," Cady said.

Delia brought us chicken cordon bleu, roasted eggplant, and potatoes au gratin. My stomach was still in knots, so I shuffled the food around on my plate while Cady ate.

"What's wrong, baby boy?" Delia asked, observing my full plate.

"We think he's got mono," said Cady. "He hasn't had an appetite for weeks."

Delia placed the back of her hand on my forehead. "You don't have a fever."

"It's nothing," I said. "Just a bug."

"Or stress," Delia conjectured. "As a kid, you always lost your appetite when you were worrying over something."

Delia knew me too well.

"Yeah," I said. "Could be final exams coming up."

Cady blinked. "Finals aren't for another month."

"You got something on your mind, baby boy?" Delia asked.

"No," I said. "I'm just tired. I think I'll turn in early."

I left Cady and Delia in the dining room and collapsed onto my old bed. I had really thought that with enough time, the feelings of guilt and shame around Freddy's death would start to fade. But they only seemed to be getting more pronounced with each passing day.

I buried my face in my pillow and cried. About an hour

later, there was a knock on my door.

"What is it?"

Delia opened the door a crack. "Miss Cady has turned in for the night."

"Okay," I said.

"Is there something you want to talk about?" Delia took a few steps into my room.

"I think I did something terrible," I blurted.

Delia patted down her apron. "What did you do, baby boy?"

"I can't say," I cried. "But I think I'm going to be in huge trouble."

"Well, if it's as bad as you say, best to own up to it and accept the consequences. You won't feel better until you do."

Delia put a hand on my shoulder. I winced.

"Look, Herbert," she said. "I know you don't want to tell me what you did, and I don't want to know. But hiding it from that girl out there is a sure way of ending up alone. You should tell her sooner rather than later."

"I know," I said.

But I couldn't bring myself to tell Cady. We hung around the penthouse for the next few days, vegging on Delia's famous snickerdoodle cookies and HGTV. My father appeared a few times and made an attempt at getting to know Cady a little. Asked her what she was studying. Why she wanted to go to Mars. He seemed to like her answers.

Mother stayed in her room until Sunday. When she appeared for Easter dinner, she was in decent spirits. She even shook Cady's hand, which surprised me, because she didn't like touching other people. I can remember maybe a dozen times in my life that my mother actually touched me. So I took it as a good sign that she was willing to extend her hand for the sake of my girlfriend. I learned later that she had taken a Valium with her afternoon cocktail.

Yum!

After dinner, my mother returned promptly to her room. My father stayed at the dining room table and drilled Cady on her plans for the future. Were there many botanists on Mars? What did being a botanist on Mars entail? Did it make good money? That sort of thing. When it had gotten sufficiently late and my father felt he had done his fatherly duties, he locked himself in his office and didn't come out again.

The following morning, Delia packed us sack lunches and hugged us goodbye. My parents did not appear to see us off. I didn't expect them to. Cady and I caught the six o'clock train back to Bridgeport, and while Cady scrambled to finish her microbiology homework on the train, I tried to muster the courage to tell her about Scepter and Gavel and the zoo prank and Freddy's death.

In the end, I couldn't do it. But I needn't have worried. Frank Harding was already hard at work on his exposé for *Vanity Fair*. I learned later that Lee had given him the Order's URL and Jake's login information at the start of spring break.

So while Cady and I had been on a *House Hunters International* watching spree, Frank Harding had been sifting through nearly a decade's worth of correspondence between gavelmen.

The rest is history.

CHAPTER 32

THE FOOD POISONING passed overnight, so I went into the hotel today for my shift. During break, Albert and I shared a reefer, and he explained that Lee Knowles comes in every week or so to book a room. The same room every time. An executive suite on the fifth floor. Room 512.

"He always pays in cash," Albert said.

Now, why would Lee do that? I think it sounds a little fishy. Albert says a lot of people do that if they're having affairs. They book a room for one night, pay in cash, and nobody is the wiser. Except Albert. Albert knows.

Lee isn't married. I don't even think he has a girlfriend. So I don't know why he would need to hide a romantic relationship from anybody, even if he is in the spotlight because of the gubernatorial campaign. I asked Albert to pull up the hotel records, and it looks like Lee has been reserving room 512 once every week or so for almost nine months now. Albert says he never sees Lee coming or going with anybody of any gender.

Yesterday, Lee made a reservation for Sunday of next week, which happens to be exactly eight days from now, which happens to be the same day as my next shift at the hotel. Check-in time is three o'clock. I'm usually still cleaning rooms at that time. And I do typically work the fifth floor. So . . .

Cady says to stay out of it. What does it matter if Lee is having an affair? But Lee is sneaky. I don't think it's that simple. And I can still hear Jake's words ringing in my ears: "If Lee were to kill someone, he'd be smart about it."

Lee is a clever little bastard. First, he hands over a bombshell story to Frank Harding, an up-and-coming writer, then he attaches himself to the political career of that same man. Now he's about to be elected lieutenant governor of Mars. This is what he's wanted since we were stupid kids. He was always very ambitious, which is why he resented our initiation into Scepter and Gavel. Before Lee interfered, gavelmen were destined for greatness. Now Lee is the one on a rocket to the top of Martian society.

* * *

It was after Cady and I returned from New York that I had my first shift back at the zoo. I was sick all morning preparing for my return to the site of Freddy's death. I should have quit the zoo gig after the jailbreak, but I thought it might look suspicious. So I put on my candy-striped vest and showed up that Saturday at noon for my shift.

"Hola, Herbert," Geoffrey said, flashing a new gold grill at me. "Bernie wants to see you in his office."

Bernie was the HR director. All my organs sank to the pit of my stomach. They knew. Bernie knew. He was going to turn me over to the authorities. It was all over for me.

The administration building was quiet. Somber. The tension following the jailbreak hung thick in the air. It had been a stressful couple of weeks for the zoo staff, wrangling the animals and investigating Freddy's death. As I crossed the main floor of the complex, I thought I could feel the eyes of every office employee on me.

I knocked on Bernie's door.

"Come in," he called.

I entered. Bernie stood at a file cabinet with his back to me. He was rifling through some files and did not acknowledge my presence right away. I closed the door behind me and stood, feet shuffling on the blue carpet, waiting. Finally, Bernie found whatever he was looking for, pulled it from the cabinet, and turned to face me.

"You want a water or something?" Bernie opened the door to a mini fridge in the corner of the office.

"No thank you," I said. He had an excellent poker face.

"Look," he said. "You've been here for a while."

I nodded. "Since September."

"And Geoffrey says you're reliable."

"Hmm."

"After the incident a couple of weeks ago, we've decided to increase security here at the zoo. Replace all the locks with electronic key cards. Fortify the gates. That sort of thing."

What was he getting at? I stood there in silence.

"We're also hiring more security personnel. Geoffrey applied to be a night watchman."

"Oh," I said.

"And he recommended you take his place. Selling tickets. Working the register. It comes with a fifty-five cent pay raise. If you're interested, Geoffrey will spend the next two days training you on the register."

I thought of quitting right there, on the spot. I didn't want to be in another zoo as long as I lived. But instead I said, "Sure. Yeah. That'd be cool."

I left the admin building feeling disconnected from my body. There I was, going through all the motions of a regular employee, taking a promotion. Meanwhile, my mind was a million miles away, trying to hide from itself. I could hardly bear the guilt.

I passed Jinx. She was pacing in her enclosure. I couldn't bring myself to meet her gaze. She knew. All the animals knew.

"So?" Geoffrey asked as I approached the ticket counter.

"Yeah," I said. "We can start training today."

"You still have to operate the carousel until they get a new ticket-taker. But I'll teach you how to ring up customers between rides."

"Sounds good."

I joined Geoffrey in the booth. He had stuffed a Ferragamo satchel under the counter. I wondered how he would afford his luxury goods if he couldn't poach from the cash register anymore.

"Security pays seventeen dollars an hour," he said, as if reading my mind.

"Cool." I wasn't one to judge. My friend died because I stole the keys to the bison paddock. Whosoever casts the first stone, etc.

I spent the rest of my shift bouncing between the ticket counter and the carousel. I'd sell a ticket to a guest, Geoffrey watching over my shoulder. Then I'd follow the guest to the carousel, where I would promptly take the ticket back. I could tell the guests thought I was an idiot for going through such a silly ritual. But, hey. It was a living.

Cady took me out later to celebrate my promotion. We've taken to referring to dinner that night as the Last Supper because I would spend the next month eating nothing but beans and rice in jail.

Geoffrey was a surprisingly good teacher. I think it was because he wanted out of that ticket booth as soon as possible.

By the next day, I was processing most of the transactions with guests while Geoffrey scrolled through his phone.

It was about two in the afternoon, I think, when Geoffrey punched me in the arm and said, "You'd better check your phone."

I had eighteen missed calls. Ten of the calls were from Cady. Three were from members of the track team. The other five were from people I knew back in high school.

"What's going on? Did something happen?"

Then Geoffrey thrust his phone in my face. On the screen were the words SECRET SOCIETY FOR MARTIANS IMPLICATED IN DEATH OF STUDENT.

Vanity Fair had just published its May issue with Frank Harding's article about the Order of the Scepter and Gavel. My name was among those listed, along with a screenshot of the note I had posted on the private message board just before the jailbreak: "Don't forget your keys. And whatever you do, don't get eaten."

"Thankfully, nobody was eaten that night or the following day," Frank Harding wrote. "But a young man with his whole life ahead of him was gored by a bison. When a ranking member of the secret society suggested turning themselves in to the authorities, their ringleader, Prescott Harrington, class of '41, replied, 'Everyone sit tight. It'll blow over eventually.'"

Not to be. Not to be.

A cop showed up at the ticket booth an hour later and shuttled me down to the police station, where I was fingerprinted and tossed into a jail cell to await bail. But bail would never come. My father made sure of that. He said I deserved to be locked up for what I'd done, and he dissuaded anyone who might post bail on my behalf from setting me free. Even Cady's hands were tied. When she visited me at the station the next day, she said, "Your father doesn't want me to try to get you out of here. He said he would disown us both if I did."

"Fuck him!" I said. "Let him disown us. Post the bail, and I promise I'll pay you back."

"You can't alienate your father right now," Cady said. "Who's going to pay for your lawyer?"

Turned out my father wouldn't put a single cent toward my attorney fees. But Cady was doing the best she could with the little information she had. It was Jake's dad who eventually sorted out all the legal fees. He respected my father's wishes to leave me in police custody on principle, saying he should have let Jake wait out the trial in jail, too. But at least he hired the best lawyers in the country to defend us when the trial came.

That's a loving dad.

CHAPTER 33

WORD TO THE WISE: Trust your instincts, even when your wife tells you to drop it.

I had my last shift at the hotel today, and boy what a shift it was! The union struck a deal with the hotel bargaining group, and the housekeeping staff will be returning to their posts with newly negotiated hourly wages and improved health benefits. Makes me think maybe I should apply for a work transfer to the hotel. I don't know if the Martian Labor Bureau would allow it, since I'm legally restricted to working the jobs nobody wants thanks to the settlement reached in our trial.

Hence the mopping up of toxic waste in the physics lab.

Anyway, I made the best of my last day at the Westin, and I think we may be getting somewhere in the Adolf Dussel murder investigation.

Let me explain:

I usually start top-down, meaning I service the rooms on the sixth floor first and work my way down. There's nothing so miserable as having floors and floors of dirty rooms looming overhead while you work a lower floor. So I go in descending order. As you can imagine, the Westin isn't very tall, only nine floors and a basement level due to permitting constraints. Nevertheless, it's the tallest building on Mars, and the ninth floor nearly scrapes the great glass dome that encloses Sector 2. So instead of building up and up, the hotel is a sprawling thing with three wings of about seventy rooms each. I'm typically assigned to the north wing, floors four through six, which has about eight rooms to a floor depending on whether there's a fancy suite or a gym or something on the floor. And since the north wing is situated squarely between the west and east wings, I pretty much work on rooms numbered nine through sixteen on each floor, roughly.

I'm simplifying for the sake of clarity.

Suffice it to say, I happen to service the executive suite on the fifth floor of the north wing. Room 512.

I typically start my shift at 8:00 a.m. and work to 4:00 p.m., with a fifteen-minute break and a half-hour lunch in between. But today I did something out of the ordinary. I started with room 512, then resumed cleaning top-down in the normal fashion.

Why would I do this? I wanted room 512 to be ready for early check-in, which starts at 11:00 a.m. Albert Ni at the front desk can see which rooms are ready after I check them off on an app on my tablet.

I also stole the Do Not Disturb sign from room 512.

Then I skipped lunch and break time, and finished all my rooms early, 3:00 p.m. on the nose. Why? Well, regular check-in starts at 3:00 p.m.

Guests can check in using our mobile app, which will tell them when a room is available or whether the specific room they requested is ready. So Lee would have seen that the room was ready first thing in the morning. Whether he would check in early or after 3:00 p.m. I did not know. Albert could have given me that information in a split second, but I didn't want to know. So long as I was still on the clock, I could technically be in any of my rooms—so long as I knocked first. Always knock first.

If room 512 was occupied at 3:00 p.m., my story was going to go like this: I left some cleaning supplies in room 512 (which I did for consistency), and I went back to retrieve them, and when I knocked, nobody replied. That would be my story.

This is what really happened: At 3:00 p.m. I walked straight up to room 512. There was no sign on the door, naturally. So I knocked. Always knock.

A woman's voice answered my knock. "Occupied."

I pretended not to hear and knocked again, hard, calling out loudly, "Housekeeping!"

Proper protocol.

Again the woman yelled, "Occupied!"

I pretended not to hear. And until I die, I will claim I didn't hear the woman, not a peep.

So, since it sounded like the room was unoccupied (that's my story, anyway), I deployed my key card and entered the room *to retrieve my cleaning supplies* (air quotes).

And there they were: her sitting on top of him, him on his back moaning in ecstasy, her fully undressed with long blonde hair down to her hips, him still in a crisp button-up dress shirt with no pants.

Governor Harding and Polly Platt.

I shielded my eyes. Pretended not to see anything. "Sorry, sorry!" I said, backing out of the room.

Then I went down to the front desk and told Albert everything.

"So what do you make of it?" Albert asked. He's been on Mars only a year or two, so he has no sense of the politics of the place.

"Well, first off, Governor Harding has a wife. And that woman was not his wife. That was an administrative assistant down at city hall. Secondly, Harding is running for reelection, and a scandal like this could pummel him in the polls."

"Then probably don't say anything. You don't want to get the guy in trouble."

"No, Al." I am calling him Al now. "Frank Harding is the scoundrel who ratted me out to the police back in college."

"Ohhhh." Albert's eyes widened. He was catching on.

"Yeah," I said. "Frank Harding screwed me over real bad."

Albert flashed his most potheaded smile. "So it's time for sweet, sweet revenge."

I nodded. "And this implicates Harding in the murder of Adolf Dussel."

"I don't follow." Albert scratched the long, pale scar on his arm. He got it skateboarding on Earth, he says.

"Polly Platt—the woman up in room 512—was Adolf Dussel's fiancée. She may have been sleeping with Harding while she was engaged to Dussel!"

"So she's the murderer?"

"I don't know. Could be Polly. Could be Harding. Could be both."

"Whoa." Albert looked dazed. Then: "Wanna get high after work?"

"I gotta get home," I said. "The election is in two days."

And that was how my last day at the hotel went.

Now I'm typity-typing two emails: one to Inspector Dunst with all my thoughts and suspicions about the murder case and one to Fychea Mohamed, an investigative reporter with *Vanity Fair*.

I can give as good as I get.

* * *

And boy did I get. By submitting his exposé to *Vanity Fair*, Frank Harding really gave it to us all. He gave it to us good.

But I was the only one who couldn't make bail. Most gavelmen came from money, so their parents had no problem forking over $25,000 for bail. My dad could have afforded it, too.

Not to be.

So I spent several weeks in the county jail. The trial date was set for May 17. It wasn't a lengthy trial since we reached a settlement with the prosecution fairly quickly. Because we did and said exactly as our lawyers directed, and because the public was so determined to send us to Mars, we didn't get any prison time. I got four hundred hours of community service, plus I was banned from all zoos on Earth and Mars for all of eternity. And, of course, I was put on the C-list for jobs up here.

Probably the worst punishment came from Father, though. Since he refused to post my bail, I missed all my final exams and failed all my classes for the semester. So I had to take on extra courses in subsequent semesters in order to graduate on time. That meant no more track and field. No more friends. No more fun. I barely had time for Cady.

And then there was the matter of the inheritance. I don't think I would have gotten much of an inheritance from my father anyway. But some money would have been nice.

Not to be.

And of course the Tomb was demolished and the secret society banished to oblivion.

What else?

Oh, and I didn't get that promotion at the zoo.

CHAPTER 34

TOMORROW is the big election, and Frank Harding is solidly in the lead. But that could change at any moment. There have been a few developments over the course of the last twenty-five hours (the length of a Martian day). Frank Harding really stepped in it today. Confident in his enormous lead over Best Bet Bill, he decided to hold a press conference during which he planned to express his gratitude for his supporters and make a last appeal to the voters on the fence (like my dear Cady). However, he didn't get very far before Fychea Mohamed, the investigative reporter for *Vanity Fair*, interrupted.

"Governor!" she shouted. "Is it true you are having an affair with your administrative assistant?"

Governor Harding pretended not to hear the question. "I'm sorry, I couldn't quite make out—"

"Are you having an affair with Polly Platt? For the record, please."

Harding hemmed and hawed and finally said, "Utter nonsense! Fake news. I won't even dignify that question with a response."

And he promptly retreated into city hall, where Polly Platt was probably at that very moment stocking paper in one of the office printers.

The question caused a stir, and of course everyone wanted to get a statement from Polly Platt. But not more than twenty minutes passed before Inspector Dunst arrived and locked himself away in an empty conference room in the municipal complex with Polly and his trusty tape recorder.

Inspector Dunst emailed me later to thank me for the lead. He also let a few details of the interview slip. Apparently, Polly Platt cracked under the pressure of an interrogation and fessed up fully to the affair with Governor Harding, which has been going on for nine months. She says that Harding promised to divorce his wife and marry Polly instead, but only *after* the election. This promise led Polly to break up with Adolf Dussel. She was honest with Adolf; she told him she had been having an affair for some time with Governor Harding and that she and Adolf would have to call off their engagement.

Adolf was devastated. But that was the last Polly saw of Adolf Dussel. She swears upon her mother's grave that she did not have any part in his murder.

Interesting.

Dunst says he has an interview with Harding tonight to get his side of the story. The good news is that Jake Harrington has been released from police custody since he is no longer the prime suspect.

Who is? I wonder.

"I don't understand people who have affairs," says Cady. She is reading the email from Inspector Dunst over my shoulder. "It's hard enough to be in one relationship. Who needs two?"

Cady and I were wed twenty-six years ago, on June 7, 2044. This was about two weeks before we were sent up. We had just graduated from Vanderough University, both of us on time, and we had a short window to get hitched between graduation and our flight to Mars.

The previous three years had passed without incident. I did my community service, went to class, and stayed out of trouble. I had learned my lesson. There were still some legal hurdles to clear. Freddy's family was suing me for my inaction at the moment of Freddy's death. They think I could have saved his life if I'd called the paramedics, stayed at the scene, turned myself in. But I know in my heart of hearts that Freddy was dead upon impact. No pulse. I couldn't have saved him, even if I had dialed 911.

And would you believe it? Father settled the lawsuit out of court for a few million buckaroos. He said he had no choice. His lawyer advised him to get involved so that Freddy's family didn't try to take down the entire Palminteri empire. So I suppose you could argue that I did get my inheritance after all. And I gave it straight over to the Eulers.

Lucky them.

Father may have paid off the Eulers to save his own skin, but he had no interest in dealing with me thereafter. He didn't come to the wedding. Mother came, assisted by Delia. Cady was heartbroken, since she had worked so hard to mend the relationship with my father. In the end, he did what he had always been threatening to do—he disowned me. Not in a formal way, but he stopped talking to me. Stopped caring.

Which meant he stopped talking to Cady. So we were wed in front of a small congregation of family and friends, with my father conspicuously absent. Then up we went, in a rocket ship to Mars. That was twenty-six years ago.

I believe Cady when she says she's never in the past twenty-six years considered having an affair.

"Too much work," she says.

I feel the same way. Affairs make catchy headlines in the gossip columns, so they seem almost as ubiquitous as root canals. But really, it takes a special kind of commitment and dedication to carry out an affair. Most people aren't up to the challenge.

CHAPTER 35

ELECTION DAY IS HERE, and guess what? Frank Harding and Lee Knowles are in the custody of the police. Late last night Inspector Dunst convinced Frank Harding to cooperate with the investigation. Harding sang like a canary. And he threw his running mate and campaign manager of many years, Lee Knowles, under the bus.

Here is the story he told Inspector Dunst:

After learning of Polly Platt's infidelity several weeks ago, Adolf Dussel confronted Frank Harding and threatened to make the affair public. Knowing that a scandal would ruin his political career and fearing retribution from his wife, Frank asked Lee Knowles to go down to C-Pod to see if he could convince Adolf to stay quiet.

Lee visited Adolf in his private pod and offered him a large sum of money to keep quiet. Two hundred credits to be exact.

Adolf refused. That's when Frank and Lee hatched a plan to kill Adolf.

Lee masterminded the whole thing. Working for the city, Lee had access to the nuclear waste disposal schedule, and he also knew that Arnie Sphinx had a few outstanding fines to settle with city hall. So Lee typed out the anonymous letter to Arnie requesting one spent nuclear fuel pellet in return for two hundred credits, which would pay his fines ten times over. Too bad Arnie had to spend the extra cash on an attorney.

Que será, será.

Anyway, Lee understood that anything he printed from his personal account would be traced back to him. So he logged on to a public computer as Jake Harrington, which was a cinch since Jake was still using the same password trick he used back in college. Lee printed the letter from Jake's account, knowing that Jake would take the fall for the murder. To strengthen the case against Jake, Lee disguised himself in the Scepter and Gavel cloak and hood that later showed up on the CCTV footage.

Where the hell did Lee get the Scepter and Gavel cloak?

Apparently, he found it under my bed after I moved out of our dorm years ago. God knows why he kept it. I can only imagine he thought it'd come in handy someday. Sneaky little bastard.

Police have retrieved the robes from Lee's pod, and they do, in fact, have my initials on them.

Once Lee had possession of the spent nuclear fuel pellet,

he visited Adolf Dussel in his pod again and promised triple what he had already offered for Adolf's silence. Adolf wanted to think it over. But it was too late for Adolf. Lee had slipped the radioactive pellet under Adolf's mattress, knowing full well that Harding didn't have six hundred spare credits lying around to pay off his enemies.

Nobody knows what Adolf Dussel would have done in the end because before he made up his mind, he was dead.

The last crucial part of this puzzle goes like this:

How did Lee avoid the security cameras coming and going from Adolf Dussel's private pod? There are cameras all over C-Pod. If you were to step outside our pod right now, you'd see the cameras on the ceiling, clear as day.

Turns out those cameras are phony. Bogus. Fake. They are simply meant to be deterrents to would-be thieves. None of the cameras in the residential blocks do anything since nobody is really worried about crime in residential pods. It's not like we keep anything of value in our cramped living quarters. So even though security in other parts of Pod City is tight, the cameras in C-Pod are just for show. They aren't even real cameras. They are shells of cameras. Cheap 3D printouts from our materials lab.

Being high up in government, Lee Knowles knew all this while he was coming and going from C-Pod.

So that's how it happened.

Ta-da!

Somehow Fychea Mohamed got ahold of Harding's salacious confession and published a four-thousand-word exposé in today's edition of *Vanity Fair*. So now the whole planet knows Frank Harding and Lee Knowles are murderers. It's a pretty big story on Earth, too.

People of Mars: Cast your ballots!

As my friend Albert Ni would say, "Sweet, sweet revenge."

Or as my dear Cady would say, "Payback's a bitch."

AFTERWORD

CADY AND I finally took that trip down to Joshua Beach, about a week after the election. Best Bet Bill won handily—not that Frank Harding would have been able to serve another term even if he had won. He and Lee were both convicted of first-degree murder and sentenced to life in prison without parole. We don't have the resources up here to sustain any kind of prison population, so Frank and Lee are currently on a transport ship back to Earth, where they will be caged men for the rest of their days.

Yippee!

Jake Harrington is a free man, and he credits me for that. He says, "Thank god you're such a scatterbrain. Of all the rooms to leave your Windex in, you left it in that one. What are the chances?" He means room 512. Jake doesn't know I planned it all. And it wasn't to exonerate Jake as much as it was to get revenge.

Sweet, sweet revenge.

We've renewed our friendship, Jake and I. Jake has been out to dinner with me and Cady a few times. He has really grown up since college, even if he still leans a little to the right. His views are more progressive than they used to be. He says it was Ursula who made him "woke." I guess before she died, Ursula made Jake promise to vote Democrat for the rest of his life in her stead. And he swears he has. So that's progress.

Cady is trying to set Jake up with Rabbi Renata Sachs from Temple Beth Hillel. Sadly, Renata is recently widowed. Her husband, Bob, had a heart attack at the age of fifty-three, just after the election. Bob lived long enough to cast his vote for Best Bet Bill. Then he was done. That was about six months ago. Now Cady is trying to organize a sneak-attack double date, just like she did thirty years ago with me and Francine, the nun.

"A good man is hard to find," Cady says. "You gotta strike while the iron is hot."

I'm not so sure Renata is ready to "strike." But I guess there is no harm in introducing her to Jake under the guise of friendship.

What else do you want to know?

Oh! I did get that transfer approved. Cleaning hotel rooms is apparently considered a shitty enough job for a lowlife like me. But I love it at the Westin. I get to hang with Albert and hear all the latest gossip, which Cady loves, too. Plus it pays better.

Wine with every meal!

Kidding.

Delia's been here for two weeks, and she's having a ball. She got over the gravity sickness and the time change and everything really quickly. Cady and I try to see her every few days for lunch or dinner or an outing. She spends most of her time at the spa or in the hotel pool. This is the first instance in her life that she's had any time to herself.

"Is this what retirement feels like?" she asked me the other day.

"I don't know," I said. "Maybe if you retire to a luxury suite at the Westin Resort."

Delia laughed. "It's good to see you again, baby boy."

I guess I can forgive Wesley. If he's willing to fork over the big bucks to make Delia comfortable in her old age, then maybe he deserves my inheritance. I'm not sure I'd have been so generous. I know, I know. I'm an ass. The point is, the money is being put to good use. That makes me a tad less bitter about the whole thing.

Besides, what would I do with $523 million on Mars?

As Cady likes to say, "Even the most expensive clock has no more than sixty minutes."

A NOTE FROM THE AUTHOR

IF YOU ENJOYED *The Secret Order of the Scepter & Gavel*, please take the time to visit Amazon and Goodreads to rate this book. Hearing from readers like you is the best part of putting a book out in the world. If you are interested in joining my author newsletter, in which I announce deals, giveaways, and other noteworthy news, please email info@booleanop.com and request to be added. And check out my other titles.

Novels:
Do Not Resuscitate
The Maiden Voyage of the Destiny Unknown

Novellas:
Cuckoo Cuckoo

Short stories:
The Button
Three Wishes: And Other Stories
The Misshapen

ACKNOWLEDGMENTS

THANK YOU to Crystal Shelley at Rabbit with a Red Pen Editorial Services for whipping my book into shape and to Emily's World of Design for a fantastic cover. A huge thanks to all my backers on Kickstarter who made it possible for me to release this book into the wild. And a final thank you to the Monkey, for whom I'd make the journey to Mars and back any day.

ABOUT THE AUTHOR

NICHOLAS PONTICELLO is an educator and writer in Los Angeles, California. He graduated from the University of California, Berkeley, with degrees in mathematics and astrophysics and later earned his master's degree in education from the University of Pennsylvania. Mr. Ponticello is interested in exploring the intersection of science, sustainability, mental health, and education and hopes to encourage more systems thinking and sustainability-themed curricula at the secondary school level.

For more titles by this author, please visit www.booleanop.com.